SOUTHERN RAIN

A NOVEL OF
SEVENTEENTH CENTURY
CHINA

HARRY MILLER

EARNSHAW
BOOKS

Southern Rain

By Harry Miller

ISBN-13: 978-988-8273-37-9

Cover design: Jason Wong

FICTION / Historical

EB100

Published by Earnshaw Books Ltd. (Hong Kong)

For Yuka

PART ONE

1

FEBRUARY TO MARCH, 1644

IT IS THE SEVENTEENTH year of the Chongzhen Emperor's reign, the first day of the first month – Spring Festival – and smoke is rising over Nanjing, as its people celebrate the New Year by lighting things on fire.

Half the city's population are setting off firecrackers, to the delight of the other half. In groups of young and old, they hang clusters of the paper-wrapped cylinders like bunches of red bananas from the eaves of temples and taverns. With the touch of an incense stick, the fuse commences to hiss and everybody scatters. If someone chances to round the corner unawares, on his way to visit relatives, he comes abreast of the little bombs the moment they begin to explode and finds himself engulfed in a thundering maelstrom. His chest thumps like a kettle drum hammered by madmen. He flails his arms about his head and staggers away as the crescendo continues, a blur of incandescence hanging in the air near which he passed, casting billows of smoke heavenward. Then, as the last charge on the string gives up its ghost and the echo rolls over the city and disappears into the hills, the celebrants clap and jump for joy, and even the rattled pedestrian grins and waves, signifying no hard feelings. He too is enjoying himself.

In addition to the hanging clusters, some firecrackers can

be thrown, and some are miniature rockets. Explosives of these sorts transform Nanjing's streets and alleys into gauntlets of spark-trailing missiles, air bursts, and ground bursts. Young boys in particular are fond of launching pocket rockets from their hands, to watch them ricochet off buildings and passers-by. Their favorite targets are peddlers on donkey carts, because they pretend nothing is happening. They go right on hawking their snacks – "Steamed buns! Dumplings!" – while projectiles bounce off their bellies or lodge in the folds of their robes, sending sparks cascading from their torsos. The pinnacle of fun is to toss a cherry-bomb into the street, timed to explode when a cart passes over it. There it lies, its fuse sizzling, while, say, the noodle-man approaches, crooning "Thick noodles! Thin noodles! Sesame paste! Black bean paste!" and just as his cart reaches it, *Bang!* off it goes in a cloud of sulfur. Both man and beast jolt from the concussion but emerge unfazed, the peddler resuming his hawking, the donkey his hauling, showing no sign of distress. Onlookers beam and the young pyrotechnicians make ready the next barrage.

Not all that is set alight that day contains gunpowder. Nanjing's denizens also burn joss paper – play money – as offerings to the gods or to their deceased ancestors. Clan after clan of them, Chens, Wangs, and Zhangs, gather in their kitchens or courtyards to burn wad after wad of the heavenly currency, which takes to the air in particulate form. The offering of joss paper is less likely than fireworks to involve the occasional victim, unless it takes place on the ground floor of a storied building and some poor soul is caught upstairs. In such a case, the unfortunate one, as soon as he realizes he is suffocating, makes a desperate dash to the nearest window and thrusts his head outside. Gasping for oxygen, not even this man complains but rejoices in the good cheer and bonhomie of festival time.

4

Thus does Nanjing exude mirth and merriment, acrid, dark, and thick. Smoke rises over Cock-Crow Temple, a nunnery on a hill. Smoke curls about the Drum Tower, whose beating of the time that day is drowned out in the din. Smoke mushrooms over Three Mountain Street, Nanjing's always-bustling bazaar. Smoke hangs above the Qinhuai River, its famous pleasure quarter. Every tiled roof, every bridge and pagoda, every curvy street and winding canal is enveloped in haze. To the gigantic Peng bird of legend, soaring far above town on this New Year's Day, Nanjing might appear as an exquisite incense censer made to resemble a fairyland. To Nanjing's human residents, the column of smoke dwarfing their city is yet another of its many superlatives; Nanjing wears it like a plumed crown. The vast metropolis, ringed by a wall of eighteen gates, is the pearl of the Yangtze River valley and original capital of the Current Dynasty. It is opulent and lively and crammed with attractions, the subject of rhapsodies by songsters and poets who call it a paradise. If Nanjing's celebrated "kingly air" is now tinged with ash, its people breathe it in even more deeply and feel all the more regal for it. They are as proud and prosperous as any people have dared to be. In a consuming exuberance, they revel and roister, until their city is choking with smoke.

🔲🔲🔲

Watching Nanjing fume from the sky or from the ground, neither Peng bird nor human would have noticed the elderly nun on a donkey cart making her way through the smog from Cock-Crow Temple on the north side of town to outside Treasure Gate, the southernmost portal of the city wall. Though missiles whizzed by her, she maintained her dignity, as did her cart driver, who seemed to have absorbed a bit of her gravitas. The nun was called

5

One-Eyed Jingang, for partially blinding herself while studying the Diamond (*Jingang*) Sutra, and she was Cock-Crow Temple's abbess. While unaccompanied women raised eyebrows if they ventured abroad on most days, the Spring Festival provided One-Eyed Jingang not only with the cover of smoke but also with an excuse to be out, for clergy were often called upon to offer prayers for the New Year. In fact, One-Eyed Jingang was expected at another place of worship, a monastery named the Temple at the Edge of Heaven, where a prayer meeting was planned for that morning. Before the chanting began, however, she wished to consult with the abbot on a matter of some delicacy.

Arriving at the Temple, One-Eyed Jingang alighted from the cart, paid its driver a little extra for the New Year, walked through the main gate, and ascended the stairway to the Mahayana Pavilion, where the abbot, whose dharma name was Baichi Shi'ai, or "Idiot in the Service of Love," greeted her with ebullient good cheer. Fearless of gossip, he invited the nun into his office.

"Wisdom to you," he saluted her, offering some tea. "Big Sister is a bit early. Have you come to help me choose today's reading?"

"No, Big Brother," the abbess returned, as she sat down on a stool. "I'm sure you've already found something appropriate. As it turns out, I've come to discuss something...inappropriate."

She placed on Baichi Shi'ai's desk the bulging sack she'd been carrying, which the abbot had assumed to be filled with boxed or string-bound folios of sutras. She untied the twine at its neck, just as somebody in the neighborhood set off another string of firecrackers like a drumroll.

The sack fell away, revealing a statuette of the Guanyin Bodhisattva, sculpted from rosewood. The carving stood about a foot tall, but its subject did not stand, nor did she sit cross-legged

6

in stolid meditation. Rather, she lolled in a sultry position with one leg arched upward at a right angle, her arm draped over her knee. Although she was Guanyin, the Goddess of Compassion, she posed in the style of Tara, Mother of Liberation; but whatever compassion or liberation she offered her worshippers, it was of a primal, physical sort. Her sexuality was total, not of parts. It sprang not from flaring hips or curvaceous breasts but from her unworldly air of assurance and utter lack of inhibition. Against all convention, this Guanyin held her eyes open, inviting her faithful to advance and be saved. A mandorla of fire radiated from her body, a manifestation of the power of her love.

Baichi Shi'ai knew better than to resist the goddess's charms. Instead, he gave rein to his native enthusiasm. "Oooh! Hail, Guanyin Bodhisattva!" he crowed.

"Yes, she does rather demand devotion," observed One-Eyed Jingang. "I'm surprised you haven't fallen to your knees."

"Whose hands crafted such a powerful image?" asked the abbot. "Or was it a bolt of lightning striking a grateful tree that did the work?"

"Actually, it was created by one of my novices, a brilliant girl. Always reading, trying her hand at something new. I noticed her chiseling away at a hunk of wood from that old column we had replaced and decided to give her a bit of rosewood to see what she could do with better material. This is the result."

Baichi Shi'ai nodded, still absorbed in Guanyin's smoldering expression. "Where will you display it?" he asked, after a while.

"Display it?" the abbess exclaimed. "Good brother! It's hard enough to protect the reputation of my convent without having something like *that* on a pedestal. Why give the next scandalmonger a chance to start yapping about the 'lewd nuns of Cock-Crow Temple'?"

Baichi Shi'ai rounded his mouth. "Oh? You think this Guanyin

7

is lewd?"

"No, I do not, but a lewd man would, and I'm tired of hearing lewd men talk nonsense about decent nuns." One-Eyed Jingang cleared her throat. "So I was hoping that you, Teacher, would take this Guanyin off my hands."

"And keep her here?" the abbot giggled. "My monks would explode! Even if I hid her away, they would sniff her out like tom cats."

"You have that little faith in your brothers?"

"I have that *much* faith in my brothers."

One-Eyed Jingang slumped. "Yes, I suppose we face the same difficulty. Since our calling is to free people from desire, it's bad policy to introduce an object of desire into either of our sanctuaries. So what should we do with it?"

Baichi Shi'ai grinned. "You talk as though she were a problem to be gotten rid of, but Guanyin Bodhisattva cannot be a problem. Yes, neither of our temples is the proper place for her, but remember: Guanyin embodies compassion for the world." He raised both his arms, in an encompassing gesture. "Let's put her out into the world, then, where her compassion can do its work. If some starry-eyed lad falls in love with her, so much the better. Everyone in the world needs to be receptive to compassion, after all."

One-Eyed Jingang thought for a bit and then nodded. "Yes, Brother, you are right. We should allow this Guanyin to play her part. I will consign her to the marketplace, to await the first receptive soul that comes along."

She put the Guanyin back in its sack and tied it closed.

"So what will be today's reading?" she asked, but her host didn't answer, and both devotees of dharma continued to stare at the enshrouded idol for a long time.

🔳🔳🔳

The boy bore the surname Ouyang, with the given name Nanyu, meaning "Southern Rain." He lived with his widowed father, Ouyang Gen, across from the Temple at the Edge of Heaven. Ouyang Gen was a carpenter by trade, who maintained the buildings and all the woodwork at the temple, and he also made furniture, which he sold to the ambitious students who lodged there as they studied for the civil service examinations. Ouyang Nanyu, however, was an aspiring painter and calligrapher. Realizing that "There is nothing that cannot be learned," he had begun practicing with brushes and ink when he wasn't helping his father. Ouyang Gen, for his part, was not at all displeased, especially after it became clear that Nanyu's bold and original style had become popular among the students at the temple, who seemed to prize his son's work as much as his own. By the time Ouyang Nanyu was seventeen (in the year this story begins), he had already sold a few paintings, supplementing the small family's income.

Shortly after New Year's Day, during the Lantern Festival, the Ouyangs hired a cart and brought into the city a large four-poster bed they had made, which they hoped to sell to one of Nanjing's revelers that night. It was constructed of rosewood and adorned with mother of pearl inlays in the shapes of paired mandarin ducks, the symbols of marital fidelity and felicity. Reaching the night-market at Three Mountain Street, they unloaded the bed from the cart and soon had it on display among the merchandise there, between a collection of folding screens and an assemblage of drums and gongs. Ouyang Gen drew back the curtains and tied them to the posts, to show off the interior.

"As the bed is made, so the net is cast," he said. "Let us hope a big fish swims into it soon."

Despite the coolness of the evening air, they were both perspiring from their exertions. Ouyang Nanyu produced a cloth and wiped his father's brow and then his own. Ouyang Gen looked at his son and noticed for the first time how tall he had grown. He gestured toward a storyteller's gallery nearby and said, "Don't you have some business to attend to?"

Ouyang Nanyu nodded and walked the few steps to where the storyteller was in the middle of a performance. He was mimicking a conversation between a beautiful woman and an arrogant official trying to seduce her. The audience chortled as the storyteller voiced the official's boastful recitation of his merits — his family, money, power, and associates — and the woman's contrapuntal rejection of them all. As he narrated, he pointed with a stick to various pictures hanging from a string, which showed the faces of the proud beauty and the odious lecher, as well as those of the influential friends he was alluding to, scenes of her modest dwelling and his gaudy mansion, and other images of places and things that the storyteller used to accompany his yarns. Many of these illustrations had been drawn by Ouyang Nanyu, and it was to deliver his latest commission that Nanyu now arrived at the little gallery. He waited until the story was over (the beautiful woman hanged herself), exchanged greetings with the storyteller, and removed from his sleeve a picture of a group of brigands attacking a boat on a river (perhaps in the next retelling, she would be waylaid by the official's henchmen while trying to escape). The storyteller received the drawing with satisfaction and gave Nanyu a few copper coins. Ouyang Gen watched the transaction from his place.

Nanyu returned and made to surrender his wages to his father, but the latter shook his head. "Keep the money for the time being," Ouyang Gen said, "and give it to me later, with interest. I have made a decision: From now on, you will no longer assist me in the workshop but will cultivate an alternate trade—painting, if you like."

Ouyang Nanyu regarded his father blankly and then sank to his knees. "Is Papa unhappy with me?"

"Leave off the tearful pleading," said the elder Ouyang. "I am neither unhappy with you nor foolish enough to send my only son away before I even reach old age. As I've often said, I expect you to care for me when I am no longer able to care for myself, and as a professional painter, with wealthier patrons than the students at the temple or your friend the storyteller, you will be able to do so more…filially than as a carpenter's lackey or porter."

"But what about the workshop?"

"That will remain my concern, until I turn it over to you, and then you will have two trades—with which to support your old father—instead of only one. After I am gone, you may manage as you see fit. Confucius may have said, 'The filial son does not alter his father's way for three years after he has passed,' but if you really want to be filial, you'll do as I say and find your own way now. You'll recall," he continued, "that my own father was a farmer. I was always handier with the mallet than with the plow, and so I helped him more by building things than by working in the fields. When he died, my two older brothers got the best of his land. I sold them my share for a few ounces of silver, which I used as capital to set myself up at the temple. With the proceeds from my business, I do my part to keep Father's tomb in good repair."

He paused and smoothed out the cover on the bed.

"So you see, my boy, there's no need to be alarmed at this bit of freedom I'm giving you. I have no intention of watching you fly away on the back of a crane."

Ouyang Gen shared a laugh with his son, before he

remembered something and grew serious again.

"There is only one occupation I forbid you to choose," he said. "You must never, under any circumstances, sit for the civil service examinations and become an official. You will increase our estate through hard work only and never seek to gain by plundering others; for if you do become a 'breaker of families,' you will not only suffer in the next life but also stir up jealousy and resentment in this one, and then you will never be safe. 'The stolen mansion is naught but the cage of anxiety.' Promise me you will never wear official robes."

"Rest easy, Father," Nanyu said. "I promise."

"Good boy. Now take those coins and buy yourself a few new brushes and some ink."

Nanyu rose, took his leave, and turned to the street.

What greeted him first was the noise, the droning clamor of the throng, talking and calling and yelling to itself, punctuated by spills and crashes and firecrackers and even by the strains of *pipa*s that somehow cut through the din from the open windows of crowded banquet halls. It baffled all his senses equally, overburdening his eyes as much as his ears, as though the stimuli entering all four apertures surpassed some aggregate limit beyond which he could not process them. In time, though, the hubbub subsided in his consciousness until he was scarcely aware of it, and as it did so, the swirling panoply of fashionable people and exquisite things arrayed before him came into focus, bathed in festive light in the night air.

To his left, he espied tables of exotic stones and crystals, arranged to resemble sacred mountains and valleys in miniature, among which moved in train small parties of the young and the old, examining, criticizing, and appreciating; a man with a pointed goatee was appraising a statue of a seated Buddha; two shiny-headed monks admired a large blue-and-white ceramic urn. In front of him were caged deer, peacocks, and cranes, surrounded by oglers; two youths held aloft at the ends of sticks their tissue-paper cuttings of auspicious, fat fish, one red, one orange; an even younger boy wielded a paper monkey, perhaps the legendary Sun Wukong; a groom led a pair of ponies. To his right, in the middle of the street, was a towering replica of Mount Penglai, with its golden palaces and jewels growing on trees, illuminated from the inside by lanterns and candles, which cast flickering reflections on dozens of upturned faces.

All the men were hatted, with most, like Nanyu himself, wearing cloth head-wraps; but many wore the tall gauze cap once reserved for officials. Everyone, regardless of his headgear, seemed to be similarly occupied, with the wearers of cloth hats and square ones discoursing together on the desirability of various curios or gathering to watch impromptu chess games or wrestling matches. One man, whose patterned robe and respectful retinue marked him as an official, was nonetheless conspicuously out of uniform, for he wore bright red shoes — until recently worn only by women. Another man — a man of taste, with neither official robe nor deferential attendants but with two beaming grandsons crowding upon him — sported a square cap and red shoes, too. Under his plain outer robe, he wore a garment of magnificent orange, far more splendid than anything worn by the official. Yet another gentleman attired himself in the "paddy-field" robe of a monk or abbot, its patchwork design, formerly betokening monastic rusticity, now affording its wearer the opportunity to show off an opulent mélange of silk. The monk-masquerader also displayed in his upraised hand an elegant folding fan with a tassel. Many in the crowd carried such fans, though they remained folded-up (it was, after all, a chilly night in early spring). Small groups of women, attended by their male relatives, had come out to enjoy the festivities, and they brandished folded fans, too. Nanyu noticed two tattered beggars getting shooed away from a restaurant, but otherwise, the scene was one of plenty and potential.

Plunging into it, Nanyu skirted the edge of the group admiring Mount Penglai and worked his way around the precious tabletop landscapes. Finding a space opening in front of him, he rushed forward, only to hit his head against a chime stone that some merchant had hung from a pole. Recovering himself, he gained the other side of the street and began pressing through the knot of people gathered around the tables arranged there, which displayed ritual vessels of bronze, porcelain, and lacquer. Behind the tables were stacked numerous blue-boxed volumes of scholarly and popular books, as well as more folding screens, with ubiquitous painted landscapes of cloud-enshrouded mountains, pagodas, and rivers. With his attention focused on the merchandise, Nanyu jostled absently against the other men in the crowd, who jostled just as absently against him; yet he soon bumped against the wrong gentleman's arm and was suddenly at the center of a flapping barrage of complaint, having disturbed a prize falcon perched there. Taking this beating, too, in stride, Nanyu extricated himself from the raptor's abuse and continued down range, but he promptly came face to face with what seemed to be a human owl. It was a man wearing spectacles.

Finally, Nanyu stood over a low writing desk, empty but for a vase of young peach blossoms heralding the new season. He watched as an old man with silvery hair began opening a series of travel boxes and removing the Four Treasures of the scholar's studio — brushes, paper, ink, and inkstones — and placing them on the desk. Nanyu selected four brushes of varying thickness and an inkstone that fit into his pocket. Inspired by the peach blossoms, he also chose a sampling of inks in springtime colors. Putting down a few of his coins as payment, he made ready to wade back into the human sea, but then he noticed, still packed in one of the travel boxes, something gleaming white. The old man, following Nanyu's gaze, reached down and brought out a bound album of four blank paper leaves, mounted on stock in the size and shape, Nanyu reckoned, of a mandarin square—the insignia showing paired birds of ascending degrees of majesty, which officials wore on the chests of their robes, to indicate their rank. The gray-haired proprietor smiled as Nanyu handed over the rest of his commission money (and a bit more), nestled the album in the lose folds of his robe—over his heart, right where a mandarin square would be—bowed farewell, and wondered how he would make it back across the street to rejoin his father.

At that moment, however, something new caught his eye: a wooden statuette of the Guanyin Bodhisattva seated in a very casual, almost sultry pose, with one leg arched upward and one arm resting on the knee. Her eyes were opened wide, and she was surrounded by a flaming mandorla, which seemed to radiate a cosmic power. Nanyu moved toward her as though drawn to a female sun by planetary attraction. Insensible of anything else, he reached out and touched his fingers to her lips.

Nanyu had never reacted to the female form in such a way before; in fact, he had never had any dealings with women at all. He'd seen them in discreet groups on Nanjing's streets (as on this night), through the windows of restaurants, where they played the *pipa*, or, more frequently, in paintings, including his own. Wherever he sighted them (or imagined them), they had seemed to be little more than innocuous elements of scenery, two-dimensional and round of countenance, with inexpressive little dots for their eyes and mouths. The religious statuary he'd seen before this evening had done little to deepen this impression.

Nanyu was unprepared for this awakening of interest, and he wondered how to account for it. Could it have been that his father, who had just set him the task of choosing his own occupation, expected him also to choose his own wife? If so, Nanyu mused, why couldn't he have someone like this alluring bodhisattva? He began making inquiries for the idol itself, taking care to avoid such words as "buy" and "how much?" — one did not "buy" religious artifacts or sutras; one "asked for" them — but the reality was that he was short on cash. He regretted having splurged on the Four Treasures and the album, but even had he not done so, the demi-goddess would have remained beyond his reach. Suppressing his desire for the time being, he collected himself and began his journey back across the street, reflecting that he now had something to work for

He had not taken three steps before he was confronted and stopped in his tracks by two burly men waving sticks, runners clearing the way for a scholar in an unenclosed sedan chair borne by four more hulks, which followed close behind. The litter's corpulent passenger wore a draping blue robe and appeared to Nanyu to be levitating above the street. The floating blue-bodied beast was crowned by a black official's hat, with its stiffened straps jutting straight out from his head, and wore on his imposing visage a thick, black beard. He seemed to be issuing instructions to someone walking beside him, a tall youth who looked even taller than he was, owing to the towering horsehair hat he wore.

Even as they gave the scholar, or at least his runners, the wide berth he demanded, most people in the crowd followed him with fascinated stares, and Nanyu was no exception. He was on the verge of making eye contact with both the grandee and his attendant when he heard a hissing sound, and a gray line of smoke cleft his field of vision. As soon as he realized that a little rocket had flown by him, it exploded, and all he could see was white. Nanyu staggered, temporarily blind. His ears were ringing too, though he could still make out the sound of children's laughter.

He would sleep with his father in the marketplace, on the unsold four-poster bed, which they carted back home in the morning.

喧喧 喧喧 喧喧

A few days later, the Ouyangs, father and son, paid a visit to the Temple at the Edge of Heaven, to see if any work needed doing there. They found the abbot, Baichi Shi'ai, in the Mahayana Pavilion. The monk greeted them with a grin so beatific as to suggest abysmal ignorance.

"Would you like a cup of spring?" he sang. "Have a cup of spring!"

He spilled his own unfinished drink right onto the stone floor and withdrew from a small drawer a pouch of dried tea leaves. Replenishing his cup with them, he added boiling water.

The three sat silently, the Ouyangs awkwardly, the abbot still grinning, as they watched the steam rise. A good ten minutes later, Baichi Shi'ai helped himself to the first sip and then passed the cup to Ouyang Gen, who took a few quick swallows before handing it off to Nanyu, signaling with his eyes that he wished his son to leave the older men to talk business. While the carpenter resigned himself to spending the greater part of the day attempting to tease a work order from the flighty abbot, Nanyu, raising the cup to its owner and taking it with him, stepped out.

He climbed a planked stairway up a little knob and soon reached one of his favorite places, the stand of Verdant Immortal Pines, which marked the western edge of the temple grounds. From there, he could look back upon the entire hillside complex, with its succession of tree-shrouded shrines — the Hall of the

Heavenly King, the Precious Hall of the Mahavira, the Hall of the Three Holies, The Dari Rulai Temple — each rising behind the last. He could also enjoy the view to the west, where Rain Flower Terrace was now catching the midmorning sun. Nanyu wrapped both hands around the warm teacup and lifted it toward his lips. As he sipped, the rising steam bathed his face and cleared his lungs as well as his head, and the brew itself seemed to spread through his body, relaxing his muscles and heightening his senses. He took a deep breath, closed his eyes, and turned toward the sun. Slowly exhaling, he beheld a sightless display of swirling, pulsating orange.

Nanyu still carried the brushes, ink, and stone from Three Mountain Street, as well as the blank four-leaf album. Arranging his Four Treasures on a flat rock, he realized he lacked water for mixing ink; but then he recalled something that Baichi Shi'ai often said: "The sage recognizes a 'this,' but a 'this' which is also 'that,' a 'that' which is also 'this.'" Spilling a bit of his remaining tea onto the inkstone, he quickly concocted a pallet of spring colors, using the surrounding view as his guide.

As the sun climbed toward its apogee, Nanyu created, on the first page of his album, a cicada, emerging from its nymph shell, on the limb of an oak. Climbing out of its old skin, it seemed ready to fly at once, with its sleek body, silver wings, and opaque red eyes. Nanyu added a broad smudge of green, representing the outline of mountains in the distance, but he included no additional landscape, and the cicada dominated the picture. To the insect's right, in bold, italic curtains of characters that seemed to radiate from its body, he wrote an inscription, using the popular name for cicada, *zhi liao*, which sounds like its piercing call and also like the (Chinese) phrase "I know."

In spring, their backs split,
Then, your ears:
'Zhi liao! Zhi liao!
I know, I know...'

In mountains
And in city streets:
'Zhi liao! Zhi liao!
I know, I know...'

Bustling, swarming,
Always rising:
'Zhi liao! Zhi liao!
I know, I know...'

From cast-off skins,
On up to Heaven:
'Zhi liao! Zhi liao!
I know, I know...'

Nanyu put down his brush and blinked. He peered down at the Mahayana Pavilion but found neither his father nor Baichi Shi'ai there. He continued looking downslope, past the temple's drum tower (whose announcements of the passing hours Nanyu hadn't noted), to the "new cells" where laypeople often lodged, including several of the students among his fledgling clientele. There, he was surprised to spot not his father but the young man with the horsehair hat whom he had seen taking orders from the blue-robed heavyweight in the sedan chair on the night of the Lantern Festival. He carried a pole across his shoulders with large wicker baskets hanging from each end. He was circulating among the new cells, greeting every young student he met and presenting him with meats and other delicacies from the baskets. Each of these transactions was accompanied by a nodding banter, and then the youth in the tall hat would produce a calling card from his sleeve and hand it to the student. The latter would receive the card with both hands, making obeisance. Occasionally, a student would also be given one or more of the Four Treasures, as well as books.

Nanyu observed the young man at this business for a good while, long enough for the smell of the meat to waft its way up to where he was standing and to make him hungry. Just as he was pondering how late he was for lunch, he realized that the horsehair-hatted youth was staring up at him. Their eyes met, and the visitor in the new cells turned his head sideways to consider Nanyu in the pines, his horsehair hat leaning accordingly and accentuating not his height but his apparent fascination. Suddenly the hat righted itself and then, as Nanyu watched, the young man placed his burden against a wall, vanished briefly from view, and reappeared directly below, climbing the planked steps toward him. Nanyu didn't move and neither man smiled; nor, after the newcomer had reached Nanyu's place, did either man speak.

The young man in the horsehair hat surveyed the temple and the terrace and then turned his attention closer at hand, to Nanyu's album. He studied it a while. Finally, he said, "Did you paint that?"

Nanyu motioned with his eyes at his ink and brushes and smiled helpfully.

"It's a cicada," said the other.

"I know."

"That's a weird way to write the inscription, right in the picture like that."

"I guess it is."

"Are you going to sell it?"

"I might. Maybe a few of the students here would like it. I've sold pictures to them before."

"So you're an artist?"

Again, Nanyu only smiled.

"But you don't look like a student, yourself."

"I'm not a student. My father is a carpenter, and I'm...maybe I'll be an artist."

The young man in the horsehair hat looked back and forth at Nanyu and at the cicada. Then he said, "You shouldn't sell it to any of the bookworms here. They're poor and can't pay much."

"Do you know some of them?"

"I know that they're poor."

"What were you doing at the new cells, just now?"

"Favors. Helping them out."

"That's nice of you."

The youth in the horsehair hat raised his eyebrows. "You're pretty sarcastic," he said. "Can't I be nice if I want to?"

Nanyu held his tongue. They were both about the same age, he reckoned, and they were equally tall, minus the hat. In brawn, too, they were evenly matched. Nanyu was intrigued, furthermore, to see a bit of himself in the other's expression: intense, slightly dour, but with a tinge of optimism, befitting someone who habitually expected the worst while hoping for the best, which policy Nanyu now adopted.

After a similar pause, the other one asked, "You've never seen me here before?"

"No," replied Nanyu, truthfully.

The horsehair hat grew even taller. "Cui is my surname. I am the chamberlain of His Excellency Wei Su, who passed the metropolitan examination last year."

"Oh."

"Are you being sarcastic again?"

There was another brief standoff and stand down. "Anyway, you can call me Big Brother Cui...Aren't you going to tell me your name?"

"Ouyang."

"Ouyang? Do you have a sister?"

"Sorry. I'm an only child."

"Don't misunderstand me. I was just curious, mind you. Ouyang is an unusual name."

"It's not that unusual."

"Where are you from?"

"Here."

Cui looked down at the temple.

"*Near* here," Nanyu said. "I'm not a monk." He removed his hat and emphatically mussed up his hair.

"All right, then. Neither monk nor student. Maybe an artist."

"You still haven't said what you were doing down there."

"I said I was helping the students out."

"And I said that was nice of you."

"It's not nice of me. It's nice of His Excellency Wei Su."

"Oh."

"'Oh.' 'Oh' for Ouyang." The horsehair hat shook from side to side. Cui faced toward the Temple at the Edge of Heaven and spread his arms. "You have *clients* down there, don't you, Ouyang Oh, the artist? Well, so does His Excellency."

"Clients?"

"Clients."

"Oh."

Cui let his arms fall to his sides. "Don't sell the cicada, little brother." Then he began walking back down the stairs toward the new cells.

🝔🝔🝔

The Ouyangs lived in a row house across Shakyamuni Street from the temple. Through their front door was the kitchen, where the brick stove was built against the front wall, permitting ventilation through a large, paneless window, opening back onto the street. Here, the Ouyangs stored, prepared, and ate their food, mostly vegetables but sometimes a little beancurd, pork, or chicken, with rice. The next room heading in was a small sitting and storage space, with a ladder leading up to a sleeping loft, which was where Ouyang Gen retired each evening. Ouyang Nanyu slept in the third room of the house, the cluttered workshop, which opened onto a communal courtyard in the rear.

The day after he drew the cicada, Nanyu was eager to return to his spot under the Verdant Immortal Pines and perhaps add another creation to his album, but the weather was threatening, and he decided not to risk his work getting wet. He leaned against the front door frame, wondering what to do if not to draw, for his father, laboring in the workshop, now refused his assistance. Just as he figured he might as well visit his clients at the temple, he noticed Cui of the horsehair hat coming up Shakyamuni Street.

Nanyu moved aside, and Cui stooped through the door. He inspected the kitchen, before turning toward Nanyu. His dour face then arrayed itself, and his eyebrows jumped once.

"Congratulations!" he said. "His Excellency Wei Su has taken an interest in your work! The emerging cicada you painted is a good omen for him as he embarks on his official career. He leaves in a few days for Beijing, where he will receive his first appointment. He would like you to follow him there and to join his entourage. You can live at his mansion and paint more pictures—anything that suggests *rising* or advancement. When you finish the album, he'll pay you four ounces of silver, and who knows what opportunities there'll be after that!"

Nanyu swayed in his shoes. "Beijing?" he said. "He wants me to go to the capital, just like that? I've never even met him."

"But you've met me, right? I told His Excellency about the cicada, and he wants it. He has a good eye for art. You're trying to make it as an artist, aren't you? Don't you want a rich patron, or are you doing well enough with the whelps at the temple?"

"I also sell to the storyteller on Three Mountain Street."

"My, you've really made it big." Cui looked sideways at Nanyu, his face a masterpiece of amusement and derision. "So, that's enough for you, huh? The storyteller on Three Mountain Street."

"Wait a minute. I can't just leave. What about my father?"

"Of course—your father. Well, let's put it to him and see what he says. Besides, I gotta take a piss." With that, Cui invaded deeper into the Ouyangs' house, through the sitting room and the workshop, where Ouyang Gen looked up from the board he was planing, and into the courtyard. Since other families were watching, he turned around to face the Ouyangs (Nanyu having followed him into the workshop) and began peeing against their outer wall.

"Mr Ouyang," he said, keeping his attention trained downward, "My surname is Cui. I am the chamberlain of His Excellency Wei Su, who recently passed the metropolitan examination and will soon be journeying to Beijing to take up his post. His Excellency has noticed your son's work and wishes to employ him. He's offered four ounces for your son's album of auspicious images, as soon as it's finished. Ah…finished." He closed his robe and reentered the workshop.

"Four," Ouyang Gen said. "Such an unlucky number."

"One album of four leaves at one ounce apiece. Have you seen it yet?"

"No."

Ouyang Nanyu nipped into the sitting room, returning with the album, which he presented to his father. Appraising it, Ouyang Gen became very serious and still. He remained impassive, while both artist and presumptive patron awaited his verdict.

Cui broke the silence. "Not bad, eh? I'll bet you didn't know your son had such talent—enough to make a living, even. Four ounces of silver for a little doodling is nothing to sneeze at. Plus, you're both as good as in His Excellency Wei Su's household."

At this last remark, Ouyang Gen frowned. "That doesn't enter into it," he said. "But now that you mention Wei Su, I don't think a picture of a cicada is going to bring him much luck under the circumstances. This is a bad time for anybody to be heading north to start a new career."

Cui flashed a smile. "Are you worried about the Dashing Prince?" he asked, referring to Li Zicheng, the furloughed postal courier turned bandit. "He's far away, in Xi'an. Grand Secretary Li Jiantai will be leading an army against him soon, and that'll be that."

Nanyu tried to imagine the geography. He also wondered how roving banditry could be a problem anywhere in China, when Nanjing, at least, seemed so prosperous.

Meanwhile, his father was asking, "You're going up on the Grand Canal?"

"Yes," Cui said. "His Excellency sets out in a few days, and we'll follow with the rest of his accoutrements. We've got a nice boat all fitted out, just for little brother, here, and for His Excellency's new wife—I almost forgot: Her name is Ouyang, too. Hey, what's that?" He was pointing at the four-poster bed that nobody had bought during the Lantern Festival.

"A bed."

"Did you make it?"

"Yes."

Cui walked over to it slowly, cocking his hatted head. "Mandarin ducks, huh?"

"Mmm."

The Ouyangs' visitor inspected the bed all around. He placed both hands on one of the posts and shook it, to ensure it wouldn't wobble when used. Finally he said, "His Excellency will be wanting this, too. Eighty-four ounces of silver."

"Eighty-*four*? Oh, I get it. Twice forty, plus four. How generous."

"You'd prefer eighty-three?"

Ouyang Gen rested his hands on his hips and looked at his son, who looked at the floor. "Mr Cui, you'll have to let me think about it."

"You'd better think quickly. I'll be by tomorrow for your answer. We leave in four days."

"Four days. I see. Son, show him out."

Nanyu wordlessly followed Cui, who walked through the house to the front entrance and wordlessly exited. Without stopping to watch him go, Nanyu turned on his heels and doubled back to the workshop where his father stood, leaning against a cabinet.

Ouyang Gen shook his head and issued a caustic snort. "He's probably going to get five for the album and a hundred for the bed from his boss and then deduct a little handling fee for himself."

"Yes, Father. I suppose he will."

The carpenter again seemed to be trying to suspend time. Finally, he shrugged. "Even so, the lout isn't wrong. It is a lot of silver. The Dashing Prince is still off to the west, but even if he gets out of hand—especially if he gets out of hand—a little extra money would be useful. I'd rather have a bag of silver than a bed to lug around, in case we have to go somewhere in a hurry. I don't like you getting tied up with that official in Beijing, but we don't want to get on his bad side, either." He looked at his son.

"No, Father, we don't."

"Well...Maybe he'll be so happy with his new wife that he'll forget all about you. Just get in and get out. Finish the album, however he wants it, and earn whatever money you can. Let me know where you are, and I'll write to you and say that I'm sick. He'll have to let you come home then. Both he and his horsehair-hatted puppy will be in Beijing for the three years of his posting at least, and that should give us time to sort things out. We'll muddle through this."

"I know we will, Father. Please don't worry about me; I can take care of myself. I'll come home as soon as you write, and then we'll be together again."

Ouyang Gen's eyes fell on the album, still open at the page with the cicada. He nodded, and his son withdrew to the kitchen to prepare lunch. Soon came the sound of something sizzling in the wok, and only then did the carpenter resume his planing.

2

March to April, 1644

Nanyu embarked on his northward journey four days later (the same day Grand Secretary Li Jiantai's army left Beijing for the front and immediately began disintegrating). His father brought him and the four-poster bed to the Longjiang dockyard, early on that gray morning. The horsehair-hatted Cui, leaping back and forth from pier to boat as he oversaw the preparations for departure, noted their arrival. He called together a squad of porters, ordered them to unload the bed from the Ouyangs' cart, and handed Ouyang Gen a sack containing eighty-four ounces of silver. Then he withdrew, to allow father and son to say their goodbyes. The Ouyangs only exchanged meaningful looks. Ouyang Gen then got back on the cart and rode away without looking back, and Nanyu watched him go.

The boat was a shallow-draft junk with one sail and a modest cabin amidships. What was now Wei Su's four-poster marriage bed was partly disassembled, lashed in a low pile to the afterdeck, and covered with a tarpaulin. Nanyu counted a crew of six men and surmised that they would spend most of their time on the foredeck, when not handling the sail, manning the sweeps, or poling or pulling the boat. It occurred to him that he would have to eat and sleep among them, for it seemed unlikely that he, a mere artist, would be housed in the cabin. Also, wasn't there supposed to be a woman on board? Sure enough, Cui soon rode off, accompanied by a hulking attendant, leaving Nanyu with nothing to do but to get in the way of the crew and dock hands. When Cui returned, over three hours later, he was escorting the boat's sole female passenger.

She was dressed like a nun, with a bulky gray over-robe that reached to the ground. Her head was shaved, and she wore no cap. In the moment between her arrival via donkey and conveyance into the boat's cabin, Nanyu observed that she was rather tall and that she was about his age. Nanyu also, despite his inexperience with women and the brevity of this near-encounter on the dock, was able to discern in the new arrival's face two things: that she was extremely intelligent and that she was seething with rage. Apropos of nothing, he made a mental note that he could not legally marry her because she had the same surname as he. He recalled something about sixty strokes of the bamboo for any same-surnamed couple who tried it.

Cui took Nanyu's album and stored it in the cabin, with the woman, for safekeeping. "How am I supposed to work on it," Nanyu asked, "if it's locked away like that?"

"You're not, little brother. His Excellency will tell you what to paint when we get to Beijing. You can make sketches if you want, for practice. Otherwise, just enjoy the ride."

With its treasure secured, its crew on board, and with Cui and Nanyu now ignoring each other on the foredeck, the boat cast off from the pier and entered the current of the Yangtze, a slight breeze filling its sail.

While he had lived beside it all his life, Nanyu had never been on the river before, but as all traces of Nanjing receded from view, he found that water travel suited him. The rocking of the boat was soothing, and as long as Cui and the boatmen stayed out of his immediate space, the experience was almost meditative. The

Yangtze itself was broad and open and featureless. The overcast offered protection from the glare of the sun, muted the colors and sounds, and provided a comforting sense of cover beneath a vast ceiling. The human habitations along the shore were far enough away for him to appreciate quietly as they rolled by, like the dreamlike scenes of a horizontal landscape painting, scrolling from left to right. Occasionally a grain barge or two-masted ship would pass jarringly close by, overtaking Nanyu's boat or moving in the opposite direction; but it would soon fade into oblivion, leaving Nanyu's vista as it had been, mercifully devoid of stimulation.

The afternoon lolled by, and then Cui distributed some Nanjing pressed duck for the evening meal. Nanyu noticed a tray of it placed outside the cabin and then disappear within. Cui ordered one of the crew to retrieve and empty the woman's chamber pot, but it was not forthcoming, as she was apparently able to dump it overboard herself. When it became too dark for the boat to proceed, the crew dropped anchor and then began hoisting up buckets of river water for washing bodies and clothes, and one bucket was passed through the curtained window of the cabin. Then, after posting a watch, the remaining crew spread blankets and lay down on the foredeck. Nanyu looked up for a while at a single bright star shining through the thinning clouds, so silent and far away that it made him feel lonely and a little afraid. He turned over on his side, but the sight of the entwined bodies of the other men repulsed him. Finally, he curled up against the cabin. He thought he heard sounds of life within, which soon dissolved into a dream.

Soon after the raising of the anchor the next morning, Nanyu realized that his Yangtze River idyll of the day before was not to be repeated, for boat traffic increased, and then, just before Guazhou, the entrance to the Grand Canal appeared on the north bank. Cui ordered the boatmen to make the port turn, and the scenery changed considerably, as the boat was now traversing a narrower waterway, pressed on both sides by quays, warehouses, and bustle. The men were laboring with sweeps and poles, and Nanyu felt obliged to lend a hand. However, Cui wouldn't let him, decreeing, "There's no need for artists to do such work," thus creating resentment toward Nanyu amongst the crew. They anchored for the night below Yangzhou, at a bend with a pagoda. Cui sent into town for some steamed buns, stuffed with crabmeat. The canal water was too dirty even for the washing of clothes, and so Cui had to obtain water from shore as well.

The next day, Cui arranged for the boat to be roped together with other northbound vessels, mostly smaller passenger craft, to be pulled by a team of oxen. Nanyu now felt crowded from the front and rear, as well as from the sides. He wished he could get up higher, for a better view of his surroundings, but he decided against climbing atop the cabin for fear of attracting too much attention and so resigned himself to the uncomfortable, disorienting ride. Lacking sufficient work space and subject matter, and unwilling to put up with the mockery of the crew, he couldn't so much as sketch anything.

For seven days, the little flotilla bumped along northward, past the towns of Shaobo and Gaoyou, negotiating its way through locks and gates every few hours, while the men on board tried to keep provisioned. Despite Cui's best efforts as forager, the unbalanced diet of too much greasy meat and not enough vegetables soon gave Nanyu and his shipmates diarrhea, and so the men spent much of each day hanging their *pigu*s over the side. The crew boiled water obtained ashore in a kettle over a small stove on the foredeck, but they now drank most of it to combat dehydration, leaving less for washing clothes. Cold breezes blew in from the west, over the big lakes that kept the Canal supplied with water. As most of the men, including Nanyu, had neglected to bring warm clothing, they were forced to huddle together when they could, in an increasingly pungent mass. Finally, they reached the inland port of Huai'an, where the convoy broke up, and Cui called for the vessel to be docked for an extra day, permitting a little rest, washing, and securing of healthier victuals and warmer clothes. With a clean robe and padded jacket provided by Cui, Nanyu stretched his legs on shore but was careful not to wander off into the strange, dusty city. When it was time to set out again the following morning, he felt refreshed but also experienced and disabused of any picturesque illusions about traveling by boat.

Nanyu's newfound stoicism equipped him admirably and, ignoring Cui's protestations, he began to help the crew in the handing of the ropes, as the boat was winched through a series of locks that conveyed it into the Yellow River. Nanyu was not so much impressed by the pathetic muddy stream as he was by the width of dry riverbed and the height of the dikes surrounding it, which attested to its legendary propensity to flood. Even after the waterborne party crossed the river and the Canal turned left to run upstream behind its northern bank for a couple of days, earthworks towered on either side. At length, they passed beyond the Yellow River's potential tyranny. The levees became lower, and Nanyu could see that they had entered a less densely populated country, lined with streams and with tufts of little mountains in the distance. There was still the occasional lock to traverse, however, and Nanyu would not spare his own labor to capture the scene in ink. He kept himself busy and useful as the boat passed out of Nanjing Province and crossed into Shandong.

Just beyond a tributary called Witch Mountain Spring, Nanyu noticed two white cranes flying upstream and then perching on the embankment. When the boat drew close to them, they took off again, swooping on ahead, before coming to a new resting place at the side of the Canal. Nanyu reckoned that the cranes moved ten times this way over the course of an hour—leading and waiting, leading and waiting—as though luring him ever onward. They didn't seem to be feeding, and if they were migrating north, Nanyu wondered why they didn't just get on with it, without waiting for him to catch up. If they wanted to stay on the Canal but were afraid of the boat, then why didn't they fly to the side, to allow it to pass? For the rest of the day, Nanyu was sometimes invited to share food, sometimes asked for help maneuvering through a lock, and then, he would forget about the cranes; but whenever his activities were finished, he'd look up and there they would be, still scouting out the route.

Nanyu continued to see them after he closed his eyes that night, but in the morning, they were gone. Missing them, he took up a vigil on the bow and was surprised when the boat rounded a bend and a cascade of water appeared on his left, pouring into the Canal over a dam from a huge lake. They were entering the country of the Four Southern Lakes, named for their situation in southern Shandong. Nanyu turned his face toward the cool breeze and shimmering water, and the day drifted by. They tied up for the evening in what was once the middle of Zhaoyang Lake, though there was now dry lakebed on the right (the Canal's embankments acting to hold the water back), permitting scattered settlement. Zhaoyang, meaning "Shining Sun," now reflected only the moon, at least on the western side, and Nanyu fell under its influence. He remembered the disassembled marriage bed on the afterdeck and thought he would try to stretch out on it, using the tarpaulin as a mattress. When all but the watch were asleep, he disengaged himself from his slumbering shipmates, tiptoed around the cabin, and curled up on the tarp, with one of the flat-lying posts serving as a decent pillow. The watchman in the stern was snoring, and Nanyu began to drift off too, under the unblinking stare of the rabbit in the moon. Water lapped against the hull and poured into the Canal through spillways, lulling him further, and soon his eyes were closed.

Sometime later, Nanyu felt, through his sleep, something bonking him on the head. It wasn't heavy, nor was it hard; in fact, it was rather soft, yet substantial. It seemed to burst apart, sending little balls, like marbles, rolling down his face and bouncing onto his chest. He flickered his eyes open but found it difficult to see, for there was a piece of cloth on his brow. Sitting up, he grabbed it away, and several more of the little orbs rolled off his body. The piece of cloth, he discovered, was a cotton kerchief, and the round pellets were dried cherries.

"Are you awake?"

It was the voice of the woman in the cabin, whispered through the fluttering curtains. In the initial misery and subsequent stoicism of his Grand Canal experience, he had almost forgotten about her.

"Um, I think I am. What was that?"

"A kerchief full of cherries."

"You threw it…out the window…at me?"

"Yes."

"Oh." Nanyu continued to shake his head and blink his eyes, as more of the moonlit scene came into focus. He estimated about twenty cherries.

"Do you get the reference?" the woman asked.

"The what?"

"The reference."

"What reference?"

"The cherry reference. About the handsome poet in ancient times. Women would shower him with kerchiefs of fruit wherever he went. Nowadays, it's a way for women to pick the men they like…although in most cases, it's still usually the women who get picked by men."

"I'm handsome?"

"It's just a reference. I've been sealed up in this chicken coop for over a week, and I want someone to talk to. I had nothing else to throw at you."

"Can I eat the cherries?"

"Yes."

Nanyu began to gather and munch on the cherries. It occurred to him that the woman wanted to talk, not to listen to him eat, but he couldn't think of anything to say. At any rate, she spoke first.

"You're the other Ouyang?"

"Yes. I'm Ouyang Nanyu."

"Ouyang Daosheng…Sixty strokes of the bamboo!"

"Is that another reference? I think I got that one."

"Good for you. So you're an artist?

"I guess."

"A cicada, huh? Emerging, rising, joining voices, making a lot of noise. Not bad."

"So you've looked at it?"

"Not much else to do in here."

"I kind of forgot all about it. All I can think about is this little boat ride."

"And what's waiting for us at the end of it."

"Actually, I haven't thought about that part at all."

"You haven't?"

"No. There's no point. My father already told me what to do. He said to wait until he sends for me. He'll write to say he's sick, and then I should be able to get away."

"Good for you again…and thanks for telling me. Aren't you afraid I might betray you to Cui or to Wei himself, tell them that you're planning to escape?"

"Oh…I don't know. I didn't think of that. I thought you said you liked me."

"I said the bit with the cherries was just a reference. Why shouldn't I tattle on you? Anything to placate them would probably be a good idea. They might go easier on me. You and your dad have it all worked out, but what am I going to do? We're not in the same boat."

Nanyu remembered how vexed she had seemed, that day on the pier. "I guess you don't want to go to Beijing?"

"Heavens, you're smart."

"You don't want to marry Wei Su?"

"How could you even ask me that? Cui is dragging me up to Beijing to be his master's young wife, just like he's dragging you up to Beijing to be his master's young artist. You can't imagine a bit how it feels? Why would I like it any more than you do?"

"But Wei Su is rich and can take good care of you."

A punishing silence emanated from the cabin.

Nanyu twisted in the wind a bit, and then he tried to restart the conversation. "All right," he said. "I guess I don't quite understand your situation."

There was a pause, as Daosheng seemed to be weighing the value of continuing. Finally, she said, "No, I guess you don't," and then she tried to tone down the sarcasm by starting again: "No, I guess you wouldn't. How could you have? My situation…" she proceeded slowly, "is that I was kidnapped by Cui on the morning of our departure from Nanjing. I have never met Wei Su, but I've heard his name. I think he must have been jilted by my mother before I was born, and now he's getting back at her by taking me for his concubine. I don't know how many 'wives' he already has."

Now it was Nanyu's turn to pause. He looked out at the lake.

"Who is your mother?" he asked.

"My mother is a former courtesan named Ouyang Zhenli. She lives on the Qinhuai River, in the entertainment district. Do you know it?"

"Yes—I mean I know *of* it."

"I did not grow up there. To hide me from Wei Su, she entrusted me to the nuns at Cock-Crow Temple, and they educated me. Mother would often come see me, taking care she wasn't followed, and I suppose it's amazing that I remained beyond Wei's reach for so long. It was Cui who finally found me. He had been paying frequent visits to the temple to discuss Wei Su's making a donation."

"That's interesting," said Nanyu. "Cui visits the Temple at the Edge of Heaven too, to gather 'clients.' That's how he found me."

"Evidently His Excellency buys friends from your temple and karma from mine. At any rate, during one of his calls, Cui must have heard about the apprentice nun named Ouyang, and then he and his master put two and two together."

"But how could Cui just take you away?"

"That's the part I'm not sure about. He had a piece of paper which he said was my contract with my mother's house—making my mother my madam, if you know what I mean—and which he said that Wei had bought out. Whether the abbess accepted the proof or not—and I doubt that she did, knowing Mother's and my situation—there was no point arguing with the 'chamberlain to His Excellency Wei Su' and so I was taken away, with almost no time to pack anything. It's very odd, though. I can't imagine that Mother would sell me to Wei like that, after going through all that trouble to keep me from him, and I don't think I had a contract at all. But the truth is I don't really know what Mother's plans for me were. We never had enough time to discuss it. I learned how to read and sing and play the *pipa*, and I always assumed," she struggled for words, "that I would have at least a few *choices*, that I would be able to attract a man the way Mother did, or write poetry, or just weave, or become a true nun."

"What about your father?"

"I don't know anything about him."

"What do you think you'll do?"

"Well, that's a simple question with no simple answer. Under the circumstances, I'm not even able to control what I *won't* do."

Nanyu said nothing. From the way her voice sounded, he could imagine her looking down at her hands in her lap, thinking out loud.

"I suppose that on the first auspicious day after we get to Beijing, Wei will hire some musicians and invite his creepy friends over for a party, and they'll write poems and drink themselves silly, while he 'combs my hair' in the next room."

"You don't have any hair."

"It's an expression. You're not very learned, are you?"

"I never said I was."

"Well, you might want to work on that. You taught yourself to paint, after all. Maybe you could try opening a book or two."

"But we were talking about you."

"No, I was talking about me...and my hair....Well, in the short term, it looks like I'm fucked, wouldn't you say?...No, you're too shocked to say. Have no fear, though: In the long term, poor, helpless Ouyang Daosheng has a few things going in her favor."

"She does? I mean, you do?"

"Yes. One of them is the Dashing Prince."

"Huh? You mean Li Zicheng?"

"Yes. Whatever they call him, he's going to be causing a lot of confusion in Beijing pretty soon, and maybe I'll be able to slip away. Maybe I'll even join him. I hear that one of his generals is a woman—a former general, actually, because she ran off with another man, but so much the better."

"But the Dashing Prince is still far away from Beijing."

"So goes the official story. Was it Xi'an, where he was supposed to be, before we left? Perhaps it's still true, but it sure doesn't feel that way. Haven't you noticed that the northbound canal traffic has slacked off, the past few days? Maybe people know things we don't, or at least they're not taking any chances."

"I hadn't noticed. I guess you're right."

"You're not very observant, for an artist."

"I guess I'm more of the dreamy kind of artist."

"Are you also more of the dreamy kind of boatman? You've been mixing in with the crew, lately. Don't you hear them complaining about the extra tolls we've been paying, 'to equip the local militia'? Haven't you sensed how worried they are about being pressed into service or having the boat commandeered?"

"No. But now that you mention it..." Nanyu's voice trailed off. The night suddenly seemed darker, as he belatedly appreciated various menaces all at once. Yet the more Daosheng frightened him with reality, the more she also intrigued him. There was something reassuring in her capacity to disturb. "You said you had 'a few things' going in your favor," he said. "Are there more?"

"Ah, indeed there are. Two more, in fact. Only, I'm not going to tell you what they are. You're going to have to notice them. You're going to have to pay attention."

Nanyu began to glance about, at the boat, the lake, and the shore, looking for any hint of what Daosheng meant. He heard her rise inside the cabin and begin pacing, which he took as an expression of impatience. In the moonlight, he searched the deck, looking for a note or some other kind of clue that Daosheng might have thrown out for him. He found nothing. Daosheng began pacing faster, more insistently. Growing flummoxed,

Nanyu stood up and scanned the horizon for the answer. He looked up at the sky. Had she made some sort of astrological reference? From the cabin came the sounds of Daosheng skipping, in stockinged feet only, to keep from waking anyone else, but unmistakable. Nanyu became frantic. He had no idea what he should be looking for and just stood there wringing his hands. He was almost crying. Daosheng began dancing a jig, as though to drive him into a panic with the tapping of her feet. His heart was racing with stress, and he would have done anything to silence her foot beats, for he could think of nothing else but them; and then his heart almost stopped altogether, with a feeling of being punched in the chest, and he turned in the direction of the cabin and gasped: "You have unbound feet!"

"Very perceptive of you."

"*Gross!*"

"Very poetic of you."

"You…you have men's feet! You're not a real woman!"

"I guess it is gross, isn't it? And that's the idea."

"Huh?"

"Well, when His Excellency Wei Su beholds these monstrous dogs of mine, it'll ruin his party. He may even be too upset to comb my hair."

"How come he doesn't already know that you've got men's feet?"

"Cui was so eager to verify that my *yumen* was intact he forgot to ensure that my feet were maimed. Of course, he assumed that they were, as did Wei. As did you."

"But why didn't your mother bind your feet, like she should have?"

"She wanted to, definitely. Her own 'three-inch golden lotuses' took her a long way, from the backwater village where her grandmothers were big-footed farmers, to the Qinhuai River 'flower district,' with all its art, opera and poetry, where she could choose whichever man she wanted. I have to admit, it worked out very well for her, and I know that she loved me too much not to give me the same opportunities."

"So what happened?" asked Nanyu, lying back down on the tarpaulin.

"As I told you, I wasn't raised by my mother; I was raised by nuns. 'In dharma,' they said, 'there is no male or female;' so they were quite unconcerned about whether I should have 'ladies feet.' In fact, Mother brought the bindings to the temple several times, around when I was seven or so, and she softened my feet with oil and wrapped them up good and snug. But the abbess, old One-Eyed Jingang, always ordered the bindings removed as soon as Mother left. Mother was furious, but Jingang wouldn't budge, and of course, what could Mother do? She couldn't risk drawing attention by making more of a fuss or by moving me. I was very perplexed at the time, as you can imagine, but Jingang taught me a rhyme:

> "'Real men' and 'real women' — why split hairs,
> If Guanyin Bodhisattva doesn't care?
> Would you peel off the Bodhisattva's skin,
> Just to see if it's a man or a woman?

"Not a bad way of looking at it, it seems to me. What do you think?"

By now exhausted and slipping into dream, Nanyu grasped at female images, from his unremembered mother's, to unseen Daosheng's, to that of Guanyin Bodhisattva, recently enthroned in his mind as the quintessential woman — right down to her unbound feet.

"I'm confused," he said.

"Good," Daosheng whispered. "And goodnight, Other Ouyang. I hope your bed is comfortable."

☐☐ ☐☐ ☐☐

They travelled another ten days, with Nanyu deciding against further conversation with Daosheng, for fear of inciting gossip if discovered. Finally, at the Canal's northern terminus of Tongzhou, the passengers disembarked and the cargo was offloaded. Daosheng was whisked onward by sedan chair, and Nanyu, with his four-leaf album restored to him, rode with Cui atop the still-collapsed bed, on a donkey cart. In time, the walls of Beijing loomed before them. They worked their way along the eastern rampart, heading north, until they came to the Dongzhi Gate, which they entered. What struck Nanyu most was the dust. It seemed to lend everything—the streets, the buildings, the people, and even the air—a dreary, beige tint, and he felt it grinding between his teeth. Donkeys were everywhere, as was their shit. Affecting Nanyu most directly, though, was the smell of charcoal, used by the myriad denizens of the capital for cooking and heating. Breathing in its soot, along with all the other dust, gave Nanyu a feeling like pneumonia, as his lungs became clogged. He soon began hacking and coughing up gobs of charcoal-streaked phlegm, which he splattered onto the ground, among millions of other splatters of charcoal-streaked phlegm.

They turned onto Bell Tower Street, which was narrow and lined with tall, gray walls, making Nanyu feel claustrophobic. There were portals through the walls at irregular intervals, and the cart stopped at one of them, along the northern side of the street, which was decorated with festive "double happiness" banners in red. Four porters emerged, and Cui ordered them to unload the bed.

Chamberlain Cui conducted Nanyu inside, through an entrance hallway with a screen wall at the end of it, upon which was a large medallion showing a *taotie*, a mythical creature known to eat everything in sight. Walking toward it, Nanyu prepared to be devoured himself, but Cui steered him to the left, into the first of the mansion's three courtyards, the one intended for servants.

Cui bade him deposit his belongings in a little cell and then join the other menials for a bit of dinner. From a cauldron on a charcoal stove in the courtyard, a cook ladled out a bowl of wonton soup and grudgingly presented it to Nanyu. Most of the others were unhappy at Nanyu's presence as well, yet when they understood that he was "His Excellency's new artist," they became deferential. From their subdued chatter, Nanyu gathered that the Dashing Prince had attacked Datong, just a few days' march away, and that the troops of its garrison had killed their commander — a prince of the blood — and surrendered the city. The rebels' final advance on Beijing appeared imminent. Some of Nanyu's messmates expressed confidence that the capital could withstand a siege, but others were not so sure. In addition to the military situation, Nanyu learned that His Excellency's new marriage bed had been set up in the main hall of the third courtyard, and he imagined Daosheng sitting on it, waiting. Her deflowering party had been planned for four days' hence. Nanyu finished his meal, took a much-needed splash bath, and retired for the night.

Wei Su was said to be extremely busy and never met with Nanyu to discuss his plans for the album. Nanyu felt useless and bored over the next few days, and he wasn't sure whether it made more sense for him to settle into his new surroundings or to flee. Though the idea of staying in Beijing was growing less appealing by the hour, an easy return to Nanjing seemed quite beyond hope, for Nanyu had no travel money. The original plan—writing to his father, waiting for a summons home, and applying to Wei Su for an honorable discharge—also appeared pointless, as events would probably be overtaking him, forcing a quick decision. Nanyu finally determined that it would be worth it to get a message to his father anyway. He rose from the charcoal-heated *kang* in his quarters and moved to the little cabinet where he had stored his Four Treasures. Noticing the four-leaf album leaning against it, he suddenly craved the sight of his cicada and whatever comfort and encouragement it might bring. Nanyu opened the cover, and what he saw bewildered him. His cicada was no longer alone. The second leaf had been completed.

Facing Nanyu's portrait of the cicada, there was now a depiction of a group of lotuses in a pond or lake. The flowers were in full bloom, with yellow centers surrounded by pink-and-purple-tinged petals. The brushwork followed Nanyu's sharply-defined style, but the composition was more complete, including the still water of the lake, scattered clouds, and lush, distant hills, all watched over by a daytime moon, odd but not entirely incongruous. Looking closely, Nanyu could see two insects on one of the lotuses: another cicada, inert and dull; and a mantis, creeping up behind it, preparing to strike.

"Daosheng," Nanyu said out loud.

He had no idea how she'd managed to create such a luxuriant summer scene, confined as she had been in a canal boat cabin, heading through the barren north in early spring. He did, though, catch her reference to the common saying, *The mantis stalks the cicada, unaware of the sparrow behind*, which warned of the dangers of supposed impunity. However, Daosheng had omitted the sparrow. Did she mean that the cicada really *could* be devoured with impunity, that no timely rescue by the sparrow, or punishment of the mantis, should be expected?

The inscription, which seemed to shine from the moon, read:

Summer's shrill chorus comes alive
It splits our ears
'Zhi liao! Zhi liao!'
You say you know

A long way from the muddy farm
This lovely lake
Where now we pause
We think we know

We're not the only ones to claim
This precious place:
Far bigger bugs
Come stalking us

Our only hope, the sages say
Lies in the present:
Live for today
Is all I know.

3

April to May, 1644

The day of Daosheng's deflowering party came gray and chilly. The mansion was astir with sweeping and the preparation of food in anticipation of the arrival of His Excellency's guests — fellow officials and a few musicians — scheduled for mid-afternoon. Nanyu, as usual with nothing to do, hung around through lunchtime. Soon there came the sounds of fussing from over the external wall as a succession of sedan chairs arrived and boisterous greetings — "Long time no see! You old rascal!" — rang out. The partiers made their way in through the door and up the corridor, heading to the master courtyard. Their raucous laughter settled into a low rumble, accented by the muted plucking of a zither, the clattering of dishes, and the barking of orders at servants. Nanyu grew restless, took up his four-leaf album, and went out.

The mood on the street was as tense as Nanyu's own, even though he was wandering aimlessly, looking at the ground, while everyone else was scurrying to get home, some with armfuls of foodstuffs and other necessaries. The sounds of humanity's rushing, however, were muffled by the air, which was hanging especially heavy; the occasional candle or lantern, flickering in the diffused afternoon light, also had a calming effect. Nanyu soon found himself on a little footbridge, one of several that spanned a weedy creek running through the neighborhood. Though it was little more than an open sewer, Nanyu paused to contemplate it, and he was cheered to notice a couple of lotus buds rising above the muck. He opened his album and rested it on the railing, comparing the flowers drawn by Daosheng to the struggling plants in the stream below. It was still very chilly in the north, but Nanyu supposed that the sun's heat, stored in the city's bricks, or perhaps the warm waste water, had tricked the summer plants into early wakening. Here in this unlikely place, he tried not just to fathom but to feel the potential hidden in those buds, soon to burst open.

"Marvelous!" came a voice from over his right shoulder. "Extraordinary!"

Nanyu looked and saw an enthusiastic young man, near his own age, dressed about as he was.

"Where did you buy it?" the youth asked, and when Nanyu was slow to answer, he blurted, "Oh, please forgive me! Of course, you have executed the drawings yourself. A fresh-born cicada for spring and lotuses for summer, drawn from your observations of—or should I say inspired by—this little stream. I must say I especially appreciate how you have rendered a more sophisticated picture of the summer as compared to the spring, just as the ten thousand things of creation all mature as the seasons progress."

"Thanks," said Nanyu, and then he became conscious of the need to elevate the tone of his conversation. "Though I dare not accept such unmerited praise."

"Don't be modest!" said the other. "Might I inquire as to your honorable surname?"

"My undistinguished surname is Ouyang, with the personal name Nanyu. And your honorable surname is..?"

"Zhu, given name Ningxin. I've longed to meet you."

"And I you."

"You are clearly a great talent."

"Again, sir, you flatter me."

"Not at all. I assume you are also a scholar?"

"Not officially, no."

"But that is impossible. Your work shows remarkable insight." The young man paused and regarded the painting again. "You have invested an old proverb with new meaning, substituting for the sparrow a daytime 'moon and water,' which symbolizes the Guanyin Bodhisattva and salvation—salvation through resignation or perhaps even faith. Thus, cicada, mantis, and absent sparrow are all one, and the notion of lurking danger is all an illusion, for, once separate existences are discounted, what need has one false self to fear another? The answer, of course, is none; and the best policy, 'living in the present,' as advocated by Wang Yangming, you endorse in your inscription, just in case there is any doubt."

"Ah, so you are a devotee of Wang Yangming?" Nanyu managed.

"Naturally. Who isn't?"

At that moment, a low rumbling echoed from the northwest, as Li Zicheng began attacking the Xizhi gate and Beijing's defenders responded with artillery. The sound of the cannonade intensified and became more general and sustained, so that Nanyu and Ningxin felt themselves surrounded by pulsing vibrations, and the reports of individual guns could no longer be distinguished. The street was suddenly deserted, leaving the two new friends standing alone on the footbridge.

"So now it's come to this," said Zhu Ningxin. "The Dashing Prince is now dashing against the gates of our Sacred Capital."

"Ah, the Dashing Prince. I'd forgotten."

"You had?" Ningxin grinned. "I must say, brother, your

powers of detachment are formidable! 'When your mind is elsewhere, your body follows.'"

"Yes," Nanyu chuckled. "My thoughts have indeed been elsewhere."

"But then again, what else should I have expected from the author of this painting, which illustrates so well the virtue of fearlessness? I consider myself very fortunate to have met you. Here we are, an island of 'tranquility in the tempest,' discoursing on art in the middle of a war. We'd make an interesting picture ourselves."

Nanyu smiled with genuine affection. It was indeed a singular experience they were sharing, which yielded a bonding effect.

Zhu Ningxin said, "Ah, philosophy aside, what are you planning to do? Surely the garrison will hold." (Unbeknownst to him, many of the defending artillerists, in cahoots with the rebels, were firing blanks.) "But if it does not, do you intend to die with the Emperor? I detect a bit of the 'south of the River' in your voice. Will you be trying to make your way back home?"

"Yes, I'd like to, were there a way."

"There is. I myself am from Xinchang, near the mouth of the Yangtze. I came here with my three brothers and three housemen to collect debts, before…well, it seemed like a good time to collect our debts. We're returning tomorrow, and not a moment too soon, I'd say. There should be enough of us to defend our boat from any desperate ruffians, and my older brother Zhu Xiangsun is a provincial degree holder; so he should be able to get us past any *official* obstructions. I'm sure he would be pleased to have a talented lad like you on board. You would be most welcome to join us."

Nanyu dipped his head in thanks. "That would be a great favor," he said. "However, I am not alone. My twin sister is a novice here in Beijing, and I'd like to take her home. Our father wishes to be reunited with both of us."

"Your 'twin sister'? That's an odd way of putting it. How can you convey the correct order of precedence, if you say it like that? Are you her senior or her junior?"

"I was born a few minutes earlier," Nanyu said.

"So she's your *meimei*, then. Please bring her too. You and she will have to stay in the cabin, for you to protect her and for her to serve you."

"We would be most grateful."

"Come to the Bridge of the Great Thoroughfare, ten *li* outside the Dongzhi Gate, tomorrow afternoon."

"Again, brother, you are too kind."

"Think nothing of it. I could not in good conscience abandon such a superb artist and fast friend. Now, I'm afraid we must part for a while. Please stay out of danger."

"And you too, Zhu Ningxin." They exchanged scholars' salutes, raising their arms before their chests as though carrying invisible baskets, with their fingers curled inward and opposing knuckles pressed together. Zhu Ningxin knitted his brow and trotted away across the bridge, keeping his head down. Nanyu lingered a few moments longer, noting how the concussions of the gunfire disturbed the surface of the stream. Then he exited via his side of the bridge and made his way back toward Wei Su's mansion.

He almost walked past the entranceway, for the ostentatious red banners that had marked it had been removed. However, the party in the third courtyard was still going on, despite the bombardment. If anything, it had grown noisier, as though competing with the gun batteries in a contest of volume. Anxious servants hovered in the corridors, afraid to ask whether the festivities should be curtailed. Nanyu salvaged some food from unwatched serving trays. He also pocketed a few extra steamed buns and liberated a flask of tea. After collecting all his clothes, he gave himself a quick splash bath and purloined the soap. Back in his cell, he secured his Four Treasures and wrapped up his and Daosheng's leaf-album in a cloth, for protection in case it rained. Then, Ouyang Nanyu curled up on his *kang* and fell into a deep and determined sleep.

When he awoke the next morning, the artillery had stopped. Confusion, however, permeated the relative quiet. Nanyu could hear in the house the sounds of argument. The voices were unmistakably those of servants, unaccompanied by the haughty declamations of Wei Su or anyone of his ilk. Nanyu doubted even that Cui was still at home, for such an uninhibited discussion would be unlikely in the presence of any authority. Nanyu gleaned that a faction of Wei's menials had decamped at dawn, shortly after the deflowering party had finally broken up, and that they had taken some of the lighter furniture and valuables with them. Those who had failed to act were now debating the wisdom of following the others' example. Consensus seemed remote, and even the advocates of looting were showing by their preference for talk that they would take no action. They seemed, at any rate, to be gathered on the far side of the first courtyard. Outside, in the street, Nanyu heard the scrambling of people, donkeys, and carts. He took a deep breath and rose. He nestled the album into his robe, in front of his heart, bundled up the rest of his belongings, and placed them by the door.

"Well, I guess I'll be reincarnated as a dog, then."

He sallied from his room, paying no attention to the conferees in the courtyard, who reciprocated his indifference, and made for the main corridor, where, instead of turning right, toward the outside, he turned for the first time to the left and walked past the unused second courtyard, right to the entrance of the third. Peering in, he saw a horrendous mess, though he couldn't determine if it was the result of looting or the detritus of a typical deflowering party. Among the overturned tables and scattered food platters on the brick floor tiles, no one was to be seen. The sliding door of the master's residence was open. Nanyu advanced across the littered courtyard, climbed the stairs, and jumped over the threshold. He found himself in the altar room, with closed doors to the left and right. Choosing the left, or western, side, Nanyu opened the door and beheld Wei Su's study, wrecked. Picking through it to the door on the other side, he turned the handle, pushed it open, and there was the gray-robed nun, sitting on his bed.

"Let's go!" Nanyu called to her.

Daosheng remained silent and inert for a few seconds, which was all the time Nanyu needed to see in her the sullenness he had somehow hoped he wouldn't find.

"Go where?" she finally muttered.

"Home."

"How?"

"I found a boat."

Something began to rekindle in her eyes, but still she spoke slowly. "Why?"

"Because it's time. Do you really want to stay here?"

"No," said Daosheng, who now rose to her feet. "But I meant why are you doing this? Do you really want to rile up His Excellency, just so you can get tied up with me, a piece of damaged goods with men's feet?"

Nanyu was prepared for the question. "Are you really going to stand on ceremony now, of all times?" he said. "Let's just get the fuck out of here!"

At his words, and in spite of everything, Daosheng broke into a full smile, which Nanyu had heard in her voice but never before seen. It was brighter than ten thousand suns.

"Ah! So you've come to life," she almost laughed. "Yes, let us by all means adopt your sagacious and manly stratagem!"

Daosheng picked up a few articles of clothing, wrapped them in a bundle, and left the room, without a backward glance. Nanyu, however, stopped to take one more look at the felicitous marriage bed before following her out.

Passing through Wei Su's study, Daosheng said, "Wait a minute. Maybe I can solve the mystery of my alleged contract."

She rifled through the drawers of an overturned desk, inspecting the papers she found. One of these, she paused to read with some interest.

"Not what I was looking for," she said, "but it might come in handy." She folded it and tucked it into her robe. "I've every right to help myself to a few ounces of silver, equivalent to what my trousseau would have been, to make up for being kidnapped; but why fill my purse, just to reward the highwaymen we're sure to meet?"

They exited the master's hall, leapt down the stairs, and hurried along the main corridor. While Daosheng waited, Nanyu reentered the first courtyard, where the debate on looting was still in progress, grabbed his things from his room, and rejoined her. They rounded the *taotie* medallion, skipped through the door, and were out of the house.

The scene on the street was as desperate as Nanyu had imagined. Itinerants, mostly peddlers from the suburbs, traveling merchants from other cities, and uprooted people like Daosheng and himself, were endeavoring to flee, taking as many of their possessions as they could. Those with no place else to go — the vast majority — were gathering available supplies to await their fates in their homes. Many of them had painted "Surrendered Subjects" or "Long Live the Dashing Prince!" on their doors. On a few street corners, Nanyu and Daosheng thought they saw groups of Beijing's citizens prostrating themselves before individual scruffy swordsmen, but they never stopped to ascertain what was happening. The streams of refugees merged into rivers as alleys emptied into bigger streets, and Nanyu and Daosheng floated out through the Dongzhi Gate, at around the time that breakfast would have been.

By then, the Emperor – whose reign title, Chongzhen, meant "Aspiring to Virtue" – was dangling from a tree on Coal Hill, having spent the previous night bewailing the faithlessness of his officials and ordering his women to hang themselves first. (Some complied. Others, including two of his daughters, Chongzhen hacked at with his own sword. One was killed; the other, his favorite, maimed.)

Li Zicheng occupied the Sacred Capital.

Nanyu and Daosheng hurried away east from the fallen city, along the road toward Tongzhou, in the midst of other fleeing people who were too preoccupied to wonder at Daosheng's unbound feet and ease of movement. It was windy and drizzling. Sweat beaded on their faces and rain on Daosheng's uncovered fuzzy scalp. They ate two contraband steamed buns on the run.

When they were finished, Daosheng said, "You're probably wondering how things went down last night."

"No," said Nanyu. "I caught your reference to 'damaged goods,' believe it or not."

"See? You learn fast."

"Anyway, you don't have to say anything about it."

"No, I don't have to say anything about it, but I also don't want any taboos hanging between us, and besides, what else are we going to talk about, Tang dynasty poetry?"

No one else nearby was focused on anything but the path ahead, so she continued, albeit in a low voice. "Yep, the *wang ba dan* combed my hair," she said. "My big old feet didn't faze him at all. I guess he'd invested too much in his scheme of getting even with my mother to be put off by them."

Marveling at her dispassion, Nanyu likewise tried to adopt a clinical tone. "Do you think you're pregnant?"

"I doubt it," Daosheng said. "The bearded pig relied a bit much on his prize edition of *Plum in the Golden Vase* to get in the mood. In fact, he ended up sticking many of his favorite pages together. He was fairly spent by the time he turned his attention to me." She tittered. "I only wish I could get that damn zither music out of my head."

Objectivity was one thing, but levity was another, and Nanyu balked at it. He looked down at his tramping feet for a long interval and then could only summon a grunt; whereupon the defrocked nun put out her arm and stopped him in his tracks. The stream of other refugees moved around them.

"Listen to me, Other Ouyang," Daosheng said. "Are *you* going to be the one moping for the whole trip?"

Nanyu raised his eyes to hers. She was still the most radiant thing he had ever seen. After a few moments, he smiled and asked, "So how did that zither tune go?"

"Are you trying to make me throw up?" She hit him playfully on the arm. "I think it was something along the lines of 'Bodhisattva Barbarian,' but they were too drunk to get it right. Do you know the tune? Maybe we can fill in some choice lyrics."

They began marching together to the tune of "Bodhisattva Barbarian," giggling and poeticizing filth. Their libretto ultimately assumed the following shape:

"Gross, black-bearded *wang ba dan*
Summons his perverted clan.
To the sound of guns,
He will fuck a nun.

"As his kingdom falls,
Higher duty calls:
Dirty books to read —
Oops! He spills his seed."

No one paid them the slightest attention.

The road now ran parallel to a tributary canal, and after about an hour of mirth in flight, they saw the Bridge of the Great Thoroughfare looming over it. Composing themselves, they began looking for anyone who appeared to be waiting for them. Before long, Nanyu spotted Zhu Ningxin and waved. Zhu waved in return, and Nanyu and Daosheng rushed to where he was standing. Zhu was a bit taken aback at the sight of Daosheng running; he looked down at her feet but passed no comment.

"I'm extremely pleased to see you, especially so early in the day," he said. "We won't be staying here much longer. Rumor has it that the capital has fallen, though the fate of the Emperor is unknown. We'll talk later. For now, please follow me."

They descended the bank to the waterline, where the Zhu family's canal boat was moored. It was larger than the craft in which Nanyu and Daosheng had traveled north, with a fairly tall aftercastle. As they came aboard, Zhu Ningxin introduced his three older brothers. The eldest, Zhu Jinqing, had inherited the family business, which, the Ouyangs learned, involved the marketing of finished silk and cotton garments, as well as curios and books. Jinqing was around thirty, though his hair was already turning gray at the temples. Next in seniority, at around twenty-six or twenty-seven, was Zhu Xiangsun, who held the provincial civil service degree. He stood atop the aftercastle, a picture of stern contemplation. Seeing Nanyu arriving on deck, he nodded formally, saying, "Ah, Ningxin's artist is here." He ignored Daosheng. The third older brother was Zhu Zaixin, who was in his early twenties. Nanyu guessed that they had not all been born of the same mother, hence Jinqing's and Xiangsun's dissimilar names; though perhaps a family tutor was responsible for the incongruity, by assigning scholarly names of his own choosing. The births of children who didn't survive, or of daughters, probably accounted for the broad differences in ages among the four sons. As was the case in many gentry households, the brothers' occupations alternated between commerce and study, with Jinqing and Zaixin keeping to the business end of things, enabling Xiangsun and Ningxin to indulge in philosophy. Of course, it was Xiangsun's status as a provincial degree holder that solidified the family's fortune.

Also on the boat were three housemen, surnamed Zhang, Fang, and Qiao. Nanyu couldn't determine whether they were tenants, bondsmen, or some other kind of retainer. They carried halberds and seemed most displeased at having had to wait for Nanyu and Daosheng. Rounding out the ship's complement were four unnamed deckhands.

As Nanyu familiarized himself with his fellow passengers, he overheard the conversation of Jinqing and Zaixin, which was marked by great concern at being stuck on a canal boat during a time of instability. It couldn't be helped, though: As it was, they had closed accounts in Beijing just in time, and now the silver was hidden below. Lest they themselves become the agent of any panic that might endanger their passage, Jinqing and Zaixin determined to keep the news of Beijing's fall a secret, assuming they could outpace it. Speed, in any case, was of the essence, and they ordered the boatmen to cast off immediately.

The smiling Zhu Ningxin tried to keep Nanyu and Daosheng at their ease, but he was reluctant to make any major decision, such as to provide them with food, now that he was in the presence of his older brothers. In the event, it was Zhu Xiangsun who descended from his perch and said to Nanyu, "Little brother Ouyang, please take some boiled water and some turnips and rice and then retire to the aftercastle. The task falls to you to protect your *meimei* from outrage." He darted his eyes at the three halberd-bearing housemen.

Nanyu bowed his head, thanked Zhu Xiangsun and his family for their trouble, and withdrew with Daosheng into the cabin, where the first thing they did was to close the shutters.

🔳🔳🔳

Their boat reached Tongzhou in an hour and entered the Grand Canal. It was the next day, by which time they had gone over eighty *li* downstream, that two officers surrendered Tongzhou to a group of Li Zicheng's horsemen. Later on that same day, however, as the boat drew near Tianjin, the Zhu brothers were mortified to descry a huge yellow banner with the words "Surrendered Subjects" fluttering above the city walls. All appeared lost, as the barge approached a group of milling soldiers, but they turned out to be the bodyguard troops of loyal generals who had just been evicted from town by mutineers in a bloody battle. The loyalists were exhorting them to make a heroic dash back in through the main gate, to no avail. In the gloom of defeat and indecision, neither officer nor common soldier thought to stop the southbound boat, and thus it slipped by. Over the next several days, the travelers passed through a succession of towns, whose inhabitants were too intent on maintaining guard against each other to offer any harassment. However, just past the Si River junction, in Shandong Province, the travelers' luck ran out.

Nanyu had ventured out on deck, to see if there was enough water to wash his and Daosheng's clothes. It was another gray day, but Zhu Ningxin perked up at the sight of him.

"Good morning, brother," he said. "You'll be pleased to know that we are making excellent progress and are about halfway home. I trust that you have been comfortable in the cabin. I must say, though, that you and your *meimei* are making a terrible racket in there. Are you playing at mahjong or chess?" His question was affable and devoid of sarcasm.

"Ah," Nanyu replied, jiggling his finger in his ear. "As it turns out, we don't sleep very well while aboard ship."

Ningxin smiled. "It is fortunate that the girl has her older brother to entertain as well as to protect her. Do you still sleep together at home?"

Before Nanyu could respond, the Zaolin Lock slid into view, along with a company of soldiers, lined up along the bank. Officers called on the boatmen to stop. While Zhu Jinqing demanded an explanation, the soldiers tied the craft to some pilings. Several tense moments passed, with the canal water flowing by and no answers to Jinqing's insistences forthcoming.

Finally, a rather slight man wearing oversized armor appeared at the top of the embankment.

"My name is Ni," he said. "I am the Confucian Drill Instructor of Zou County, concurrently captain of militia. Regrettably, it has become necessary for our Righteous Braves to assemble a river flotilla to protect the good people of this vicinity in these uncertain times. This vessel will serve our purposes, and my men will be taking possession. You and all your passengers will remain in place as crew, porters, and other auxiliaries, and your cargo will be appropriated. Prepare to be boarded."

Zhu Jinqing threw up his hands in disgust, but Zhu Xiangsun strode up beside him and laid a restraining hand on his shoulder. Addressing Captain Ni, he said, "My surname is Zhu, with the given name Xiangsun, and I am a graduate of the provincial examination. For shame that a Confucian drill instructor should turn plunderer of canal traffic! As you are well aware, no gentleman can be conscripted to perform manual labor, and my family is likewise exempt. These deckhands are bound to me, and the boat, too, is part of my estate, immune to the demands of mere militia. No matter how uncertain the times, there is no excuse for lawlessness!"

Captain Ni removed his helmet. "My apologies, sir. I had no intention of imposing on a scholar."

"That's more like it, Captain Ni. I'm glad you have remembered your learning." Zhu Xiangsun made ready to return Captain Ni's obeisance. Captain Ni seemed to be deep in cogitation, however, and offered none. After a few moments, he said, "I'm sure you can appreciate my position, though. Orders are orders. Besides, how can I be certain that you are the scholar you claim to be?"

"More insolence!"

"Careful, sir. A true gentleman would not be so quick to anger. You say you are a provincial degree holder. I suppose your indignation is some proof of your claim, but again, how can I be sure?"

"Can you not see that I am dressed as a scholar?" Zhu Xiangsun said, trying to manage his temper.

"I can see it very plainly, sir," Ni said. "Yet you know as well as I do that the underlying cause of today's myriad troubles is the tendency of the lower orders to put on airs and ape their betters. Common peddlers have been dressing—and acting—as learned men for several reigns, leaving no ready means to distinguish high from low, noble from base, straight from crooked."

At Ni's words, which seemed to deny Zhu Xiangsun's standing and hence his argument, Jinqing, Zaixin, Ningxin, and Nanyu all groaned and looked down; yet Xiangsun himself brightened, as though his persecutor had suddenly thrown down a friendly lifeline.

"Yes, Captain," he said. "Your diagnosis of our empire's sickness is quite correct. In fact, I am quite confident that someone of your penetrating insight will be able to recognize the veracity of my claim and thus to resolve this unfortunate impasse."

Ni smiled. "Very well, then. You will please submit to an oral examination, on the learning of my home county's most famous son."

"Mencius," said Zhu Xiangsun, returning the smile. "I am conversant with every chapter of his teachings. Name any one of them."

"Chapter Three: 'Duke Wen of Teng.' You have committed it to memory?"

"Naturally."

"Excellent. You may begin when you are ready."

"*Duke Wen of Teng, while still crown prince, was once going to Chu,*" Zhu Xiangsun started off. "*While passing through Song, he saw Mencius, who talked to him about the goodness of human nature, always citing as his authorities the sage kings Yao and Shun.*"

"Fine," said Ni. "Why is this first passage important?"

"It is important because it describes how Mencius made his first impression upon Duke Wen, how he planted the seed of enlightenment in the young Duke's heart."

"Correct. And the significance of what Mencius talked about, the 'goodness of human nature'?"

"The Way of Confucius and Mencius, following that of the sage kings Yao and Shun, is nothing more or less than human nature, which is inherently good."

"Right again. Please continue."

"*Duke Ding of Teng died. The crown prince said to Ran Yu, 'I have never been able to forget what Mencius once said to me in Song. —'*"

"Evidently, Mencius made quite an impression indeed!" Ni said. "However, I am interrupting you. Go on."

"*'Now that I have had the misfortune to lose my father, I want you to go and ask Mencius's advice before making funeral arrangements.'*"

"Let's stop right there. Why on earth would Duke Wen need to ask Mencius's—or anyone's—advice on how to mourn for his own damn father?"

Zhu Xiangsun staggered at the unexpected skepticism and vulgarity. After pausing to recover, he said, "The point of this whole episode is to show that Duke Wen was dependent on Mencius's counsel."

"All the more reason to ask why Mencius's counsel was necessary. You just said that the Way is nothing more or less than the way of human nature. Duke Wen was a human being. Why couldn't he simply follow his own nature and mourn his father as his natural feelings would surely have dictated? What point was there to ask for guidance?"

"The point, Captain," Zhu intoned, "is that only the Ancients—the sage kings Yao and Shun—understood human nature and that only Confucius and Mencius understood the Ancients. Duke Wen needed Mencius's advice precisely because the Way of human nature had been lost, except as preserved in the person of Mencius. That is the essence of the degenerate age, of all human experience since the days of the sages, right up to our own time: The Way of human nature does not prevail. The only hope is to receive the transmission of the Way from Mencius and thus to begin to reorder human society, by restoring it to its true nature."

Captain Ni considered Zhu's words and then nodded. "Well

explained, sir," he said. He and Zhu Xiangsun both took a few moments to reestablish themselves under the churning clouds and amid the shuffling soldiers. Presently, Ni said, "What's next?"

"*Ran Yu went to Zou to ask Mencius's advice. 'Splendid,' said Mencius.*"

"Damn right, it's splendid!" Ni again interjected. "Heaven knows how long Mencius was waiting for such an easy customer to come along."

By now accustomed to Captain Ni's challenging style of discourse, Zhu continued, unperturbed. "As Mencius was saying, '*The funeral of a parent is an occasion for giving one's utmost. Zengzi said, "Serve your parents in accordance with the rites during their lifetimes; bury them in accordance with the rites when they die; offer sacrifices to them in accordance with the rites; and you deserve to be called a good son." I am afraid I am not conversant with the rites observed by the feudal lords. Still, I have heard something about funeral rites. Three years as the morning period, mourning dress made of rough hemp with a hem, the eating of nothing but rice gruel – these were observed in the Three Dynasties by men of all conditions alike, from emperor to commoner.*'

"*Ran Yu reported this to the crown prince, and it was decided to observe the three-year morning period. The elders and all the officials were opposed to this and said, 'The ancestral rulers of the eldest branch of our house never observed this; neither did our own ancestral rulers. When it comes to you, you go against our accepted practice. This is perhaps ill-advised. Furthermore, the* Records *say, "In funeral and sacrifice, one follows the practice of one's ancestors."' 'I have authority for what I do.'*"

"Just a minute," said Ni. "Who utters that last sentence?"

"'I have authority for what I do'? The crown prince, the future Duke Wen, says that."

"Really? The text doesn't give the subject of the sentence. It could just as easily be 'We have authority for what we do,' spoken by the elders and officials."

"Yes, but –"

"Don't you just love the ambiguity!" Ni was bouncing with excitement.

"Ambiguity in Mencius?" Zhu was incredulous.

"Why not? The ambiguity could be designed to draw attention to an elusive but important truth, in this case, the confused nature of authority. The crown prince wants to adopt a three-year mourning regimen. The elders and officials object, on the grounds that doing so would violate ancestral practice. So which side, after all, does have the authority over how to conduct the mourning? Is it the crown prince? Or is it the elders and officials? That is the question, made all the more intriguing by the fact that the text doesn't answer it."

"The text does answer it," Zhu said. "It's just that neither the crown prince nor the elders and officials possesses the authority. Mencius does."

"Precisely!" shrieked Ni. "Brilliant!"

"The plan to adopt the three-year mourning regimen," Zhu continued, noting the more than sixty armed men now staring at him in awe, "originated with Mencius – or actually, with the sages. Thus, only so long as the crown prince listens to Mencius may he be said to wield any authority at all. In other words, the crown prince's – or anyone's – authority is conditional upon his following the Way, as imparted by Mencius."

"Sir, your explication is so thorough as to leave me no opportunity for comment," said Ni. "Kindly proceed."

"*The crown prince said to Ran Yu, 'In the past, I have never paid much attention to studies, caring only for riding and fencing. Now the elders and all my officials do not think too highly of me, and I am afraid*

64

they may not give their best in this matter. Go and consult Mencius for me.'"

"Uh-oh," said Ni. "The young man is wavering. Time for another dose of Mencius."

"Ran Yu went once again to Zou to ask Mencius for advice. 'I see,' said Mencius. – "

"I see that the crown prince is a weak-willed little twerp!"

"'But in this matter, the solution cannot be sought elsewhere.'"

"Indeed it cannot. Mencius's Way is the only Way."

"'Confucius said…'" Zhu went on, but the unwashed members of his audience, the militia and boatmen, had lost interest. What Confucius said, or what Mencius said Confucius said, was after all none of their concern. Nanyu, however, though he also found Zhu Xiangsun's recitation hard to follow, was fascinated, and he struggled to unlock its mysteries. At length, Zhu raised his finger for emphasis, and Nanyu focused on what he said:

"'"The gentleman's virtue is like the wind; the virtue of the common people is like grass. Let the wind sweep over the grass, and the grass is sure to bend."'"

Captain Ni allowed the words to sink in. Then, looking over his men, he said in a low voice, "Indeed. The grass is sure to bend." He scanned the horizon, apparently in reverie. Then he returned to Zhu Xiangsun. "All right. After Mencius quotes Confucius, how does he send off Ran Yu?"

"He sends him off with *'It rests with the crown prince.'*"

"And how does the crown prince respond to that?"

"He responds by saying, *'That is so, it does indeed rest with me.'*"

"Beautiful," said Ni. "So what do you suppose has happened?"

"What do you mean?"

"Well, here goes the crown prince again, claiming that the authority rests with him. Does he realize that his authority is derived wholly from Mencius, or is he now asserting it for himself? You notice how the crown prince fails to consult with Mencius face to face but instead relies on Ran Yu as an intermediary? Perhaps he has misconstrued the nature of the Way, having received the transmission of it only indirectly. Perhaps he is enthralled by the idea of the gentleman and his power, and he presumes to cast himself in the role, without understanding it."

"I'm not sure how to answer your question," Zhu said, "or what the question is."

"Just thinking out loud," Ni said. "Maybe the final description of the funeral will clarify things."

"*For five months, he stayed in his mourning hut, issuing no orders or prohibitions. The officials and his kinsmen approved of his actions and thought him well-versed in the rites. When it was time for the burial ceremony, people came from all quarters to watch. He showed such a grief-stricken countenance and wept so bitterly that the mourners were greatly delighted.*"

"My!" Ni said. "How strange. How weird."

"There's nothing strange or weird about it," said Zhu.

"No? Don't you see that the ambiguity has come back, in the form of the same unanswered question: Who has the authority? We know that Mencius *might* have conferred it, through Ran Yu, upon the crown prince; but the crown prince might simply be pretending to it himself, driven by a mistaken sense of his own worth. With these two possibilities in mind, we can read the final passage in two ways."

"Two ways?"

"Yes. The first way assumes that the crown prince listened to Mencius and adopted the three-year mourning period. Accordingly, for the five months before his father's funeral, he remained in seclusion and took no part in public affairs. *The officials and his kinsmen approved of his actions*—because they were the correct ones, learned from Mencius—*and thought him well-*

versed in the rites — because he was. *People came from all quarters to watch*, drawn by the power of the crown prince's — that is, Mencius's — virtue. Then, at the funeral, *he showed such a grief-stricken countenance and wept so bitterly* — the natural manifestation of his true feelings — *that the mourners were greatly delighted* — that their new duke was such a filial son and humane man."

"How else is there to read it?"

"By assuming that the crown prince did *not* listen to Mencius. According to this version, the crown prince merely went through the motions of seclusion. *The officials and his kinsmen approved of his actions* — because he'd finally listened to them and not to Mencius — *and* thought *him well-versed in the rites* — out of their shared ignorance. *People came from all quarters to watch* — drawn by the promise of a cheap spectacle; and at the funeral, *the crown prince showed such a grief-stricken countenance* — counterfeit and ostentatious — *and wept so bitterly* — crocodile tears — *that the mourners were greatly delighted* — at the vulgar farce."

Zhu Xiangsun, bewildered at Ni's exegesis, stood there with his brow wrinkled and his lips moving, without managing to say anything. His brothers and Nanyu looked at each other in anticipation. The family lackeys Zhang, Fang, and Qiao, as well as the soldiers on the shore, drummed their fingers against their weapons and stared at Zhu Xiangsun with disenchanted eyes, understanding only that he had somehow been shown up. As for Captain Ni, the silence deadened his enthusiasm. He inclined his head and seemed to grow sad, almost tearful. After a few pregnant moments, he looked up and smiled grimly.

"Never mind, Your Honor," he said. "I can perceive very clearly that you are a bona fide provincial graduate, fully as perspicacious and enlightened as any scholar I've ever met. These are troubled times, as I need not remind you. Keep to the Way, sir, and your influence will remain undiminished, a force for good and for...order. Please proceed now, and be careful."

He nodded, and his men threw the boat's ropes back onto the deck. Of all those ashore or afloat, no one made a move to push the vessel away; instead, each group kept looking at the other, as it drifted out of sight. Presently, the deckhands began poling the boat forward again. Nanyu nodded to the brothers and retired without a word into the cabin. Zhu Xiangsun remained in place the longest and then, with a shake of his head, crossed the deck to his luggage, rummaged through it, and withdrew a worn and faded blue box containing the works of Mencius, which he opened and began reading.

回回 回回 回回

As it turned out, the Zhu family (and their guests and servants) only made it a few *li* beyond their encounter with the Righteous Braves of Zou County before they were stopped again by troops under the command of the Shandong governor and forced to carry about twenty of their number to a rallying point downstream. According to their recounting, the governor had in the past few days executed several of Li Zicheng's agents, who had come to the province to encourage defections, but he was now finding it difficult to distinguish the loyal counties from the renegade. Retreat southward seemed to be the safest course. Nanyu and Daosheng lost their domestic sanctuary, as four officers made their headquarters in the aftercastle cabin. All that was left to the supposed brother and sister was a small corner of the room, partitioned off by a sparse curtain of laundry. From this uncomfortable position, they saw that they were entering Zhaoyang Lake, where they had had their first conversation, under the moon.

"'Romantic setting of moonlit deck; bliss of wedding night;

68

how to describe this joy?'" Daosheng pouted.

"We're lucky we haven't been drafted or stranded," said Nanyu.

Indeed, the Shandong soldiers were reasonably well-behaved (helping themselves only to all of the food) and disembarked at the southern side of the lake country. The travelers managed to buy more provisions at inflated prices and in another couple of days passed Suqian, where loyalist troops were busily fortifying the town. Finally safe behind friendly lines, the refugees found that the tense atmosphere had lifted, though they remained liable for heavy tolls. Soon they reached the Yangtze. Although Xinchang, where the Zhu family lived, was well downstream, Zhu Jinqing turned the boat upstream, to Nanjing, where they would drop off the Ouyangs and do a little trading besides. In one more day, on a warm and sunny morning, they had reached the Longjiang docks, from whence Nanyu and Daosheng had first set out.

With the housemen Zhang, Fang, and Qiao looking on, the Zhu brothers lined up for the formal leave-taking. The Ouyangs expressed their gratitude in as dignified and scholarly a way as they could.

"We cannot thank you enough for preserving us from chaos," Nanyu said.

"Not at all," returned Zhu Ningxin. "To render assistance to such an insightful artist as you—how could we have done otherwise? Perhaps our empire will enjoy a resurgence in the southland, with enough talent such as yours now safe here. I hope we might correspond, and please do visit us in Xinchang. I would like to see more of your work as you continue to perfect it, and I especially await the lessons of the remainder of the four seasons." He and Nanyu made the same obeisance that they had exchanged on the footbridge in Beijing.

With Zhu Xiangsun, things were more awkward. "That Captain Ni had a very peculiar understanding of Mencius," he said, "even though he accepted my viewpoint in the end. I have made a few margin notes in this old traveling copy, which I would like you, please, to 'accept with a smile.' My youngest brother is impressed with your artistic abilities. It is important that you assimilate the correct interpretation of the Way, as your understanding matures." He held out the weathered blue box, which Nanyu, after the customary refusals, accepted. Nanyu made it a point to call Zhu Xiangsun "Your Honor."

Again, none of the brothers had anything to say to Daosheng. As it became obvious that they were waiting for the Ouyangs to leave before they could prepare themselves for the day's business, Nanyu and Daosheng made one final bow and left the quayside.

As soon as they were out of sight, Daosheng drifted closer to Nanyu, so that they were walking shoulder to shoulder, though not as hurriedly as during their escape from Beijing. In the early morning foot and cart traffic, with people carrying vegetables and other goods, no one payed them any notice, as long as they were careful not to smile. They also found it possible to carry on a quiet conversation.

"'Man and wife together, we have reached Nanjing,'" Daosheng said. "'With little ado, we have become man and wife.'"

"Are you speaking in references again?" Nanyu asked. "I can almost catch where your speech leaves off and someone else's begins."

"Your sense of hearing is growing very acute," said Daosheng. "I am, in fact, quoting from *The Peony Pavilion*."

"And to what," Nanyu said, "do these lines from *The Peony Pavilion* refer?"

"Why, to sex, of course—'the clouds and the rain,'" said Daosheng, with neither emphasis nor expression on her face. "See if you like this one: 'Now that Feng Yi the River Spirit comes to strike his drum / I understand the flute-playing skill of the noble daughter of Qin.' Not bad, huh? My favorite is actually 'And when my dream reached the summit of delight / There came flower petals showering down.'"

"Not bad, as you say," said Nanyu. "But 'With little ado, we have become man and wife' refers not just to sex but to marriage."

"Yes, it does," said Daosheng, "and it implies that the one is the foundation of the other."

Nanyu breathed in. "So are we married, then?"

"Do you want to be?"

"Yes."

"As do I."

They looked for the briefest instant at each other and then ahead, at the Nanjing city wall, specifically the section of it that was constructed upon its ancient foundation and called by the locals "The Stone Wall." Although the Qingjiang Gate was nearby, they decided not to enter the city there but instead to make their way southward, along the outside of the wall, and to head for the Temple at the Edge of Heaven. The detour would give them a chance to prolong their togetherness, either by a few hours, should they be separated, or forever, should they not be.

"'Little ado' you say," Nanyu pursued. "Is that really all there is to it?"

"In practice, Husband, there's a bit more ado," said Daosheng. "As chance would have it, you are carrying a copy of the rules in your bag."

"You mean Mencius?"

"Yes. I recalled the relevant passage from my earlier studies and found it in Zhu Xiangsun's travel edition—yours now—

while you were dozing last night."

Daosheng fished the book out of Nanyu's carrying sack and began thumbing through one of the middle folios.

"It's in Chapter Three, though a bit later than the business with Duke Wen and his dad's funeral. Here it is: *Those who bore holes in the wall to peep at one another, and climb over it to meet illicitly, waiting for neither the command of parents nor the good offices of a go-between, are despised by parents and fellow-countrymen alike.* Hmmm."

"I'd say we've already done a bit more than to peep at one another," Nanyu said.

Daosheng pondered the text. "This is clearly an injunction against fornication and elopement," she said, "although in this particular context, it's being used merely as an example of unseemly haste, part of a larger warning against the over-eager seeking of government office." She closed the book. "The general lesson is that everything—whether getting married or becoming an official—must be done according to the Way."

"So have we gone against the Way?" Nanyu asked.

Daosheng didn't answer immediately. They walked past an outdoor food vendor, with stuffed buns steaming in a column of baskets on a stove, and realized that they hadn't eaten any breakfast, nor did they have any money.

"Well," she said, "whose Way is it? I don't think we've gone against our own Way, do you?"

"No," said Nanyu, "but I reckon that's the whole problem. Our Way isn't the Way of most people, and there're more of them than there are of us. We don't need Mencius to tell us that we'll be 'despised by parents and fellow-countrymen alike.'"

"No, I don't suppose we do."

Nanyu and Daosheng trudged on, as the morning sun continued to rise. They exchanged brave little smiles to stave off despair and walked in silence for a few minutes. Then they simultaneously widened their eyes and exclaimed: "Sixty strokes of the bamboo!"

The difficulty of their situation now loomed so completely that it assumed preposterous dimensions, and Nanyu and Daosheng could only laugh at it.

"As if the displeasure of parents and fellow-countrymen weren't enough," Daosheng said, "we are also incurring the wrath of the magistrate. What delightful folly!"

After their laughter had subsided, Nanyu said, "I remember, Wife, how you had a few tricks up your sleeve, when you seemed to have fallen into the hands of Wei Su. And here you are now, a world away from him."

"One of those tricks up my sleeve was named Ouyang Nanyu."

"And a very neat trick I turned out to be."

"Wasn't I clever to have played you?"

"The point is that maybe things aren't quite so hopeless, if we keep playing our game well…By the way, what happens in *The Peony Pavilion*? Does the book have a happy ending?"

"It's a play, not a book, and yes it does have a happy ending. The eloping man and woman get married in the end."

"And I bet they had a lot standing in their way at first?"

"Well, yes, they did have a lot standing in their way at first, especially the fact that the woman was dead."

"So I guess we're in much better shape, then, seeing as how you're still breathing."

"Infinitely better shape, Husband," said Daosheng. "Yes, we can certainly look on the bright side, as we consider our situation: We're guilty of fornication, elopement, and statutory incest. As Mencius promises, we are sure to be despised by parents, fellow-countrymen, and no doubt the magistrate as well."

"Speaking of parents," Nanyu said, "welcome to my home."

They had come around to the south of the city and were walking along Shakyamuni Street in Nanyu's neighborhood.

"Let's not go in, just yet," said Daosheng. "We still have some thinking to do — and some eloping."

They crossed to the other side of Shakyamuni Street, afraid even to look at Nanyu's father's house. Fortunately, none of the neighbors called out, perhaps unable to recognize Nanyu in the company of a woman, and Ouyang Gen was absent from the front-facing kitchen for the moment. Reaching the Temple at the Edge of Heaven, they stepped through the main gate — which Nanyu noticed for the first time was called the Entrance to the Practice of the Benevolent World — and turned immediately to the right, avoiding the central buildings and entering instead the wooded area to the east, with its web of secluded pathways. They could hear the assembled monks chanting the morning lesson but encountered no one. Holding hands, they ascended a planked stairway to a pavilion housing the Altar of the Twin Cassias, which was just then bathed in the rays of the morning sun, slanting through the trees. Forgetting their cares, they took in the scenery as they turned toward each other. Daosheng was smiling radiantly again, and Nanyu basked in the vision of her, even as he savored the fragrance of the dew on the pines. The chorus of the monks trailed off, and a gong sounded.

"Good morning!" came a songlike voice from inside the pavilion.

It was the abbot, Baichi Shi'ai, stepping around the altar. Nanyu and Daosheng turned to face him, too surprised to unjoin their hands.

"Oooh, as you were!" the abbot said. "I see you are enjoying this beautiful day as much as I am — how sunny it is! Ouyang Nanyu! So you are back from Beijing. You stayed just long enough to pluck an apricot blossom!"

Apricot blossoms referred not only to young scholars just graduated from the examinations and awaiting their first official appointments in the capital but also to Liu Mengmei ("Willow Dream-of-Apricot"), the male lover in *The Peony Pavilion.* Ostensibly, Baichi Shi'ai's remark meant that Nanyu was as fortunate as an emperor who had obtained the services of a great talent. More subtly, it alluded to Daosheng obtaining Nanyu. Nanyu didn't follow either of the meanings; Daosheng followed both.

"I wouldn't presume, Teacher," she said. "I am merely a local girl, recently a novice at Cock-Crow Temple."

"Ah!" exclaimed Baichi Shi'ai, and then he continued:

> "This nun is seventeen and her emotions in their prime.
> She's awakened to a springtime breeze of fragrances sublime.
> Her face bears naught of ceruse but exudes a shining light;
> Her lips are unanointed, yet their rouge naturally bright.

"So, you have 'come down the mountain,'" he concluded, meaning that she had forsaken her devotions.

Daosheng was half expecting a scolding but decided to trust the abbot's enthusiasm.

"Yes, Teacher," she said. "I have descended from Cock-Crow Temple; but the view is nice enough from here, isn't it? Why climb any higher? Besides, I'm afraid of heights."

Baichi Shi'ai grinned even more beatifically. "This is the Edge of Heaven!" he said. "Only Heaven itself is higher. You're not afraid of Heaven, are you?"

Daosheng and Nanyu took another look at their surroundings, smiled, and shook their heads, though as they did so, they finally realized they were still holding hands and unclasped them.

Baichi Shi'ai saw them break contact and frowned. He said, "Well, then, what *are* you afraid of?"

The Ouyangs buckled under the weight of the question. After a few moments, Nanyu said, "We were just talking about that."

"Where to start?" Daosheng added.

The abbot kept his wide-eyed stare directed at them for a good while. Then he recited,

"I beg of you, Zhongzi,
Do not climb into our homestead;
Do not break the willows we have planted.
Not that I mind about the willows,
But I am afraid of my father and mother.
Zhongzi I dearly love;
But of what my father and mother will say,
Indeed, I am afraid.

"That is from *The Book of Songs*," he said. "Does it describe your predicament?"

"It describes the first part of it," said Nanyu.

"It is not merely the anger of our parents that we fear," said Daosheng. "The list of the disapproving would constitute a sutra in itself."

"Not a sutra I would know," said the abbot, his countenance sharpening in a way that Nanyu had never seen before. "Yet perhaps the young lady's analogy is apt. It is a sutra of the world, a sutra of suffering, that lies unrolled before you now, and before you it will remain, as long as you remain in the world. As you are cursed to recite from this unpromising sutra, you may as well begin with its first verse, which, as you seem to recognize, concerns your parents. Indeed," he said, with his arms stretched toward the couple, "even those of us sworn to dharma would counsel people like you to look to your filial obligations first, for, by honoring your parents, you cultivate moral virtue, and moral virtue is a form of karma."

Having come to the end of the lesson, Baichi Shi'ai resumed his innocent demeanor. He nodded, as though remembering something, and said with his index finger raised toward the sky:

"Here is a lady I have met in love;
Here are the wedding dishes, all in a row.

"So nice and simple!" he beamed. "If you are 'met in love,' then the wedding dishes arrange themselves. What need is there for a go-between, even?"

Affected both by the abbot's inner verve and by the aura of whimsy surrounding it, Nanyu and Daosheng allowed themselves relaxed smiles and held hands again. With a final gaze at the wooded hillside and the streaming sun rays, they bowed to Baichi Shi'ai and descended from the Altar of the Twin Cassias.

回回 回回 回回

They kept their hands joined and their mouths closed until they emerged through the temple gate and onto the street, at which point they assumed again the manner of unattached pedestrians and began to discuss their next move.

"So what's your father like?" asked Daosheng.

"Now that you ask, I can't say as I really know," returned

Nanyu. "I've got only one father, so I can't compare him to any other. You know he's a carpenter, but he doesn't insist that I become one too. He's even encouraged me in my painting, as long as there's a little money in it. I guess he doesn't really care what I do, within limits."

"And we're shortly to find out what those limits are," said Daosheng. "If there is a quarrel, I hope it comes after breakfast. I'm famished."

"Maybe I should go in first."

"Yes, let's not the both of us barge in and give him too much medicine all at once."

They had reached the doorway. Daosheng waited outside, and Nanyu stepped in.

He found no one in the kitchen but heard hammering in the workshop. "Father!" he called to the rear. "Father! I'm home."

The hammering stopped, and footsteps approached. "Nanyu!" whooped Ouyang Gen, as he appeared in the doorway to the workshop. They met in the sitting room, and Nanyu fell to his knees.

"Thank Heaven you are safe!" said his father, almost tearful with relief. "The news of the fall of Beijing reached here about ten days ago. By what miracle did you escape and return home so quickly?"

He sat down on a hardwood chair that he and Nanyu had made together some years ago, and he motioned for his son to sit on a stool.

"I met a young man from a scholarly family named Zhu the very night the rebel attack began, and he was impressed by my pictures." Nanyu smiled, though he still looked mostly at his father's feet. "You were right about painting, Father. It might have saved my life. Thinking me talented, they treated me very well."

"And so you fled the Capital with this scholar family?"

"Yes, Father. They had a boat ready to leave the next morning, a pretty good one."

"So you traveled again by the Canal? You were never detained by rebels?"

"No, Father. There was fighting with the rebels going on all around us, but we somehow made it through. Militia stopped us once, but Zhu Xiangsun is a provincial graduate, and he was able to talk them into letting us go."

"But leaving Beijing…" Ouyang Gen said. "What about Wei Su? Did he dismiss you?"

"No, Father. I never even met him. On the night Beijing fell he vanished, along with about half his household and a lot of his furniture. It was a confused scene, and there didn't seem much point in staying around; so I just left."

Ouyang Gen was silent for a while. Then he said, "So Fate has played its part. At least you are safe. Are you hungry? You look thin."

"Thank you, Father, I am quite hungry…But please tell me how it has been with you."

"It has been like every other springtime here," said Ouyang Gen. "Until ten days ago, that is. Since then it's been pretty edgy, and rice is even more expensive than it used to be."

"But you are in good health, Father?"

"Yes, I am," the elder Ouyang said. "Good boy. Now fetch some turnips."

He gestured toward a basket in the corner, and Nanyu pulled out four turnips, two in each hand.

"You're even hungrier than I thought," said Ouyang Gen. "I'll have to send you out later to buy some more foodstuffs. I don't have enough for two. Didn't they feed you on their boat, that scholar family of yours?"

"Yes, they did, Father, but they didn't give us any breakfast this morning."

"'Us'?"

Nanyu let his father's question hang in the air long enough for it to accumulate its desired import but not long enough to invite suspicion that he'd been concealing anything.

"Yes, Father. I've not been alone."

"Oh?"

"I've been with a woman."

Ouyang Gen was in the process of rising from his chair. Coming to his feet, he took one step and then froze, looking at his son with one eye narrowed and one agape. Nanyu was determined to maintain his poise, but he couldn't help glancing past the kitchen to the street, and his father saw it.

"She's outside, isn't she?"

"Yes, Father."

"Call her in."

Nanyu called, "Daosheng!" and she walked in though the kitchen.

"*Aiya*! Her feet got here before she did!" said Ouyang Gen.

Daosheng knelt at the threshold of the sitting room.

Ouyang Gen gave her a long look. "Your name is Daosheng?"

"Yes, Father."

"You came from Beijing, with my son, on the boat?"

"Yes, Father."

"You were the only woman aboard?"

"Yes, Father."

"Why would you get on a boat, the only woman, with so many men?"

"It seemed desirable, Father, to get out of Beijing by any means available. Besides, Nanyu was with me, in the cabin."

"Why did this scholar family allow you into the cabin with

my son?"

"Because they thought we were brother and sister."

"And why would they think that?"

"Because my surname is Ouyang."

The eldest Ouyang of the three fell back into his chair. After a brief reflection, he said, "Son!"

"Yes, Father?"

"So you decided to let this Zhu Xiangsun, or whatever his name is, continue to believe that you and this girl were brother and sister, and no one would be the wiser."

"Yes, Father."

Ouyang Gen actually started to smile and seemed about to burst out laughing, when his face turned ashen, and he cried, "Wait a minute! That lummox Cui said that Wei Su's new concubine was named Ouyang. Is this the same girl?"

"Yes, Father."

Ouyang Gen shot up from his chair and stomped his foot. He flailed his hand in the air and slapped it against his thigh.

"Fool!" he shouted. "You've brought a 'breaker of families' to our doorstep! I warned you to be careful about him! You don't think he'll miss this girl, and come looking for you, looking for us?"

"Father," Nanyu said, "There's no need to be so angry."

"No?" His father walked back in a circle, unable even to look at Nanyu. "You've ruined us! That Cui will be here any day now, with a whole pack of Wei Su's goons. Why on earth would you dare to provoke such a man? He won't be satisfied with all the money we have. He'll finish us off for pride."

"No, Father, we think he won't," protested Nanyu, who had sunk back to the floor beside Daosheng, at the beginning of his father's tirade. "Hand Father the letter," he said to her.

While Ouyang Gen smoldered, Daosheng removed from her sleeve the paper she had found in Wei Su's desk. She raised it upward with both hands and approached the irate man on her knees. He snatched it and began reading.

"It's a letter from Wei Su to Niu Jinxing, who calls himself Li Zicheng's prime minister. Niu's answer is appended," Daosheng said to the floor. "Wei Su is a traitor. Not only was he in communication with the rebels, expecting a higher post from them, but he also helped them to get into Beijing. He bribed some of the garrison to fire blanks. This letter proves it, though the proof will hardly be necessary. It will soon be known all over Nanjing that he's joined the bandits."

Ouyang Gen took his seat again, the better to puzzle over the evidence.

"Wei Su is finished, Father," said Nanyu. "When Li's rebels are put down, he'll be executed. His family here in Nanjing will be disgraced, and Cui is a marked man, too. No one will be bothering us anymore."

"How did you get this letter?" Ouyang Gen asked, handing it back to Daosheng.

"I found it in Wei Su's study, Father," she answered, "and I took it with me."

Ouyang Gen was quiet, the fire of his anger half quenched, half spent. He put his elbow on the armrest and his chin on his fist, thinking and continuing to calm down, while Nanyu and Daosheng waited at his feet. Presently, he said, "You are clever, girl. I'll give you that."

"Is that a good thing or a bad thing, Father?" Daosheng said. "Am I a 'fast-mouth' who doesn't know her place?"

Again Ouyang Gen took his time. He looked at the young ones, and after a while, he said, first to Daosheng, "As my son may have told you, I don't put much store in 'knowing one's place.' Why should we be the only ones to be content with our lot, when so few others are?"

Then he turned his eyes to Nanyu. "Be reminded, Son: your obligations to me are to provide for me, as I have for you, when I can no longer work. The particulars I leave to you — except that I forbid you ever to become an official. Of course, you must also have a son of your own, and a clever one, to carry on our line."

He paused for a few moments more.

"Before you left, I instructed you to choose your own profession, so that you might better serve me, by serving yourself." Once more, he paused. "I suppose choosing your own wife, likewise, would be…practical. Besides, doing without a go-between will save me a lot of money."

Now, all three of them remained silent for a thoughtful interval. Nanyu was the first to speak. "Uh, in that case, Father… the business about our having the same surname…"

Ouyang Gen shrugged. "I haven't heard of anyone getting sixty strokes in a long time. Count it as another unenforced law, though it still is the law, another reason for you to keep clear of the magistrate…Now, both of you, get up off the floor. I know you're hungry. Can the girl cook as well as she steals evidence?"

Saying nothing, Daosheng turned to Nanyu, who still held the turnips in his sweaty hands. Taking them, she disappeared into the kitchen.

Ouyang Gen said, "Son, tell me now: Where are her parents?"

"I don't know about her father. Her mother lives on the Qinhuai."

"Lives on the Qinhuai?"

"She was a courtesan."

"An ambitious woman, then," Ouyang Gen said. "We may not be good enough for her."

Nanyu said nothing.

"Anyway, you still need her permission, I should say her approval, for you to be considered married; otherwise, you're just eloping. Until we work out the details, the girl may not stay here, nor are the two of you to be left alone. We'll have a bite to eat, and then we'll head to the Qinhuai, to look for her mother." The elder Ouyang almost smiled again. "We could probably walk it, with her men's feet, and save a little cart money."

Daosheng made a soup with the turnips and a bit of cabbage she found in a basket near the stove. Ouyang Gen remembered some peanuts that were stored in a hamper under the table, and he put a fistful on a dish. The three of them ate in the kitchen. When they were finished, Ouyang Gen gathered together a few of the finer edibles he had on hand, including the rest of the peanuts, and put them in a couple of hollowed gourds that he had bought on Three Mountain Street. Then he said, "Let's go," and they all left the house. Though it would have been easy to hitch a ride in to town on a donkey cart, Ouyang Gen preferred that they walk through Treasure Gate and thence to the Qinhuai, which was not all that far.

Daosheng's mother, Ouyang Zhenli, was the sole owner and resident of the House of the Entrancing Fragrance, where she had formerly worked with two other girls under a madam. The house was situated on the south bank of the Qinhuai River, with its front door on Scrip Street, where in centuries past the government's paper money had been stored. The notes were long defunct as a means of exchange, and the avenue was now lined with brothels. The locals called it Agarwood Street after a certain gentleman, remorseful after taking leave of his weeping concubine, spent a small fortune on fine clothes and a magnificent four-poster agarwood bed which he brought back to her, to signify that he wished never to be parted from her again. When she affected no longer to recognize him, he tore the clothes to shreds and set fire to the precious bed, enshrouding the neighborhood with thick, pungent smoke that left its redolence for several days—

agarwood also being an ingredient of the best incense.

Nearing the House of the Entrancing Fragrance, the three Ouyangs observed that it was closed up. A passing makeup vendor told them that Madame had gone to Cock-Crow Temple to recite lessons, as had recently become her wont.

Ouyang Gen was annoyed, as Cock-Crow Temple was at the other end of the city. Since he had forbidden Daosheng from spending the night at Shakyamuni Street, however, there was no choice but for them to proceed to the nunnery at once, where at least the girl would be able to stay if her mother were unavailable or, perchance, unamenable to alternate arrangements. They made their way back to the main thoroughfare and soon hitched a ride on a northbound donkey cart, which was carrying bolts of cotton. For a few coppers, the driver took them all the way to the Drum Tower, before their paths diverged and the Ouyangs had to get off. As they were looking for another cart or wagon to take them toward the east, Ouyang Gen bought a cheap, sloppily-written handbill from an urchin who was hawking the latest news from the north. It contained a list of officials known to have defected to Li Zicheng, and Wei Su's name was on it.

"It's true, then," he said, handing the paper off to Nanyu, while looking at Daosheng. Having splurged on the handbill, Ouyang Gen decided they would walk the rest of the way to Cock-Crow Temple, and they arrived at the gate a little after midday, exhausted and hungry again.

Whereas the Temple at the Edge of Heaven was sprawling and wooded, Cock-Crow Temple was a denser complex of buildings interconnected by stone stairways and completely covering a small hill just inside the city wall. The hill was higher than the wall and open to the cooling winds blowing in from Xuanwu Lake on the other side of it. The view of the lake from the temple was one of the most celebrated in town, whether or not one ascended the Baozhi Pagoda—named for a legendary monk—that rose above it.

A portly laywoman escorted the Ouyangs up the main flight of stairs, around the pagoda, and through the door of a small room facing the lake, where they ignored her invitation to sit and instead stood in a row by the open window, savoring the panorama and the breeze. It was a pleasant while before they became conscious of someone else entering the room. They turned away from the lake and beheld the abbess, One-Eyed Jingang. Daosheng began to sink to her knees, but Jingang rushed over and embraced her, keeping her standing.

"I'm so happy to see you!" she said. "When that young jackal carried you off, I feared you were lost forever."

"Fortunately, Teacher, I was able to escape," said Daosheng.

"Very fortunately," agreed Jingang. She turned to regard the older and the younger man and understood everything. "And this would be your young champion and his father."

The latter inclined his head. "My name is Ouyang Gen, Teacher. This is my son, Nanyu."

Jingang produced a sagacious smile. "I suppose you'll be wanting to talk to your mother," she said to Daosheng. "She'll be finished with her reading momentarily. In the meantime, why don't we all have a little chat?"

She motioned the group toward four wicker-topped stools, and they sat down. The laywoman had by then brought in tea and snacks, which she arranged on a small table.

Forgoing the customary hesitation, the Ouyangs went to work on the refreshments, resisting the urge to look out the window again and trying to remain attentive to their host, who herself ate and drank nothing. After they had made some impression on the victuals, Jingang cleared her throat and addressed Ouyang Gen.

"As a matter of fact," the abbess said, "little sister Daosheng always showed remarkable discipline during times of fasting, when she was living here. Most others, even full-fledged nuns long in residence, tend to break down and sneak something to eat before the observances are completed. Daosheng could keep fasting to the end. You should know, Mr Ouyang, how strong of heart she is."

"Yes, Teacher," said Ouyang Gen. "Though I met her only this morning, I've already got an idea of her cleverness. I guess she would have to be plenty strong of heart, too."

"Success at fasting is a sign of sagehood," continued Jingang. "The spark of sagehood in Daosheng convinced me that she would prove to be a 'gentleman of a woman.'"

Nanyu cocked his head.

"A 'gentleman of a woman,'" the abbess explained, "makes it her purpose to liberate other sentient beings, as she has been liberated. If she is married, then she strives to liberate the sentient being that is her husband, even as she serves him; she strives to liberate the sentient being that is her father-in-law, even as she serves him."

The wind shifted, and the air that had been blowing in through the window now flowed out. The three Ouyangs caught a whiff of a thin trace of perfume and turned toward the interior of the room. Standing in the doorway was a fourth Ouyang, Ouyang Zhenli, dressed in a plain, gray robe, with her long hair, still raven black, tied simply back.

"*Ma!*" Daosheng jumped up, ran across the room, and grasped both of Ouyang Zhenli's hands.

The older woman cried tears of relief and tensed her jaw, as if in an effort to staunch them. She made a playful complaint to One-Eyed Jingang: "Why didn't you tell me sooner that she was back?"

The abbess, taking pleasure in the Ouyang women's reunion,

said, "There were a few things I wanted to say, not just to your daughter but to our other guests also. Perhaps you overheard them?"

Ouyang Zhenli looked past her daughter's shoulder to where the men were now standing. Daosheng stood to the side.

"Mother," she said, "this is Ouyang Nanyu, who helped me get out of Beijing, and this is his father, Ouyang Gen."

Ouyang Zhenli bowed her head at Ouyang Gen, nodded less pronouncedly at Nanyu, and glanced at the still-seated One-Eyed Jingang before she too was able to form a clear picture of what had transpired during her daughter's time away and what business had brought the families together now.

"Aha," she said to Daosheng, "So you have fallen in love with the young man."

The male Ouyangs began to fidget.

Jingang said to Ouyang Gen, "As you can ascertain, the lady is unafraid to speak of love, and since love is what you came to discuss with her, I suggest you get to it without any more delay. Of course, love is not my area of expertise, so I shall leave you. Please do remember what I said, though."

As the others inclined their heads, Jingang left with the laywoman, who had brought another cup of tea, and all four Ouyangs sat down.

"Actually," said the former courtesan, "love is best addressed in song or poetry, and I doubt that you gentlemen have come to hear me sing. I did note the abbess's mentioning marriage, and that is a very practical thing. It is usually worked out by one party asking a lot of questions and the other party answering them through a go-between, but I sense a certain eagerness to make do without one. Very well; we'll conduct the negotiations ourselves." She took a sip of tea. "Before we begin, though, I suppose I should thank you, young man, for rescuing my daughter from the clutches of Wei Su, no matter what condition you are returning her in."

Nanyu reddened.

Ouyang Gen spoke up. "Now that you mention Wei Su, let's talk about him first. What interest does he have in your daughter?"

Daosheng added, "I crave enlightenment on that point as well, Mother."

Ouyang Zhenli looked out at the lake. "Wei Su has no rightful interest in Daosheng and no requited interest in me," she said. "He was a suitor, many years ago, yet I swear I did nothing to encourage him. My affections were reserved for a much kinder man, named Wang Yin, who was a farmer and foodstuffs merchant from Liyang County. Wang Yin saw me through the window of the House of the Entrancing Fragrance, where I worked, one morning, while he was brokering the sale of rice liquor to Qinhuai banquet halls. I had just risen and was without my makeup, but he didn't care about that. He smiled at me, and I couldn't help smiling back. That's all it took." She shook her head. "Every evening, a parade of fops, hoping to win me with poems about my painted eyebrows and lip rouge, and this peddler sees me with neither, my hair all messed up, and I invite him in… Mind you, he was very respectful. We sat in the reception room on the first floor, looking out at the Qinhuai, which I remember was magically quiet after what had been a rowdy night."

Ouyang Gen exhaled. "So then…"

"So then he bought out my contract, and he purchased the house for me, too. My old 'mama' took the money and set up shop with her remaining girls elsewhere. Wang Yin spent most of his time in town with me—he was the youngest of three brothers, with no family of his own—and his business prospered, as he could see his local clients more often.

"Wei Su, however, was galled to have been bested by an upstart. He was just a stipendiary student at the time, but his father was very rich – richer than Wang Yin – and there seemed to be no stopping him. As fate would have it, the Wei family owned some of the land next to Wang Yin's, in Liyang, and that's how Wei Su got his revenge. He let a few pigs wander onto Wang Yin's farm and then accused him of stealing them. The magistrate was on Wei's side, of course, and he had my poor husband fined and flogged. Wang Yin had no political protection, and local officials and clerks smelled blood. They dunned him for special taxes and fees whenever they needed extra cash, and they had him coming and going. He lost his land and was driven out of business, and he died before we had spent even a year together."

The four were silent, especially Daosheng. After a while, she looked up, with nearly as much stifled anger as Nanyu had noticed at their first meeting.

"He was my father?"

"Yes."

"You never told me."

"No."

"Why not?"

"The answer is a question: How do you think I survived?"

Daosheng could only take a deep breath.

"I was a courtesan," her mother said. "I had to live by my reputation and talent. It was only because a few influential men continued to rhapsodize about Ouyang Zhenli and the House of the Entrancing Fragrance that I was able to inherit the place from my poor husband and avoid being evicted. Even Wei Su preferred that I stay there, as he could imagine harassing me nowhere else. For food and clothing, I relied on the rest of my admirers — but never, mark you all, on Wei Su. As you can imagine, it was best for me to play all sides and encourage everyone, and thus was

I able to accumulate enough finery to keep the game going for as long as I did. I want you to know that I remained chaste and devoted to Wang Yin and that I favored my callers with song and conversation only. They applauded my 'widow's integrity,' even as they obviously regretted it. Besides, I was known to be damaged goods, so no one could hope to win any fame by 'combing my hair.'"

Daosheng and Nanyu stirred, and Ouyang Zhenli noted their discomfort.

"As my charms faded," she continued, "I remained a sentimental fixture on the Qinhuai, and no one—not even Wei Su—has ever ventured to erase me from the landscape. Up through the present day, then, that is how I've lasted…as the twilight jewel of the Qinhuai River."

Ouyang Zhenli was crying, and her listeners were silent, knowing that she had yet to deliver the final line of her story, which came soon enough.

"And it wouldn't have been possible with a child," she declared, "especially a daughter. So I hid you here at this nunnery, not just from Wei Su but from everyone, visiting you as often as I dared."

Nanyu and his father were moved, but Daosheng was still shaking her head.

"You've explained why you hid me from the world," she said, "but not why you hid my father from me."

"Your father was taken from you," said Ouyang Zhenli. "What good would his name have done you?"

"You gave me *your* name," answered Daosheng, stomping her foot. "That was a pretty strange thing to do, if you were trying to conceal the fact that you'd had a child. Wouldn't the name Wang have been harder to trace to you? After all, it's far more common."

Now Ouyang Zhenli stomped her own foot, forgetting that it was bound, with the little toes curled underneath. The bent-under toes struck the ground, shooting pain halfway up her leg. She grimaced and said through clenched teeth, "Why is it so important who your dead father was? I'm your living mother. Wang Yin never provided for you, and I did."

No one said anything.

"Why should only men have heirs, to carry on their family lines? No: You'll be carrying on *my* line, with *my* surname."

Ouyang Zhenli's resurgent determination had dispelled her sadness, and Daosheng's air of resentment and reproach likewise subsided, never to be displayed again. Slowly she inclined her head until she was looking at her mother's tiny feet. Nanyu also lowered his gaze.

After a few moments, Ouyang Gen began nodding, in an effort to speed things up.

"Excellent!" he said. "So the girl's real name is Wang! Now we can get them hitched without worrying about the sixty strokes of the bamboo, and then she'll be Mrs Ouyang, just the same."

He bent down to pick up the gourds containing the peanuts and other snacks and, with an eager smile, proffered them to Ouyang Zhenli. The latter forced an indulgent smile of her own.

"Yes, Mr Ouyang," she said, "I will gladly accept your fine gifts. However, for a wedding to proceed on the very day it is arranged seems a bit rushed. Let us wait until the day after tomorrow, which, so the almanacs say, will be auspicious. You may pick Daosheng up at my house. Mid-morning would be a good time—and no donkey-cart, please, sir. We would prefer a proper sedan chair."

Ouyang Gen stifled his chagrin. "Yes, that will be fine," he said. Business being concluded, as far as he was concerned, he rose, glanced out the window one last time, and exited over the threshold.

Nanyu stood up as well. He aimed a meaningful look at Daosheng, who was still subdued, in the presence of her mother; yet, under the stilled surface of her countenance, he noticed her characteristic glow. He felt himself floating out of the room and down the stairs, and he remained largely unconscious of his body for the rest of the day, even as he and his father walked the entire diameter of the city from north to south, emerged through Treasure Gate, and finally collapsed in the workshop of the house on Shakyamuni Street. They woke for a midnight snack of boiled pork dumplings, purchased from a corner vendor, and then slept again, until well past sunrise.

The ensuing day was given to busy preparation. While Nanyu swept, mopped, and dusted, his father went out to reserve the sedan chair and the services of two porters. He returned home with a supply of auspicious red bunting and paper cutouts of the "double-happiness" design, and he used these to decorate the front doorway, in the hope of bringing good fortune to the upcoming marriage. Having thus unintentionally advertised his son's wedding, Ouyang Gen was vexed to find himself suddenly very popular, as neighbors and hungry students from the temple and even a few monks and pedestrians began dropping by to inquire as to when they might share in the festivities. The flustered carpenter told them to return the following day at noon, and then he had no choice but to retain the services of the dumpling man, paying in advance for a large supply of meat and dough for wrappings (the monks would be given cabbage dumplings). He bought a pre-printed guest book, in which each celebrant would write his name or make his mark and list also the amount of money he was bringing as a present. Reflecting on this last detail, the father of the groom felt somewhat consoled.

Nanyu wanted nothing more than to collect his thoughts

under the Verdant Immortal Pines, but he couldn't leave his father with his hands full and so remained at home to help with the planning. Both Ouyangs realized belatedly that they needed to borrow extra dishes and to lay in a store of rice wine and other spirits, which they kept hidden, lest a few visitors show up and begin making toasts early.

They didn't sleep until late that night and were awakened early the next morning by the expected parade of well-wishers. Appointing a well-groomed student to act as a sort of receptionist in their absence, the Ouyangs spiffed themselves up as best they could and hurried on foot to Treasure Gate, where they found the sedan chair and porters. Father and son now assumed a dignified aspect as they walked in advance of the chair, although now that they were within the city limits, they were mostly lost in the bustle and received only scant attention. It was, as Ouyang Zhenli had said, a favorable day for nuptials, and theirs was not the only wedding party making its way through the streets and alleys. By the time they entered the opulent Qinhuai district, their modest sedan chair had become unworthy of notice, and Nanyu was glad. Arriving at the House of the Entrancing Fragrance, he saw nothing but Daosheng's eyes, peering out through a window.

She was wearing a brighter-color robe than her usual novice's attire, and a wig with hairpins concealed the fuzzy scalp of a woman recently "come down from the mountain;" but otherwise, her costume was plain and her attitude no-nonsense. Though Nanjing custom dictated that the bride's mother (and not her father) give her daughter away by accompanying her to the groom's house, all Ouyangs concerned believed that she had fulfilled this symbolic duty two days previously—and Ouyang Gen might also have been a bit self-conscious at the prospect of hosting a celebrated entertainer at his humble domicile. Ouyang

Zhenli, therefore, elected to remain at home, although she did conform to local custom by contributing a flask of *gaoliang*.

Daosheng prepared to embark in the sedan chair, but then she remembered one last, customary detail.

"I don't want to go, Mother!" she cried, clinging to Ouyang Zhenli's sleeve. "Please don't make me go with them. I want to stay here with you!"

Everyone grinned at the performance, and Nanyu said to Daosheng, "All right, then. Never mind. Just forget the whole thing."

Daosheng released her mother's sleeve, saying, "You know this isn't goodbye, in any case."

Bows were exchanged all around, with genuine good humor. Daosheng climbed into the sedan chair without Nanyu's proffered assistance, and the party retreated down Agarwood Street. Cheers greeted them a short time later when they arrived at Ouyang Gen's home. The crowd of guests had decorously refrained from eating or drinking until their return. Now that bride and groom were in their places, however, the dumpling man began tossing handfuls of his creations into cauldrons of boiling water, fishing them out with a strainer, and apportioning them to large bowls, which were quickly distributed among the wobbly tables that now blocked the street in front of the Ouyangs' door. Smaller dipping bowls, and the soy sauce, rice vinegar, and sesame oil that were to fill them, had already been passed out, as had several cloves of garlic per table. Everyone had brought his own pair of chopsticks.

Nanyu and Daosheng began circulating among the guests, toasting them at every table. Nanyu recognized a few of the students and monks from the Temple at the Edge of Heaven, but the serene face of Baichi Shi'ai was not in the crowd. He looked across the street at the hills of the temple and took comfort, nonetheless, that the abbot was with him and Daosheng in spirit. As for Daosheng herself, she had to deal with several male guests who enjoyed busying her with frequent requests for more liquor, more soy sauce, more something or other. They justified their behavior by claiming to be preparing her for married life.

Much alcohol was consumed. Ouyang Gen consulted closely with his appointed receptionist as they counted the copper coins that people had brought as wedding gifts, which filled a box next to the guest book. "I just might come out ahead," he said, every few minutes.

Nanyu had been rehearsing what he would say, in case anyone asked about Daosheng's background, but he never had to field the first question on the subject. No one, furthermore, took the trouble to inspect her feet, having no reason to suspect that they were unbound. All were focused on drinking, in any case. Lunch turned into an afternoon fete, which then evolved into dinner and an evening soiree. The tireless snack chef was kept on, though he switched the menu from dumplings to noodles, served with spinach and sesame paste. Toasts gave way to drinking games, and soon the presence of Nanyu and Daosheng became superfluous — indeed, both bride and groom were forgotten. They were able to slip away, with neither formal ceremony nor leering prodding by the group. Finding the workshop unromantic, they climbed up into the sleeping loft.

Ouyang Gen was heedless of their movements, absorbed as he was in the counting of his earnings. Finally, he put the coins away and fell asleep with his head on the money box. By that time, many tired merrymakers had begun to go home, though isolated tippling continued at two or three tables. The occasional sounds of clinking cups punctuated the next couple of hours, until the last few drinkers dozed off on their stools and benches, their foreheads on the tables before them, in the crooks of their arms. All was finally quiet, as the sky began to brighten in the east.

Just as the sun rose above the hills of the Temple at the Edge of Heaven, in the middle room of the Ouyangs' home, the wooden supports of the newlyweds' sleeping loft creaked and splintered, and the whole thing fell with a crash to the floor. Nanyu and Daosheng lay disheveled and entwined amid the wreckage. They began hurriedly to dress but stopped when no investigating footsteps could be heard coming their way. Only the sounds of snoring came from outside.

Daosheng said:

"In the storeroom was the sleeping-tree;
Very delicate were its boughs.
Oh, soft and tender,
Glad I am that the thing fell down.

"In the storeroom was the sleeping-tree;
Very delicate were its flowers.
Oh, soft and tender,
Glad I am that we have no bed.

"In the storeroom was the sleeping-tree;
Very delicate was its fruit.
Oh, soft and tender,
Glad I am that we now must move."

They cleared some of the lumber away, smoothed out their bedding, and dozed off again on the floor, while the sun continued to rise. However, as light filled the room, a strange murmur seeped in with it, an eerie wail that gradually assumed both male and female cadences as it swelled. Nanyu and Daosheng, still fast asleep, turned to each other for comfort in the mournful chorus; but by the time their eyes began blinking and they lifted their heads, the lamentation had come together into a single, despairing refrain: "The Emperor is dead!"

The news of Chongzhen's death had finally reached Nanjing. It was one thing for the realm to have lost its capital. It was another for it to have lost its father.

PART TWO

4

MAY TO JUNE, 1644

THE HONGGUANG EMPEROR ascended the throne in Nanjing, to rule over what remained of Chongzhen's empire. A first cousin of Chongzhen's, Hongguang had arrived from his estate in the interior, claiming only to be seeking refuge. He nonetheless consented to be named regent and was crowned emperor twelve days later, thus making Nanjing the makeshift capital.

Meanwhile, the Dashing Prince, Li Zicheng, had led the bulk of his army back out of Beijing, leaving the city in the hands of subordinates who immediately began plundering and murdering its population. He moved not south but against Chongzhen's sole remaining general in the north, Wu Sangui, who had been guarding the Great Wall against the hostile Manchus on the other side. Confronted by enemies both before and behind, General Wu chose to submit to the Manchus, and together their allied army routed the rebel Li in a two-day battle. The victors entered Beijing soon after that, welcomed by its traumatized residents. However, since the Manchus had enthroned an emperor of their own—a boy whose reign name, Shunzhi, meant "Orderly Rule"—and since "there are not two suns in the sky," the remnant government's elevation of Hongguang in the south made a dynastic showdown inevitable.

Because the Manchus had earned great credit by punishing

Li Zicheng and restoring calm in Beijing, the rump regime in Nanjing was at a disadvantage. Upon assuming the throne, therefore, Hongguang, whose reign title meant "Liberal and Illuminating," sought to cultivate popular support. He issued a propitiating edict, in which he waived tax arrears, anathematized official corruption, amnestied prisoners, and promised an end to oppression. His proclamation contained the phrase "Our wish is to give the people a new beginning."

卍卐 卍卐 卍卐

While these events were unfolding, Nanyu and Daosheng moved to the House of the Entrancing Fragrance to live with Daosheng's mother. Ouyang Gen put up only token resistance to the idea, as it meshed with his own plan of allowing Nanyu to find a separate path. Besides, he was in no mind to repair the sleeping loft for the next generation while he himself moved to the workshop. So he gave them a rather unreluctant sendoff, the very morning after their nuptials, as news hawkers continued to wail about the dead Chongzhen.

"You're moving to a real palace," he said.

The House of the Entrancing Fragrance was, of course, a marked improvement over the carpenter's shop on Shakyamuni Street. It was a two-story, square-shaped mansion enclosing a courtyard. The front door was on Agarwood Street, while a sitting room and kitchen were in the rear, right at the edge of the Qinhuai. The bedrooms were on the second floor, following the same pattern, with one overlooking the street and one commanding a view of the river. Parallel galleries completed the square, and there was a staircase in each of these.

Ouyang Zhenli was quite happy to have her daughter and son-in-law residing with her. "Now we can make up for lost time," she said to Daosheng. However, she was also careful to let the younger ones enjoy their privacy. She yielded to them her own bedroom — the Qinhuai-facing one — as well as her own bed, a kind of wicker platform, which would be good for sleeping coolly on warm nights. ("Let's hope we don't rip a hole in it and fall through," Daosheng said.) Ouyang Zhenli set up a smaller wicker bed for herself in the front bedroom.

On the first night in their new home, Nanyu and Daosheng realized that some time would be needed to grow accustomed to it, for they were situated at the very center of the most vibrant entertainment district in China, and it came most fully alive, in all its cacophony, at night. The ill-tidings of the same day did little to disrupt the routine of nocturnal merriment and may even have added an abandoned intensity to it. There seemed to be two strata of noise. In the background was the indistinct clamor of banquet halls, opera houses, tea rooms, and street traffic. From much closer at hand, from a very immediate proximity, in fact, came sounds that infiltrated Nanyu's and Daosheng's most intimate sub-consciousness, as "flower boats" — floating brothels — drifted slowly up and down the narrow Qinhuai, right below their bedroom window, staging for them a continuing symphony of flutes, *pipa*s, arias, folk airs, poetry, philosophic discourse, gossip, feasting, flirting, giggling, and moaning. It was quite novel to experience such diverse, interwoven, performances, from waterborne platforms drifting past.

Nanyu and Daosheng lay on their bed, not speaking and indeed unable to think, with a thin darkness between them. As a boat passed beneath, the light from its lanterns swept slowly across the ceiling, and the smell of perfume invaded their noses. A woman's voice chanted,

"If you don't know how, why pretend?
Maybe you can fool some girls,
But you can't fool Heaven.
I dreamed you'd play with the
Locust blossom under my green jacket,
Like a eunuch with a courtesan.
But lo and behold,
All you can do is mumble.
You've made me all wet and slippery,
But no matter how hard you try
Nothing happens. So stop.
Go and make somebody else
Unsatisfied."

The poem, and the male and female laughter that accompanied it, had a disconcerting effect on Nanyu and Daosheng. They lay there, waiting, while the light, perfume, and poetry faded.

Soon, another boat approached. A female singer, whose voice was much softer than her predecessor's, sang,

"You held my lotus blossom
In your lips
And played with the pistil.
We took one piece of
Rhinoceros horn
And could not sleep all night long.
All night the cock's gorgeous crest stood erect.
All night the bee clung trembling to the flower stamens.
Oh my sweet perfumed jewel!
I will allow only my lord to possess my sacred lotus
    pond,
And every night,

You can make blossom in me
Flowers of fire."

Nanyu and Daosheng felt a little better and soon drifted off.

◨◧ ◨◧ ◨◧

"How do you sleep at night, Mother?" asked Daosheng, when she and Nanyu greeted Ouyang Zhenli downstairs in the sitting room, the following morning.

"I don't," returned Ouyang Zhenli with a grin, as she set a plate of steamed buns on the mahogany table. "This house really isn't for sleeping, and neither is any other house in the area. I thought you knew. You might have to change your habits somewhat. Retiring and waking early, I'm afraid, are unsuited to the mode of life here."

"That doesn't sound very promising for a new bride and groom, with a livelihood yet to be earned," said Daosheng. "How are we supposed to be industrious, if we stay up all night and sleep till noon?"

"Well, you could try the front bedroom, instead."

"Thank you, Mother. That's kind," said Daosheng, glancing sideways at Nanyu. "But who knows? The music of the Qinhuai may yet hold potential as a source of inspiration."

"It certainly may, especially for the aforementioned new bride and groom," said Madame Ouyang.

The three of them spent the day giving the house a thorough cleaning, pausing only for a siesta in the afternoon. They worked until well after the sun went down and enjoyed a late supper of cold noodles, even as the night-revelry on the river reached and passed its apogee. By the time the Ouyangs had finished their midnight tea, the Qinhuai, while still far from quiet, was beginning to settle down.

Ouyang Zhenli said goodnight and retired upstairs. Nanyu and Daosheng remained in the sitting room, watching the river. A smallish, uncovered pleasure-barge emerged from under the adjacent footbridge, to turn once or twice in an eddy, just outside the first-floor window. Its passengers were four or five young men in scholars' robes, who reclined about the deck, intoxicated though not boisterous. One of them tapped a stone on a low snack table and chanted,

"This official wears no official sash.
This farmer pushes no plow.
This Confucian does not read books.
This recluse does not live in the wilds.
In society, he wears lotus leaves for clothes.
Among commoners, he is decked out in cap and jade.
His serenity is achieved without closing the door.
His teaching is done without instruction.
This Buddhist monk has long hair and whiskers.
This Daoist immortal makes love to beautiful women.
One moment, withering away in a silent forest.
The next, bustling through crowds on city streets.
When he sees flowers, he calls for singing girls.
When he has wine to drink, he calls for a pair of dice.
His body is as light as a cloud,
Floating above the Great Clod.
Try asking the bird, flying in the air:
'What clear pond reflects your image?'
Untrammeled! The dragon, curling, leaping,
Unruled! Beyond this world — or of it?"

"I like that one!" said Daosheng, as the boat caught a fresh current and moved away around the bend. "It conveys such a feeling of…"

"Chaos?" said Nanyu.

"Freedom," said Daosheng.

"Freedom?"

"Yes, as in, 'As long as my parents are still alive, how can I have the freedom to do as I please?'" Daosheng was quoting from a popular novel.

"That's a good question," said Nanyu. "How can we?"

"We already do," said Daosheng, "and you, my hero, took the first step, by springing me, and yourself, from the clutches of Wei Su in Beijing."

"Yes, Wife, I remember. That was indeed a bold move."

"Did you surprise yourself by it?"

"A bit, but I had a former apprentice nun to inspire me."

"And you always will."

The stretch of river before the house had cleared of boats. They could hear little ripples lapping at the foundation, with the strains of two or three *pipa*s echoing from different pleasure houses. The moonlight was subdued.

After a while, Daosheng continued. "As for our parents, neither has opposed our marriage, and both seem happy to let us choose our own occupations."

"But that's just the problem," Nanyu said. "And I don't see how the freedom you hear in that poem will help us to choose. It seems to be an argument *against* choosing. An official wearing no sash? A farmer pushing no plow? Would they really count as an official and a farmer?"

"The poem means that everyone is a multitude unto himself," said Daosheng. "He can do anything, and be anything, without having to qualify himself or to accept the limitations of conventions and definitions. It's like what One-Eyed Jinggang used to say about seeing through fixed types, even obvious ones like 'man' and 'woman,' until they fall away."

Daosheng tilted her head from one side to the other.

"Still," she puzzled, "I see what you mean. That kind of freedom does seem rather negative. Even if you are able to transcend conventions and definitions until fixed types fall away, you still know only what you are not; you haven't determined what you are. If freedom means that you can be as many things as you choose, you still have to make the choices."

"Hmmm," Nanyu mused. "Baichi Shi'ai is always saying something about how 'this' is also 'that' and 'that' is also 'this.' Is that not a better way of looking at it?"

"Yes, *the sage embraces things*," said Daosheng, "while *ordinary men discriminate among them and parade their discriminations before others*. Perhaps embracing things is the sagely approach to freedom, while simply delighting in transgression — in being 'a Buddhist monk with long hair and whiskers' — is really an elaborate way of discriminating among things and parading — by flaunting — one's discriminations before others."

Nanyu thought for a moment. "But aren't freedom and... 'transgression' the same thing?" he asked. "How can you have the one without the other?"

There came a prolonged splashing sound, as someone in a house upstream dumped the night's accumulation of garbage into the river.

Daosheng smiled. "Yes, we've managed to muddle the argument pretty well, I'd say." Her smile turned saucy. "In our case, of course, embracing and transgressing were indeed one and the same." She put her head on Nanyu's shoulder. "And yet, now we are past the transgression and may freely embrace as husband and wife. Funny, isn't it? Though this freedom, perchance, was not properly our lot, it has nonetheless fallen upon us to enjoy. Does this not mean that we possessed it all along?"

Nanyu chuckled. "I thought you said I was your hero! Did we possess this freedom all along, or did I have to grab it, when I grabbed you, from the fat man?"

Daosheng ran her fingers through her short crop of hair. "I'm sure I don't know, Husband, though I'm glad you did *grab* me, if only to realize what was already fated."

They remained silent for a while, listening to the rhythms of distant drums, the lapping of the river, and their own heartbeats. Suddenly, Daosheng rose and walked across the room, to the window. She leaned her back against the frame, facing her husband.

"However we came by our freedom," she said, "it would be a pity to waste it. We would seem to have the opportunity to pursue a variety of 'this' as well as 'that,' and if we've already committed the requisite transgression, so much the better. Even if we turn out not to be sages, we can at least be clever. Things being how they are, we might not have the leisure to embrace everything at once; but we should be able to use our freedom to do something, perhaps many things."

"Like painting," said Nanyu. The half-completed four-leaf album happened to be at his elbow, on a side table.

"Yes! Let the cicada molt yet again, to emerge as the 'untrammeled dragon!'" said Daosheng. "Will you visit your clients at the temple and the storyteller on Three Mountain Street?"

"We can go in the morning."

"Excellent!" said Daosheng, who had begun to pace in the center of the room. "*This* artist actually paints pictures! I guess you don't belong in the poem we just heard." She nodded to herself, and Nanyu was pleased to note the magic twinkle in her eye.

"And why stop there?" she continued. "Here we are, in a fully equipped tea room, in one of the best-known houses, in the liveliest part of town. Why not put it to good use, and go into business?"

"You're sure your mother won't mind?"

"Well, it wouldn't hurt to ask her. Both she and your father, as I just said, have been plenty encouraging so far. Perhaps they would help us out with a little capital, for our venture."

"Hmm. You know, speaking of tea, Baichi Shi'ai shared some with me recently."

"Maybe he's found a good place to buy it."

"I thought he just summoned it into the cup."

"Really," said Daosheng. "You should ask him about it when you visit the temple. Don't forget to call on your father, too."

"We should both go."

Daosheng was gazing into space, imagining the myriad possibilities. Not wishing to disturb her concentration with further discussion, both she and Nanyu went upstairs and turned in. On this second night on the Qinhuai, it was the anticipation that made it hard to sleep.

The next morning, Ouyang Zhenli endorsed her daughter's proposal to open a tea shop. She herself now only entertained old acquaintances when they happened to drop by, and although she didn't charge them specifically for the tea or for her company, she accepted their gifts and tips. Daosheng planned to offer tea and snacks to paying customers, while providing music and singing as a draw. The two of them agreed that Ouyang Zhenli's established patrons would be treated as her private guests, that they would keep separate pantries, and that the younger Ouyangs would pay twenty percent of their receipts as rent for the venue and accoutrements, but otherwise, they didn't expect that much conflict would result from the new mode of operation. Ouyang Zhenli looked forward to playing *pipa* duets with Daosheng.

Nanyu and Daosheng went to see Ouyang Gen and found him setting the hinges in a door. He was receptive to the younger ones' business plan and expressed confidence that his clever new daughter-in-law would make it work. He brought out the box of wedding gifts from a few nights before and removed about half the coins, "For my expenses," he said; and then he handed it to Daosheng. Turning back to his unfinished door, he dismissed his guests with a "Now we've all got jobs to do."

Nanyu and Daosheng took their leave, crossed the street, and ran into Baichi Shi'ai, who was just then emerging from the Entrance to the Practice of the Benevolent World. Beaming, the abbot invited them to enjoy "a cup of summer" and escorted them into the Temple of Tea, a small tea room, built just outside the front gate. As Nanyu and Daosheng made themselves comfortable on a grass mat, Baichi Shi'ai drew water from the well and set it to boil. Sensing that the Ouyangs had come on business, he treated them to the generous silence he commonly bestowed upon Ouyang Gen.

Daosheng cleared her throat. "As fate would have it, Teacher," she said, "it is tea that brings us here," and she went on to sketch the outlines of her idea.

Baichi Shi'ai was thrilled and nodded vigorously. "Fate is indeed friendly today," he said. "My wholesaler, Mr Qian, is expected momentarily. Why not stay and see what he has in stock? You can acquire a taste for the tea I have on hand, while you wait."

The monk served them two green teas: the local Rain Flower and the much rarer Heaven's Pool, imported from Songluo

Mountain in the southernmost reaches of the province. Rain Flower was what Nanyu had imbibed on the day he drew his cicada, even as he overlooked Rain Flower Terrace. He had to admit, however, despite his fondness for the produce of his own region — and despite the fact that his name shared a common character with that of the local tea — that the Heaven's Pool was more refreshing.

When Mr Qian arrived, he brought two more green teas: Dragon Well and Heaven's Eye, both from farther down the Yangtze valley, which tasted as fresh as the ponds that watered them. Baichi Shi'ai let the Ouyangs have big bags of Rain Flower and Heaven's Pool as a wedding present and urged Mr Qian to sell them even more of those two varieties, as well as some Dragon Well and Heaven's Eye, at a discount. The resulting four-item menu seemed inauspicious, so Mr Qian recommended a Fujianese tea called Water Sprite, which was processed a newer way, yielding a darker sort of tea that people were beginning to call Black Dragon, or Oolong. Overstimulated by all the tea they had sampled, Nanyu and Daosheng thanked the abbot and merchant in turn and bounced out the door.

Back home, Daosheng found two celebratory red flags and, with her mother's permission, painted the single character for tea on each. She placed one on the street side and one on the river side, and as soon as they finished their lunch, the Ouyangs opened for business.

囗囗 囗囗 囗囗

"The Qinhuai lolls
By the flirting mansions
Waving like fine thin silk

"Waving like fine thin silk
Right below our window
Lolling, sparkling 'neath the teahouse flag.

"Her hair adorned with plum flowers and lotuses
Reflected in the summer ripples

"Reflected in the summer ripples
Sparkling, alone."

Mother and daughter sang and played their *pipa*s while seated behind low screens. Daosheng occasionally rose to retrieve tea or snacks from the adjacent kitchen, handing them to Ouyang Zhenli, who served them to the customers. The new establishment's patrons tended to be thoughtful and sober men, for those desiring alcohol would go elsewhere and neither Daosheng nor her mother were the typical singing girl who might have attracted carousers. In the resulting meditative ambiance, Nanyu's services as bouncer were unneeded, and he mostly paced the halls, ushering new arrivals into the sitting room but otherwise making himself scarce. The first evening wound up at a reasonable hour. The entrepreneurs counted and divided their coins, took down the tea flags, and went to bed.

☖☖ ☖☖ ☖☖

"On the many-curved Qinhuai
A flower boat frolic
Made fast to the quay
To the sound of the women's song

"So many boats
Hug the willow shore
Next to the pavilion in the moonlight

"The nights turn to days —
For their cotton and damask
Who will leave them a tip?

"Will it be this young man,
Steady and strong?
Alas he has no office
And he's poor, poor!"

During off hours, Daosheng devised numerous improvements. She discovered that six porcelain saucers could be fitted together on a tray so that it looked like a plum flower, with one saucer in the middle and the other five as the petals. She painted the saucers in the appropriate colors and fashioned a cover for them, with a handle on top that looked like a flower stem. Six snack foods — say, pickled cabbage, turnips, peanuts, bamboo shoots, bean curd, and sautéed spinach — could be prepared and served as a set and replenished individually, by lifting out the empty saucers. Guests admired the efficiency as much as the aesthetic effect.

Daosheng invented new dishes, by combining familiar elements, such as dried bean curd and peanuts, or soybeans and seaweed, lightly sprinkled with sesame oil. She also found an ingenious method of flavoring the tea: putting a fistful of leaves into a gauze bag, placing the bag in a lotus flower, and letting the petals close around it for the night. At daybreak, the flower would open, and Daosheng would remove the naturally-scented leaves. The House of the Entrancing Fragrance was living up to its name.

🗗🗗 🗗🗗 🗗🗗

As summer deepened, the heat became unbearable. Daosheng designed lattices for the windows and interwove them with some wisteria vines that she rerouted from a trellis outside. Though past flowering, the wisteria provided shade from the long afternoon sun while still admitting the breeze. At night, the living lattice could be moved aside for viewing the colorful boats.

"Meandering, melancholy Qinhuai
When was it? How long ago?
Where lived my clever girl?

"Only now with her gone do I miss my ruined country
A sudden gust disturbs the surface, as if speaking to me."

🗗🗗 🗗🗗 🗗🗗

After one month, Daosheng reviewed the outgoes and income:

Expenses

Teas:	Rain Flower	400 coppers
	Heaven's Pool	800
	Dragon Well	600
	Heaven's Eye	600
	Water Sprite	800
	(subtotal)	3200
Snacks:	peanuts	525
	bamboo shoots	470
	bean curd	325
	dried bean curd	450

spinach	415
cabbage	385
soybeans	325
turnips	315
seaweed	490
(subtotal)	3700
vinegar, oils, chilies, etc.	72
bamboo (for lattice), etc.	49
Total Expenses	7021
Gross Earnings	17239
less 20% rent	-3448
(subtotal)	13791
less the outgoes	-7021
Net Profit	6770 coppers

It was the equivalent of about two ounces of silver, and Nanyu and Daosheng took their earnings to a money changer to obtain the more valuable metal. Back home, they put the two ingots on a table and contemplated the shape: oval, with upturned ends, kind of like boiled pork dumplings. The metal's dull luster grew fuzzy in their gaze, as they sat for a long while. Each of the ingots reflected blurry images of each of their faces.

That afternoon, Ouyang Zhenli went off to go to Cock-Crow Temple, and Nanyu and Daosheng were slow to open the shop. They were still sitting there, absorbed in their ingots, when they were startled by a voice.

"Worshipping the god of silver, I see."

A plainly-dressed though clever-looking young man had come through the house and now stood at the entrance to the tea room. Nanyu and Daosheng shook themselves from their stupor and rose to their feet, Daosheng heading for the kitchen and Nanyu motioning for their guest to sit down in the chair she had vacated.

"Are you open for business yet?" asked the newcomer.

"We're supposed to be," said Nanyu, "but we forgot to put up the flags."

He made no effort to do so now and sat back down where he'd been, with the young man, and with the silver still on the table. "I hope you don't mind our taking a few extra minutes to get ready," he continued, realizing that he'd never had to deal so closely with a customer before. "Your first cup will be on the house…I believe we've been honored by your presence, on an earlier occasion?"

"Yes, I stopped in a couple of days ago," said the man. He removed a fan from his sleeve and began to wave it slowly at his smooth-shaven face and neck. "I had a mellow time, free of the usual banalities—so please don't be so formal, while you keep me company. My name is Gong Xian."

"I'm Ouyang Nanyu, and this is my wife, Daosheng."

"You are most welcome," said Daosheng, who had appeared from the kitchen, carrying a plum flower tray. She handed it to Nanyu over the little screen, and then made to sit down behind it.

"Actually, big sister, why don't you join us?" said Gong Xian. "That is, if you don't mind. I was just telling your husband how I have found your house, even after only one visit, to be a kind of refuge from rigid distinctions. Why sit separately, behind a screen?"

"Why, indeed?" said Daosheng. She swung her feet, one by

one, over the screen, and Gong Xian gasped when he saw them. It took him a few moments to regain his poise, while Daosheng scooped the silver off the table, put down the tray, and lifted the cover. The central saucer was empty, for the house had run out of peanuts; so in a sudden whimsy, she opened her fist, and dropped the silver into it.

Gong Xian chuckled. "And here I was, professing to be the eccentric."

"Are you an eccentric, Mr Gong?" asked Daosheng.

"I have that reputation," Gong said. "But perhaps eccentricity is the falsest distinction of all." His expression turned sheepish. "For example, I suppose I should apologize for remarking just now that you were worshipping the god of silver, when, truth be told, I'm not above praying to him myself. I just sold a landscape painting for two ounces of silver, just like these."

Nanyu said, "Oh. I was supposed to get four for a little album, but...I got distracted."

"Are you an artist, too?" Gong asked.

"Um...possibly," said Nanyu.

Daosheng skipped to the kitchen and returned with a tray holding three cups of Heaven's Pool, which she placed on the table, before resuming her seat.

"You say you were distracted from your work," Gong continued, addressing Nanyu. "Do you mean that you were disgusted by the idea of prostituting your art, of painting for money?"

Nanyu hesitated. "Uh, no, that wasn't the problem."

Gong Xian lifted his teacup to his face, savoring the rising steam. "I'm glad to hear it," he said, smiling. "Of course, it's mandatory for artists to decry the art market, but I find it quite pretentious when they do so. So-called literati artists have the luxury of exchanging paintings amongst themselves, expecting no payment but prestige; but inevitably, they become subject to each other's narrow judgements, far too concerned with what 'literati paintings' should look like. Those standards were set long ago, by self-appointed connoisseurs now dead and gone." He took a sip. "I, on the other hand, though I must exert myself in the 'inkstone field,' plowing in the morning and harvesting in the evening — at least I have the freedom to set my own standards."

"Ah, 'freedom,'" said Daosheng.

"Yes, the term is apt," continued Gong Xian. "I mean, supposing I did crave renown as a literati artist, I would have to submit to the whims of others, in the hope that they would grant me the title. However, if *I* call the tune, and *I* decide who's qualified to be a literati artist — or a sage or a worthy or an immortal or a Buddha — subject to *my* definition — that, then, is freedom; that, then, is self-sovereignty."

Gong Xian was looking out the window and speaking to no one in particular. "Once I exercise the freedom to define myself, to assign a value to myself and to my work, then the world may come to concur. In fact, few gentlemen and officials consider me a crude 'professional painter' at all. On the contrary, many of them come in person, in their tall, four-horse carriages, right to my rustic door. Plainly, those fine gentlemen and officials consider my dry brush and left-over ink to be valuable — because I considered them valuable first."

Daosheng refreshed Gong Xian's teacup. "Very well, then," she said. "You're a 'literati painter' who paints for money and a 'professional painter' whose work appeals to literati. Refusing to be labeled as either gentleman or craftsman, you are free to carry on as both."

"Big sister is most astute."

"What kind of work do you create, then, given that you set the standards and gentlemen reward you with their silver if not their anointment?"

"Anything, as long as it's original. Take landscape, for example. Paintings by other artists are all of places where people have gone. They cannot paint places where no one has ever gone. My paintings, on the other hand, are of places where no one has ever gone."

"But how can that be?" wondered Nanyu. "Where are such places, and how could you paint them, if no one—not even yourself—has ever been there?"

"The world has many wondrous and inaccessible places," Gong Xian said. "Were they not captured by artists, people would grow old and die beneath their windows, without ever being able to see them. It doesn't matter whether these places actually exist, for anything that exists in the minds of artists also exists in the world."

The afternoon sun was pouring through the window, and the three of them were baking in the heat. Belatedly, Nanyu got up to deploy Daosheng's wisteria lattice. Gong Xian finished his second cup of tea and dabbed his forehead.

"Perhaps our conversation should end on that note," he said. "Besides, the only thing in this artist's mind right now is the heat. I should probably head back to my place on Cooling Hill—fortunately, it really exists!—and take my siesta. Good afternoon, big brother and big sister."

He showed himself out, not offering to pay for his second cup of tea or for the snacks.

While Daosheng cleared the table, Nanyu decided to follow Gong Xian's example and to take an afternoon nap. Half asleep already, he stumbled upstairs and collapsed onto the wicker platform, which had been stripped of its coverings. Even so, the air moved only sluggishly over and under him.

Daosheng sat down amid the tables downstairs and was

likewise content that their shop remain closed for a few hours. She untied her robe and held it open in the front, fanning her bare torso with her other hand. Leaning back against the inside wall, she too felt ready to close her eyes, when her dimming vision caught sight of the two ingots of silver, still on the table. She sat up and grabbed one of them and pressed it against the side of her neck, hoping that it possessed some kind of innate cooling power. Perhaps it did, for she shivered at its touch. Smiling, she reached over to deposit both fan and ingot on the side table, but then she noticed the four-leaf album sitting there, together with Nanyu's bundled-up Four Treasures. With a shrug suggesting "Why not?" she took up the album and the painting supplies, and began organizing them on the table in front of her. She fetched a cup of water from the kitchen and went to work mixing several different kinds of ink, her attention focused inward.

On the third leaf of the album, Daosheng traced an outline of Cooling Hill, a familiar Nanjing landmark. Then she added a full forest of trees, eschewing evergreens and depicting instead a multitude of maples, oaks, birches, beeches, willows, and poplars. These she rendered in their autumnal colors, brilliant reds and yellows, ablaze in a cloudless sky. Crisp fall air seemed to flow through the scene, and Daosheng unconsciously pulled the neck of her robe closed. Remixing a fresh supply of ink, she paused for a moment before conjuring up the main element: a sprightly *fenghuang*, a phoenix with wings outstretched, dancing on a hillock in the foreground. Its plumage mimicked the hues of the trees, but Daosheng set it off with a golden tint; and it craned its neck heavenward, singing lustily. The inscription blared from its beak:

This pheasant's crest is an empress's crown.
This peacock's tail is her train.
This crane's legs end in sharp eagle's claws.
This hen, like a rooster, is crowing again.

This bird could be guarding mysterious Kunlun.
This bird could be scattering snakes.
This bird could embody the Five Holy Virtues.
This bird could bring peace; let there be no mistake.

Yet this queen of birds has come down from the
mountain;
This regal *fenghuang* has surrendered her throne,
Not soaring but earthbound, to Great Clod well-
rooted,
Humble, perhaps—yet her fate is her own!

That's why she's dancing on her little hillside,
Grateful for every last autumnal tree,
Cool air in her lungs, under sky crisp with sunshine.
Is this, after all, what it means to be free?

Daosheng replaced the album on the side table, leaving it
open, for the ink to dry. When Nanyu awoke and came back
downstairs, he saw it and smiled.

After a few more days of brisk business, Daosheng counted out
some newly-earned coppers and restocked the storeroom with
tea and other foodstuffs. She also hired two men to apply fresh
paint to the trim of the house. While they worked in the blazing

sun, Nanyu sat in the tearoom, studying Mencius, as had become his habit. He glanced up to watch the sweaty painters ascending their ladders, and then he resumed his reading. *"There are those who labor with their minds and those who labor with their muscles,"* his lips moved. *"The former rule; the latter are ruled."*

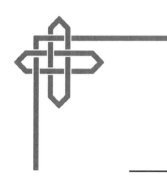

5

JUNE TO SEPTEMBER, 1644

IN THE ATMOSPHERE of dynastic uncertainty that permeated the south, social stability was proving elusive. The news of Chongzhen's death, coupled with the Nanjing regime's promise of liberality, had spread disorder throughout the Yangtze valley. Bondservants passed the word amongst themselves that they no longer had to serve their masters. In several villages in Songjiang Prefecture, thousands of bondsmen began seizing their contracts of indenture from their masters at swordpoint. Once they had obtained, and destroyed, the legal instruments of their slavery, the renegades pressed their advantage by humiliating and killing their former overlords and plundering their mansions bare. The prefect mobilized the militia and captured and executed them.

Nearby, in Jiading County, Suzhou Prefecture, a group of tavern lackeys and scullery boys rose in a riot and began threatening their masters in broad daylight. Armed with spears and cudgels, they ate and drank to their hearts' content, while forcing their erstwhile superiors to kneel at their feet. The newly humbled ones could only hit their heads against the ground and beg for their lives. In the event, none was actually killed, but their homes were robbed and burned. An official who chanced to be passing through Jiading sized up the situation, organized a militia, and killed about twenty of the mob.

Farther up the Yangtze valley, masses of tenant farmers and other unfree people began chanting, "The emperor has changed. Masters should become servants!" They too demanded the return of their indenture papers and pillaged villas and storehouses. Their leader reasoned, "We are endowed by Heaven with a special opportunity, for our masters are all weak and feeble and are not able to take up arms." In fact, the balance of power would be swinging ever more toward the lower classes, as the looming threat of Manchu invasion necessitated that they be armed for defense, a prospect which few of the better sort relished.

Many wealthy families of the south were abandoning their country estates and seeking refuge in Nanjing. In the process, they lost control of their tenants and housemen, who then came to Nanjing on their own to join the army. Often, the new recruits would find out where their former masters were lodging and show up on horseback outside the gates of these places, exultantly cursing them. Not always stopping at denunciation, the unwelcome visitors would sometimes take to vandalizing the mansions' entryways with their spears until they were mollified by gifts of food and drink.

Nonetheless, as summer turned into autumn, the gentry of the south beat back these challenges and reasserted their control. Order was restored for a time.

And along the Qinhuai, the flirtatious poetry and merry music that served as background to Nanyu's and Daosheng's waking and sleeping remained undisturbed by the discordant strains of rebellion.

🏮🏮🏮

The Mid-Autumn Festival has always been the occasion for happy family reunions. Celebrated under the full moon during the eighth lunar month, the holiday symbolizes completeness. Although the House of the Entrancing Fragrance offered not only a serviceable kitchen but also a comfortable sitting room with views of the moon and of its reflection in the Qinhuai, Daosheng could no longer imagine enjoying any form of recreational activity in the same place where she earned her living. Instead, she planned a boat excursion on Xuanwu Lake, and she wanted to invite her mother as well as Nanyu's father.

"But inviting your mother is a breach of decorum," said Nanyu, as the two of them discussed Daosheng's idea over breakfast. "As dictated by ritual, each family consists of parents, sons, daughters-in-law, and daughters yet unmarried. The natal relations of the daughters-in-law no longer apply."

"Ah, Husband," returned Daosheng. "I am naturally filled with filial piety toward your honorable father. Yet how can I dismiss my equally natural feelings toward my own mother?"

"Such is your obligation."

"Are we under no obligation to my mother, who has housed us and lent us her tearoom?"

"That is in the nature of a business relationship."

"Nonsense. Do you honestly believe, Husband, that when we turned up at her doorstep, with your honorable father, the carpenter, having decided that he couldn't be bothered with building us a proper bed—or, for that matter, with letting you build one yourself—that she viewed us only as potential business partners, with no familial affection whatever? Did she surrender her own bedroom to nondescript lodgers, thinking only to bring in a little extra cash? Do you really suppose my mother to be that wanting of human feelings, or are you the one who lacks them, since you obviously cannot perceive them?"

"But you're speaking of 'a love without discrimination, which amounts to a denial of one's father.'"

"No, Husband. I'm speaking of 'reciprocity,' which, according to Confucius himself, is the one word that should guide us all our lives."

"You keep calling me 'Husband,' yet you aren't behaving as a proper wife should. 'Between husband and wife, there should be differentiation.'"

"Oh! Is that what you call it!"

"It means that your proper sphere is within the family and mine is without. Your mother is an outsider, no longer a concern of yours."

"Rest assured, Husband, that it is you who remains my chief concern, especially now that you are acting like such an oaf. 'Only if a husband has a remonstrating wife will he avoid falling into evil ways. If a husband transgresses against the Way, then his wife must correct him. If a wife simply obeys her husband in everything, then how can she be considered a virtuous person?'"

Nanyu made ready to retort but could not, for he had run out of text. He lowered his head until he was looking only at his bowl of rice porridge. In the meantime, Ouyang Zhenli entered the sitting room, having heard everything. She exchanged knowing smirks with her daughter.

"Never mind us, Mother," said Daosheng. "We're just keeping house. I believe my husband has something to ask you."

Nanyu looked up. "Ah…Good morning, Mother. I trust you slept well. Have you any plans for this evening? Let's go moon viewing on Xuanwu Lake."

The operation was somewhat involved. Because the government stored its population registers on islands in the lake, it was technically off-limits to civilians. Discipline had relaxed in recent years, however, and a pass system was now in place, permitting access to the area to anyone who obtained a bamboo tally, which Daosheng now secured with the help of several coins. Next, she sent a messenger to Shakyamuni Street with an invitation for Ouyang Gen. By the time he arrived—on foot—in mid-afternoon on the day of the festival, Daosheng had prepared a few boxes of mooncakes, the traditional delicacies served on Mid-Autumn Festival. She also arranged for a cart, which the four Ouyangs then rode through town, past Cock-Crow Temple, and out through the Gate of Great Peace to the lake. There they found the boat that Daosheng had engaged, with its crew of two, its comfortable seats at the railing, and its spacious floor planking for lying down drunk and contemplating the moon. Heavy blankets were provided, and they were necessary, for a coolness that both presaged the coming months and recalled past years was now an unmistakable presence in the evening air, especially after the boat was launched and began cruising on open water.

Like his son, Ouyang Gen was less than thrilled at the inclusion of Ouyang Zhenli, and he mostly ignored her, although it occurred to Daosheng that he might have been anxious to avoid the appearance of any unseemly relationship with an unattached woman of his own age. Daosheng appreciated also that her father-in-law had come to rely on her to run things, and so she assumed the role of master of ceremonies. To preserve good cheer, she announced a friendly two-copper fine, payable as a contribution to the "mooncake kitty," for any mention of taboo topics, such as the loss of the north, the disturbances in the south, or the political situation in Hongguang's court. She also placed a moratorium on poetry, anticipating that the production of it would become a task set for the women by the men.

Almost immediately, however, Ouyang Zhenli broke both rules simultaneously by picking up her *pipa*, which she'd brought aboard, and singing:

"From Heaven's Peak the moon rises bright,
Over a boundless sea of cloud.
Winds blow for miles with main and might
Past the Jade Gate which stands so proud.
Our warriors march along the frontier,
While Tartars peer across azure bays.
From the battlefield outstretched here,
None have come back since olden days.
Guards watch the desolate borderland,
Thinking of home, with wistful eyes.
Tonight upstairs their wives still stand,
Looking afar with longing sighs."

No one said anything, as a twilight breeze rustled through the trees on the shore. A few seconds later, it reached their faces, bringing another reminder of the coming chill.

"Well, now I'm feeling right chipper," said Ouyang Gen. "Hey, Daughter-in-Law, doesn't your mother know the rules? I think she should pay double for that one."

"Very well, sir," said the courtesan. "If you insist, four bits it is." She dropped her fine into an empty mooncake box, and it made a clanging sound.

"Whoops, careful," said Ouyang Gen. "Let's not attract any ruffian's attention by rattling our money around." He looked up at the two hired hands, who were poling the boat. "Are these guys reliable?" He laughed with an amused bravado.

"You be careful, yourself, Father," said Daosheng, trying to manage him with a smile. "You're coming close to forbidden territory, too."

"Oh, what's the sense trying to avoid unpleasant topics?" said Ouyang Gen. "The trick is to turn them into pleasant ones. For starters, we should change the fine from paying money to drinking liquor!" He chortled again.

"Yes, Father," said Daosheng. "Such a reform would greatly alter the course of the conversation, as well as its tone. In fact, now that I think of it," she continued, "perhaps your method is altogether superior. Why not bring a little levity to bear upon uncomfortable issues? They might frighten us less."

"That's more like it, girl!" said Ouyang Gen, raising his cup to Daosheng and then to the others. "I'm certainly not the first to want to see a rosy hue around ugly things, and some folks can even pull it off without the alcohol. Have you heard the news about the Du family, who are staying up the street from me?"

Nobody had.

"They used to own half of wherever they're from," recounted Ouyang Gen, "but they got chased out by the mob, and now they're living just outside the Nanjing wall, in a place not much bigger than mine. Most of their servants abandoned them, and one of them, it turns out, joined the army." He looked toward the west, where the last traces of the sun were vanishing. The others faced the opposite way, toward the moon, looming just over the horizon. "Anyway," Ouyang Gen went on, "this guy comes by on a horse, wearing thick leather armor, and he tries to talk his friend, a servant who stayed loyal to the family, into running away too. Now, get what the other one supposedly says. He says: 'Everyone has his own allotted destiny. Your destiny is always to get what you want; so if, by chance, things don't go your way, you become indignant and take what you think you deserve. However, my destiny is ill-starred and meagre. It's my part to stay by my master's side, content to share with him all cold and hunger.' And then, as the story goes, the traitor feels so ashamed of himself, he goes away and never bothers Mr Du's exalted household again."

None of the others said anything, not because the story was

HARRY MILLER

unremarkable, but because Ouyang Gen had yet to make his point. He did soon enough, though, and he was succinct.

"Dog farts!" he said.

"How so, Mr Ouyang?" ventured Daosheng's mother. "Why don't you believe the story?"

"Because it's only what the gentry want to hear. What better taffy to feed themselves, in these troubled times? 'Don't worry! We still have plenty of loyal serfs, and they'll stick with us through thick and thin. They'll even talk some sense into the troublemakers.'"

"But not all the bondservants have revolted," Ouyang Zhenli said. "Some of them have indeed remained loyal, just like Mr Du's man in this story you find so hard to swallow."

"What's hard to swallow is how proud he is to be humble," said Ouyang Gen, struggling to remain calm. "Have you ever heard anyone argue so cleverly for his own slavery?"

"Father, I too find this aspect of the story most odd."

It was Nanyu. Ouyang Gen was becoming accustomed to his daughter-in-law speaking up but was taken aback that his son had done so. Saying nothing, he simply gestured for Nanyu to elaborate.

"If, as you suggest, Father, the gentry have disguised their own hopes as a servant's speech, in a story designed for their own ears, then their hopes are pathetic indeed."

"What do you mean, Husband?" asked Daosheng.

"Well, they're presuming for their survival upon the meekness of their underlings. It's such a strange thing to hope for."

"Husband, the vast bulk of their learning amounts to a presumption upon the meekness of underlings."

"But what if human beings turn out to be not quite so meek? By the gentry's own admission, as allegedly voiced by Du's servant, the energetic and enterprising ones will tend to revolt.

Wouldn't the preservation of social harmony, then, depend upon the suppression of energy and enterprise among the people?"

Silence followed Nanyu's question. By now even the twilight had receded, and if one looked straight up, then not only the shoreline but the entire earthly horizon dropped away. The boat seemed suspended beneath the moon and the stars, and as it rocked there, the sensation came over each of its passengers that he or she was floating in space.

Daosheng drank some Rain Flower from a flask. "Yes, Husband, it does seem a bit ironic that Du's servant would speak with such eloquence on his being *resigned* to loyalty, as though it were bad karma. Yet what disturbs me the most is what the others are doing with their freedom. They seem just as enthralled by their masters' money and power as they always were. Why do they even bother to get their contracts back? Why not simply invalidate the contracts by just running off?"

"Because, Daughter," said Ouyang Zhenli, "it was, after all, the contracts that enforced their slavery; and furthermore," she continued, reaching again for her *pipa*, "freedom by itself is not enough. Money — as you and your young husband are no doubt learning — is essential, and a little power might come in handy, too."

She raised a cup in a toast to the younger ones, as well as to Ouyang Gen, as though commending them to Heaven for good fortune in the coming months. Then she played the following song, singing:

"Are we floating on Xuanwu Lake? How would we
    know?
Chilly, chilly comes the autumn breeze.
Sparkling is the canopy of stars,
Ruddy is the shivering moon.

"Where have they gone, the ancient wall, the gay city?
Now we've only the Moon Rabbit and the Milky Way
    for company."

To enhance the feeling of detachment from the earth, Nanyu and Daosheng lay down in the bottom of the boat and looked skyward. The glowing moon and canopy of stars imparted a sense of vastness that the young ones found exhilarating. However, the thrill of being dwarfed by nature was compromised by the reality of being scrutinized by society; for, although the urban horizon had indeed fallen away, the couple's celestial view was now framed by the looming figures of Nanyu's father, Daosheng's mother, and the two hulking boat hands, all of whom looked down at them imposingly, like four fearsome guardians of the zodiac made flesh.

"'Romantic setting of moonlit deck; bliss of wedding night; how to describe this joy?'" muttered Nanyu.

"Don't be smart," reproved Daosheng in a whisper, "and I'll thank you not to recycle my ironies."

Ouyang Zhenli continued to sing and play the *pipa*, and Ouyang Gen was beginning to doze off; and so they continued quietly.

"Well, I guess it could be worse," said Nanyu.

"Yes, Husband," said Daosheng. "Such an epithet usually describes the most successful family gathering, it seems to me. However, I don't see that we had any alternative. As you recently remarked, family business is properly left to me, as your wife. I doubt that you would have preferred me to abandon our parents, or at least your father, on Mid-Autumn Festival."

"No, I guess not."

"And at least we don't have to contend with crowds, with access to the lake still being regulated."

"Once again, Wife, you have managed things very cleverly."

"And once again, Husband, you'll note that our parents are going very easy on us. Not once, for example, has either of them pressed us as to when they might expect to hear any 'good news.'"

"You might have added it to the list of forbidden topics, warranting the heaviest fine."

"I didn't want to call attention to it in the first place."

"'Good news'?" blurted Ouyang Gen, who was suddenly awake. "You have 'good news'?" Ouyang Zhenli stopped the music.

"Ah, no, Father," stammered Nanyu. "We were just discussing the good news from the Huai River front."

"Is there good news from the Huai River front?"

"Just that it hasn't collapsed yet, Father," said Daosheng.

"I thought we weren't supposed to talk about the military situation."

"Indeed we're not, Father," said Daosheng, who had risen to a sitting position, to avoid addressing her father-in-law while lying down. "That's two coppers we owe ourselves."

Ouyang Zhenli cleared her throat and smiled. "Yes, you should be careful not to get our hopes up, you two. The next time you say the word 'Huai,' it better be to report very good news indeed—nothing less than a total victory." The "Huai" of "Huai River" sounds like part of the word for "pregnant"

"Rest easy, Mother," said Daosheng. "On the Huai front, everyone involved has been exerting himself mightily. It is not through lack of trying that our efforts on the Huai have been slow to bear fruit."

Ouyang Gen seemed to be reading the stars to determine in which direction the Huai River lay.

Ouyang Zhenli pondered for a moment and then spoke up slightly to ask a question of the man poling in the bow. "Little brother, is that an island up ahead?"

"Yes, ma'am. Footpath Island."

"How very fortuitous. Mr Ouyang, why don't we stretch our legs a bit?" she said, leaving unstated the fact that her bound feet rendered her a poor hiker. Observing the other's discomfited expression, she added, "These two boys will act as our chaperones. Perhaps the view will be better from that little hill. Nanyu and Daosheng will watch the boat." Ouyang Gen agreed to the proposal without too much resistance, for in fact it was time for him to relieve himself, after his tippling.

The matter being settled, the boatmen steered toward Footpath Island and soon pulled the craft into a cove and tied it to a tree. One of them lifted up Ouyang Zhenli and deposited her on the bank, and then the four who went ashore disappeared up a wooded pathway, leaving Nanyu and Daosheng on the floor of the boat, under a pile of blankets.

After they had accustomed themselves to the silence—and were enjoying the novelty of it—Daosheng said, "Of course, I wasn't entirely truthful with Mother, just now, concerning our objectives on the Huai River front. As you know, our strategy has been limited to nimble probing and timely withdrawal."

Nanyu said nothing, and Daosheng went on.

"We should face facts, Husband," said she. "Our hit and run approach, while it has been excellent for morale, is unlikely to yield the favorable intelligence that both our parents await. Although it has been advantageous in the short term to avoid burdening our camp with additional dependents, while developing our capabilities, it may, alas, be time now to mount a frontal assault and to bring back at least one, ah, trophy, to please our superiors."

"Merciful Buddha, Wife!" ejaculated Nanyu. "What the fuck are you talking about?"

"I'm talking about filial piety, or at least the avoidance of filial impiety."

Nanyu did not need Mencius to tell him that the most serious breach of filiality was to fail to produce a male heir. He breathed in, as a queasy tightening began to develop in his stomach. "Yes, Wife, of course you are right," he said, "but are we really going to deal with it right now?"

"Why not?" returned Daosheng. "It's a family holiday, we've got a few minutes' peace and quiet—quieter than our own bedroom—and we seem to do well on boats. Besides, the business is thriving, and we've got a bit of silver saved up. There's not much reason to put it off."

Nanyu looked up again at the heavens. He was pleased to confirm that the celestial guardians were in fact away from their posts, leaving him and his Heaven-sent wife as alone as they had ever been. He took one more moment to appreciate everything, from the countless stars, to the lapping of the lake water on the side of the boat, to the cool air on his face; and then he went beneath the blanket, where Daosheng was waiting in place to whisper in his ear.

"No need to save your ammunition this time, Husband. In fact, under the circumstances, I recommend double shot. Aim carefully and make sure the payload goes where it needs to go."

The boat rocked, sending out ripples, sparkling in the moonlight.

After a decent while, Ouyangs Gen and Zhenli and the two boatmen returned to the little cove. Finding Nanyu and Daosheng asleep, they climbed aboard, broke out additional blankets, and bedded down on the side benches or on the free portion of the bottom planking. The moon continued to watch over them until morning, when they awoke, finished off the mooncakes and tea, poled back to the south bank, and off-hired the boat. Then, the Ouyangs hitched a ride on a donkey cart through the Gate of Great Peace and all the way through town to Shakyamuni Street, where Ouyang Gen got off. The other three rode back through Treasure Gate to Agarwood Street and the House of the Entrancing Fragrance, where they went back to sleep until well into the afternoon. That evening, they resumed business as usual and continued in their accustomed mode of life for another week, after which, Daosheng began to notice that everything — the tea leaves, the lotuses, and the garbage in the river — seemed to smell much more pungently than usual. Ouyang Zhenli observed how her daughter recoiled from every aroma and informed her that she was pregnant. Daosheng sent a message to Ouyang Gen, who walked over immediately, delighted, and then the four of them made offerings at a local temple, to ensure that the child would be a boy.

6

September 1644 to June 1645

In the first month, it has no form;
It has no shape, it makes not a sound,
It is exactly like the watercress drifting on the river –
Will it eventually put out roots and settle down?

　　　　　　　　　　　　　　　　　— Traditional

THE WEATHER MELLOWED as the autumn deepened. Fat, aged
dragonflies lingered for a while longer, circling and hovering in
slanting sunrays, but they became scarcer and soon were seen no
more. Mornings and evenings were growing crisp.

Ouyang Zhenli took over most of the duties as tea server
in the House of the Entrancing Fragrance. Daosheng remained
behind the screen, singing and playing the *pipa*, careful to exert
herself as little as possible and seldom moving about. The smells
of the kitchen overpowered her, however, and she sometimes
had to excuse herself to be sick. Nanyu continued to keep out of
the way, all the better to maintain his studies.

Meanwhile, the Nanjing government sent military officials to
reestablish contact with Wu Sangui, the man who had aligned with
the Manchus against the rebel Li Zicheng. Instead of receiving
them, General Wu directed them to his new commander-in-
chief, the Manchu regent, who chided the southerners for their

slowness in tendering their respects.

꿔꿔 꿔꿔 꿔꿔

> In the second month, it is an embryo,
> Fully implanted inside you.
> Your wobbly legs have no desire to walk long stretches.
> Your listless hands have no desire to do any
> needlework.

"Take some money out of the kitty and hire a maid," said Daosheng to Nanyu one day. Noting his cogitation, she added, "No, Husband, I do not mean for you to take a concubine. We simply need someone to do the cleaning."

By now, all traces of summer had given way, even in the south, and the air was cold throughout the day. It colored cheeks and noses a ruddy red and made everyone glad to be alive, though Daosheng was growing ever more preoccupied with the life inside her. One day Nanyu, anxious to prolong her devotion to just him for as long as possible, coaxed her on board a small rowboat and drifted with her down the languid Qinhuai. Clumps of trees on both banks were turning orange and yellow and the air was suffused with a tart, earthy smell, which blew past their tingling faces in sudden, rustling gusts. Nanyu drew out a cloth bundle and unwrapped two apples, delicacies from the north becoming rarer with every day. He and Daosheng bit into the pulpy fruit, which dissolved in their mouths.

"It's like the summer sun is captured inside them," said Daosheng. "The stored *yang* essence will be good for the baby, especially in the cool weather."

"What else should we be doing, to ensure a healthy son?" asked Nanyu.

"It's better to ask what we – or I – should *not* be doing," said Daosheng. "The *Classic of Filiality for Women* says, 'Pregnant women of antiquity did not sleep on their side, did not sit on the edge of a mat, and did not stand on one leg. They did not eat any forbidden foods and did not walk on the left side of the road. They did not eat what had not been cut properly' – oops – 'they did not sit on a mat that was not positioned properly' – perhaps I should avoid mats altogether. 'Their eyes did not look upon evil colors, their ears did not listen to debased sounds' – like what we hear every night from the flower boats – 'their mouths did not utter any arrogant words' – ha! – 'and their hands did not touch any evil things. At night they recited the classics, and during the day they discussed the rites and music. Thanks to this "instruction in the womb" the sons who were born to them were beautiful in body and limb and excelled all others in talents and virtue.'"

"Well, it's a frame of reference, anyway," said Nanyu, after assimilating the barrage of injunctions.

"A frame of reference to the ridiculous."

"We could at least recite the classics at night."

"I just recited a classic, and it amounted to a pile of rules that can only be broken. What are the 'evil colors' I'm not supposed to look at, and how can I identify them without looking at them? If I tried to comply with such nonsense, I'd end up so broken in body and spirit that our son would certainly be stillborn."

"So what should we do?"

"Just keep those delicious, uncut, apples coming."

"Those were the only two I had. They're really expensive now."

To the north, in Shandong Province, various rebel groups, including some former adherents of the Dashing Prince, Li Zicheng, were surrendering to the Manchus. To face this threat, the Nanjing government was amassing militiamen at Huai'an, but these irregulars proved to be good for nothing but plundering. One southern officer jettisoned them from his command, claiming that his remaining veterans could fight better without them.

❦ ❦ ❦

> In the third month, of the three meals of the day,
> You eat only two.
> You don't want any tea, don't long for any rice –
> All you crave are astringent plums and sour soup.

Frost appeared every morning on the rooftops. Nanyu and Daosheng liked to venture out, just to stand for a few minutes on the footbridge next to their house. They breathed in the piercing air until their nostrils burned, and they laughed at their foggy exhalations. Retreating indoors, they would then warm up with a bowl of soup, sometimes bitter melon and sometimes hot and sour. But they did drink plenty of tea, after first cradling the cups to warm their hands.

The Manchus moved southwards. They pursued Li Zicheng, the Dashing Prince, into Huguang Province, where he was eventually killed. They also broke off negotiations with the remnant dynasty in Nanjing and sent the bulk of their forces against it. The first southern city they captured was Suqian, just a couple hundred *li* to the north of Nanjing.

❦ ❦ ❦

> In the fourth month, slowly it grows.
> Your body wracked by pain, you can hardly walk.

If you are old, you're laid low as a cripple,
But you are still young; you will be all right.

The frost turned to snow, blanketing the pleasure district and muffling its hubbub. In the mornings, subdued conversations carried over it, and lonely footsteps trod on it. The House of the Entrancing Fragrance remained popular for its warming brews. Daosheng continued to play the *pipa* downstairs for a while each evening, her condition still hidden beneath her padded jacket. Soon, though, she would retire to her room, where the bamboo sleeping platform was now lined with cotton bedclothes. She'd wrap herself in them as though in a cocoon as Nanyu watched over her, tending the coal pans, letting her rest.

The Manchus fortified Suqian with an additional five thousand men, while no fewer than eight of Nanjing's generals milled around nearby, vowing to retake the town.

ⴰⴰ ⴰⴰ ⴰⴰ

In the fifth month, it's quite a burden,
To be heavy with child.
Had you known that being pregnant would be so
    painful,
You would have shaved your head and entered a
    convent.

The New Year brought no respite from the winter. Eight days into "spring," the southern capital was subjected to a violent hailstorm, and other parts of the remnant empire suffered blizzards lasting ten days. As for the military situation: Two of the southern generals near Suqian quarreled, with one assassinating the other before defecting to the Manchus.

Nanyu and Daosheng kept to their bedroom, spending long mornings under piles of blankets. They looked forward to the new year and the addition to their family that it would bring. One of their bed-bound pastimes was to discuss names for the baby. The most amusing possibilities combined elements of each of their own names (although children were supposed to be named after paternal relations only). Daosheng's name meant "Rising of the Way," but the most obvious combination of Nanyu's name and hers, Nansheng, or "Southern Rising," sounded like "Difficult Birth," which could not have been more ominous. The pronunciation of the next-best candidate, Nandao ("Southern Way"), was identical to a rhetorical phrase meaning "How could it be possible?" Neither Daonan nor Shengnan had pleasant rings, either. That left Yusheng, or "Rising of the Rain," as the only acceptable option, though most people hearing it would assume it meant "Born of the Rain."

"It could even pass as a girl's name," said Daosheng.

"Well, would we waste it on a girl?" Nanyu thought out loud. "Only sons are given meaningful names. Girls get names like 'Pretty Snow' or 'Pear Blossom.'"

"Or 'Rising of the Way,'" said Daosheng.

"Oh, I...hmm."

"Never mind, Husband. You're still half asleep. Let that be your excuse."

"Yes, Wife, I guess I'm a little slow to awaken."

"You are free to take your time, of course," said Daosheng, "but I wish to point out that it is getting rather late in the morning. Perhaps you should stretch your limbs, one by one. Please consider, while you are at it, that there is a possibility our child will be a girl."

Nanyu started, for he hadn't considered it at all. Then he said, "Father would be let down."

"As would I, for his sake," said Daosheng. "Yet we still shall have created another human soul. Remember what One-Eyed Jingang said about the folly of obsessing over what makes a human soul male or female."

"But shouldn't boys and girls be raised differently?"

"That depends on what they're being raised for. The ancients—a woman, in fact—advised putting baby girls under the bed and giving them bits of broken pottery to play with, to imbue them with humility and habituate them to labor. Look at me, Husband, and tell me if you truly want your daughter, if we are destined to have a daughter, to be raised for humility and labor."

Nanyu hesitated.

"You're not sure, are you?" said Daosheng. "Humility and skill at labor are virtues in a woman, so you have been told—and so you have been shown, by me, over the past months. I'll not deny that I feel a certain sense of accomplishment at how humbly and handily I've served as your wife, and if such a feeling accrues to me naturally as a woman, then so be it. Know this, however: I was not *raised* to be humble or to labor for my husband and in-laws. I am your wife out of choice, not because the underside of a bed or a shard of pottery conditioned me to be. I chose you, in fact, because you didn't choose me for my humility and handiness; and whatever compelled you to take me on, as I've said before, you took a great risk in doing so. So, once again, Husband, look me in the eye and tell me whether you would want your own daughter to be *broken* until she were nothing but a humble servant, or if you would rather that she be permitted to retain a spirit as unique as mine, for which you have already ventured everything."

Daosheng had sat up as she spoke, and the blankets had fallen away. Her legs were crossed under her pregnant belly, and her hands rested on her lap, with fingers intertwined. Her hair had grown to shoulder length but was now tousled, so that curled locks seemed to radiate away from her head. In spite of the harshness of what she had just said, her expression was a picture of peace.

Obediently, Nanyu looked into her eyes and saw himself gazing back, mesmerized.

◨◧◨◧◨◧

> In the sixth month, you burn incense and paper money
> And pray to the gods
> That they will take pity on you
> And protect you from harm when it's time to deliver.

Most of the snow had melted, but warm weather had yet to arrive. The trees were still bare and the earth gray. The government in Nanjing ordered the widow of the general who had been murdered the previous month to assume command of his troops, for it was rumored that she was uncannily quick-witted, even to the point of being able to predict the future. Another general scoffed at the superstition, claiming that it was more worthy of a historical romance than practical strategy.

◨◧◨◧◨◧

> In the seventh month, it's getting hard to go about the
>   day.
> Rising, you're grim and determined,
> But in no time, your strength is exhausted;
> You return to your bed in pain.

145

Daosheng gave up the last of her duties in the tea shop, which reverted to Ouyang Zhenli's operation, though Nanyu still earned a few coppers for doing the shopping. Daosheng kept to her bed, with Nanyu, when he had time, sitting beside her, reading.

The Nanjing court was shocked by the appearance of a young man claiming to be Chongzhen's heir. Officials who interviewed him found him not quite right in the face, though confusion persisted. While the southerners dealt with the crisis, the Manchu army was advancing on three fronts, pressing in on all the towns and cities on the north bank of the Yangtze.

◆◇ ◆◇ ◆◇

In the eighth month: a belly like a balloon.
There are all sorts of things you can't do anymore.
You'd love to get out to paint flowers once more,
But you're afraid your son might be born on the street!

Nanyu and Daosheng opened their bedroom window to savor the whiff of life in the air. They thrilled at the buds on the trees.

With Manchu columns threatening to cut them off, the southern generals gave up their attempt to retake Suqian, but it proved equally impossible to establish a stable defense. Finding himself confronted by the invaders at Xuzhou, the southern commander boarded a boat and fled. Another general abandoned Huai'an. Most of Nanjing's remaining forces north of the Yangtze fell back to Yangzhou.

◆◇ ◆◇ ◆◇

In the ninth month, it's about to be born!
The child in your belly has grown oh so heavy.
You've no strength in your arms, and your legs are
    swollen;
You never feel comfortable, no matter what you do.

Nanyu waited night and day on his wife. The heat having returned, he fanned her and mopped her brow.

The Manchu army, now incorporating even southern turncoats, descended on Yangzhou. In an early-morning attack, its soldiers overwhelmed the city's defenders and began a ten days' massacre of the population to discourage future resistance elsewhere. A few days later, they crossed the Yangtze, and late the next night, the Hongguang emperor quit his capital, taking a thousand cavalry with him.

Left to their own devices, a group of the highest-ranking ministers still serving the hollow court rode out to the Manchus' encampment in the suburbs. With the ground still wet from a heavy rain, they surrendered Nanjing.

※ ※ ※

And then, as soon as the period of labor begins,
You find yourself a paper-thin distance from dying.

Daosheng went into labor seven days later, on a silent afternoon. Ouyang Zhenli sent Nanyu out to fetch the midwife, and then she banned him from the second floor.

The pain of one contraction is enough to make you
    faint.
The pain of two contractions can cause your soul to flee.

147

Clenching your teeth, you bite through a nail,
And your hands and feet feel as icy as snow.
Even if the child is delivered without a hitch,
The fate of the mother still hangs in the balance.

The sounds of his wife gasping and crying upstairs fell upon
Nanyu like cudgel blows, and he became dizzy. The world
seemed to be whirling around him, not spinning regularly but
jarring forward and backward, up and down, closer and farther.
Barely able to walk, he felt his way along the wall, stumbling
out into the courtyard and settling to the ground at the base of
a column. He pressed the back of his head against it, hoping to
fuse with its solidity, and the veering and lurching seemed to
retreat to a more distant plane. He could perceive the square
window of sky above him, a translucent gray. He wrapped one
arm around his retracted knees and anchored his other hand
to a flagstone, and then he held on, waiting. A heavy drop fell
on his shoulder and another on his knee and another on the
left side of his nose and another in the center of his forehead.
He closed his eyes, with his face still turned Heavenward and
the after-image of the framed sky glowing on his retinas; and
the rain began falling harder, no longer in single drops but
showering, until he was soaked. He discovered that if he held
absolutely still, he lost consciousness of his wet clothes and then
of his body. He might have fallen asleep. Soon the rain tapered
into a drizzle and stopped, though it continued dripping off
the eaves, either splattering on the stone or falling into ceramic
vases and jars in individual, sonorous drops that echoed within
the four close walls of the courtyard — *plunk…plunk…plunk* — the
rhythm slowing, forcing the rate of his breathing and his pulse to
slacken apace, until he was hypnotized, aware of the shrieks that
registered somewhere above the resounding drops of rainwater

but not acutely affected by them; and he remained in this state as the sun went down. Finally, without having moved a muscle, he heard his wife give a desperate yelp.

Nanyu opened his eyes to the last of the twilight, a smoldering purple, as the sun and the clouds faded away together. He rocked forward and stood up, straightening his legs beneath him, now miserable in his drenched clothes, as panicked commands, then silence, then a wail, and then a sob poured down upon him. With a heavy brow, he climbed the stairs, pulling himself up by the handrail, passed along the corridor and entered his bedroom, his mother-in-law and the midwife both clamoring and gesticulating at him before giving up and scurrying away, frightened at his impassivity. He peeled off his damp clothes and left them in a heap on the floor. He dried himself with a cloth and wrapped himself in a thin blanket. Then, he crawled into bed with his weeping wife and stillborn daughter and fell into a dreamless sleep.

It was nearly noon the next day when Nanyu was awakened by the sounds of the Manchu army entering the city. The troops headed first to secure the Palace, and then they began settling into billets in the northern part of town, forcing the residents there to move southward in search of new homes. In spite of these evictions, the occupation proceeded without looting. The Manchu prince who commanded the army ordered the public execution of eight of his own bannermen who had attempted it.

Nanyu studied the face of his daughter. Of course she looked like Daosheng, and her fuzzy scalp recalled the day when he and Daosheng had first met. Her closed eyes and unwrinkled brow suggested the contentment of a Buddha, and Nanyu allowed himself the briefest flash of religious reflection, a feeling of peace, in the realization—or rationalization—that his beautiful daughter was now in a better place. But his feelings did not remain philosophical for long, for his attention was drawn to the eerie frown that had frozen on her face as she died. It protruded supernaturally, in engorged lips that dominated her countenance, with the ends of her mouth arched downward in an impossibly sharp angle, a horrifying grimace conveying abysmal disappointment, despair, bitterness, and rage. It was transfixing and nearly fatal, causing Nanyu almost to forget to breathe, as it communicated its mortification to him. He closed his eyes and was afraid to open them again. Silently crying and with chattering teeth, he reached out to caress the back of the girl's scalp with his hand and pulled her head toward him, nestling it under his chin, trying not to think of her dreadful expression, opening his eyes only to ensure that Daosheng was still breathing. He fell back asleep.

Two days passed.

On the morning of the third day, both Nanyu and Daosheng got out of bed and washed, saying nothing. Nanyu swaddled Yusheng's body and tied it to his chest. They went downstairs, exchanging dull glances but no words with Ouyang Zhenli, drank several cups of tea, and shared a steamed bun but ate nothing else. Then they walked out the door and continued on foot, out through Treasure Gate, all the way to Ouyang Gen's house on Shakyamuni Street. The doors of every residence had "Surrendered Subjects" painted on them.

Lowering his eyes in silent acknowledgement of his father, Nanyu handed Yusheng off to Daosheng, who sat down in the kitchen, and proceeded back to the workshop, selecting six boards and cutting them to size without the aid of a measuring stick. He nailed them together into a small coffin, which he brought back to the kitchen and placed on a bench. With sullen expressions, grinding their teeth, Nanyu and Daosheng lowered their baby into the coffin, and Nanyu, unable to resist taking one last look at Yusheng's unearthly frown, fitted and nailed down the lid. He took the box up, carrying it in front of him, and, trailed by Daosheng, left without a word.

They crossed the street to the Temple at the Edge of Heaven. Ascending the stairs, they made their way to the abbot's cell. Baichi Shi'ai was emerging as they arrived, as though already aware of their purpose. He whispered something to an attendant, and the monk disappeared into a nearby shed and returned with a shovel, which he tendered to Nanyu. Baichi Shi'ai gestured to the eastern side of the grounds, and Nanyu and Daosheng moved off in that direction.

They arrived at the Altar of the Iron Buddha. Nanyu set down his load and began digging a grave on the slope behind it, while Daosheng sat on a mossy tuft and watched. Both lost track of time, as Nanyu dug through roots and excavated rocks. When his efforts had resulted in a deep, rectangular hole, he leaned the shovel against a tree and turned toward the little coffin. He picked it up, rubbed his hand along its surface, and then lowered it to the bottom of the grave. Noting Daosheng, who continued to sit stoically, out of the corner of his eye, he paused. The sun shone down in rays through the trees, making bright patterns on the forest floor, and Nanyu noticed squirrels and chipmunks chasing each other around in circles and birds flapping through the trees, teaching their young ones to fly. He resented all of it and curled one side of his mouth into an indignant scowl. Reaching for the shovel again, he began pushing soil into the grave. He heard Daosheng sniffling once or twice as he placed rocks and tree bark on the grave, so that it was unrecognizable as one. After bending down to press his palm once more into the receptive earth, he straightened up and nodded at Daosheng, and the two of them turned away and hiked back to the area of the abbot's cell. Nanyu returned the shovel to the shed, and it felt strange having nothing to carry. He raised his empty hands to Daosheng. Then they lowered themselves down the stairs and soon stood at the Entrance to the Practice of the Benevolent World, looking out.

Undesirous of returning to their old lives immediately or at all, they lingered at the threshold. Some Manchu cavalrymen were gathered around a campfire at the side of the street, waiting for their rice porridge to cook. Their braided pigtails hung down from under their conical lacquered helmets, stretching all the way down their backs. When one of them removed his helmet to cool off, Nanyu saw that his pigtail contained all the hair on his head; the rest of his scalp had been shaved. Nanyu found the effect reptilian, and he became even more nauseated than he had been.

As he studied the soldiers, Nanyu realized that his father's house was in the background behind them. Just as he refocused his attention, to ascertain whether or not his father was still at home, he saw Cui, of the horsehair hat, appear abruptly, duck in through the door, and advance through the house, back toward the workshop. Nanyu thought he heard the braying of a sarcastic greeting.

In a very private recess of his frame, Nanyu felt the sudden manufacture of adrenalin, which coursed upward through his body, past his stomach and into his chest. Along with a full range of instincts, it restored to him the power of speech.

"Did you see that?" he asked Daosheng.

"Yes," she said, likewise reenergized.

"Looks like we may have to get out of town for a while," Nanyu said.

They retreated back through the gate and rushed again up the stairs. They bumped into Baichi Shi'ai, who sensed their new urgency.

"We spotted our enemy at Father's house," Nanyu said. "We

need to leave."

The abbot required only a moment to assess the situation. "Go to Crimson Cloud Monastery," he instructed them. "I'll ask a student to go to your house—a monk might suggest your whereabouts—to get some of your things. Then I'll send them along to you with someone else."

"Good," said Nanyu with a quick bow. "We'll need money, as much as we have saved…We'll also need my Mencius."

"And my husband's four-leaf album and Four Treasures," added Daosheng. "And the box of papers beside the bed."

"Consider it done."

"And then, when you can, please explain to Mother what's happened."

"I think she'll figure it out," said the bonze, "especially after that lummox pays a call on her, too. It's Cui, isn't it? Wei Su's henchman, who used to politick for him here? I must make sure to choose our mules carefully. I'll also try to find out what he's doing here."

"Thank you, Teacher." Nanyu and Daosheng continued to stand there, looking at Baichi Shi'ai's shoes.

"Go," he said. "Head east and then north. The abbot at Crimson Cloud is called Anshan, as in 'Peaceful Mountain.' He knows me."

Nanyu and Daosheng nodded one more time, turned away, and headed back down the path to the Altar of the Iron Buddha. With a parting glance in the direction of their daughter's grave, they continued along the wooded walkway and emerged from the temple grounds through a side portal. Keeping up a brisk pace, they threaded their way through the knots of soldiers, camp followers, and other refugees. They made their way around the outside of the city wall and then turned right, along a road that led away from it, and soon, Nanjing was behind them.

To the rhythm of his footfalls, Nanyu's addled mind turned over random lines of verse in Daosheng's voice, as though she yet intoned them in their teahouse on the Qinhuai: *So much feeling might as well be none…The candle sheds a tear at dawn – has it a heart*? In time, though, the mental echoing reduced itself to one stubborn refrain:

> I know not where I'll come to die.
> I cannot keep us both alive.

For hours he thought of nothing else.

PART THREE

7

JUNE TO AUGUST, 1645

THE HONGGUANG EMPEROR was made a prisoner. He was brought back to his former capital, shabbily dressed, in an uncurtained sedan chair, with his empress and concubine riding donkeys behind him, unlamented by his former officials, who were already rushing to offer their services to their conquerors. The Manchus forced their captive to attend a banquet, seating him below Chongzhen's false heir, who was also in their custody. Hongguang was later shipped off to Beijing and discreetly executed the following year, by which time the false heir had likewise been disposed of.

Meanwhile, the surrendered ministers of the Nanjing government presented the Manchus with the names of some three hundred associates whose concern for civic order matched their own. So recommended by the leaders of the old regime, these gentlemen quickly filtered through the Yangtze valley, to establish the authority of the new regime. Most of the local gentry, still smarting from the commoners' rebellions of the previous year, pledged to cooperate with the new magistrates. The transition of power in the region was off to a peaceful start.

Nanyu and Daosheng rested at the Crimson Cloud Monastery. They were housed in separate cells but spent most of their days together, staring into the stream that ran down the hillside at the base of Bright Moon Terrace, where dozens of little childlike

Buddhas were carved into the rock. They said little and ate less, even though the abbot, Anshan, provided for them generously. After a few days, a monk arrived from Baichi Shi'ai — it was the attendant who had fetched Nanyu the shovel that he had used to bury Yusheng — and he brought the couple a light assortment of clothes, Nanyu's edition of Mencius, his album, and his Four Treasures, a bag of copper coins, Daosheng's document box, and four ounces of silver. Daosheng was sure that there had been five ounces and assumed that the student who had retrieved their things had pocketed one of them.

The monk also brought news. Wei Su was now employed by the Manchu government in Beijing, as a senior department head in the Ministry of Revenue. It was common knowledge that he had served Li Zicheng after the bandit had taken the capital, but his role as a fifth columnist in the campaign remained undiscovered. In fact, Wei now claimed that he had joined Li only under duress. After the Dashing Prince's ejection from the capital by the Manchus, Wei was said to have attempted suicide; but his health recovered in time for him to accept his current position, the third — each under a different ruler — in the space of a year. Although tainted by opportunism, Wei's reputation was only marginally worse than that of his peers, who had all, of course, served at least one other dynasty. At any rate, Wei Su was now as powerful as he had ever been, and none dared to denounce him openly, especially not in Nanjing, where his family soon recovered and improved its position.

Baichi Shi'ai's messenger assured Nanyu and Daosheng that their parents were fine. The lackey Cui had paid them both early visits, but he seemed content merely to unsettle them and had refrained from more serious abuse.

"He's biding his time," Nanyu concluded, after the monk left. "He's hoping that our parents will lead him to us or that we'll turn up, for him to ambush us."

With Wei Su's influence spreading, Nanyu determined that they were still too close to Nanjing to be safe. He recalled Cui's abilities at marshaling followers for his patron, even at temples and monasteries, and he feared that Wei Su's reconstituted faction might soon grow to include the residents at Crimson Cloud. The Ouyangs therefore spent one last day rallying their strength, left reassuring messages with Anshan for their parents, expressed their thanks to all concerned, and took their leave.

They traveled on foot, Nanyu reasoning that no civilian watercraft would escape appropriation, given the continued military struggles in the interior and farther south. Even so, they followed the course of the Yangtze, heading downstream along the south bank. Neither Ouyang had a clear destination in mind, yet both knew that an eastward course would take them closer to Xinchang, where lived Zhu Xiangsun, who, although he lacked Wei Su's high office, was still the most powerful man they knew.

While still in the environs of Nanjing, Nanyu and Daosheng were impressed by the most sizable military encampments they had ever seen, with Manchu cavalry, Chinese pikemen, artillerists, and musketeers, together with auxiliaries, encamped in almost every field. After going only a short distance, however, they were surprised to note that all signs of the army vanished. Consulting sparingly with Daosheng, who was still prone to be taciturn, Nanyu deduced that the Manchus were deploying their forces carefully, massing them at significant points but otherwise taking pains to keep the unpredictable soldiery away from their new empire's wealthy heartland.

At first, Nanyu and Daosheng sought out temples for their lodgings; but sleeping separately, as the abbots always insisted, soon became unbearable, for both Ouyangs began experiencing forebodings whenever parted. Roadside inns proved even less pleasant, as the quarters for men and women were not only detached but crowded with strangers. The idea of sleeping under the stars briefly appealed, but when they tried it, they started awake at the sound of every approaching footstep. Finally, Nanyu learned to spot unused storage sheds, empty granaries, and even carpenters' workshops and to bargain with their proprietors to stay in them. He was accustomed, of course, to the latter type of accommodation and knew how to make the place comfortable, fashioning a bed from sawhorses and a few planks. But as natural as it would have been for him to negotiate each night's stay as a brother carpenter, Nanyu instead employed his boxed volume of Mencius as his strongest credential, and he and Daosheng were treated almost like visiting royalty.

After several days of travel in this mode, Nanyu and Daosheng reached Suzhou. They were alarmed to see a cloud of smoke rising from the center of town near the famous Tiger Hill, and they feared that the shaky peace had collapsed and that riot had resumed, perhaps in the guise of an attempt at restoring the old dynasty. Explosions echoed through the pagoda-spired city, and Nanyu and Daosheng approached gingerly. Soon, however, they noticed celebratory sky-lanterns rising amid the smoke, which now smelled reassuringly of incense, and they realized that the banging sounds were made by firecrackers.

"It's the Lao Lang Festival," said Daosheng, managing a smile at the recollection of past years' celebrations. "I'm glad they observe it here too; I'm finally hungry enough to try the food. Mind you, Husband," she added, "not to get too friendly with the cooks."

They headed to Tiger Hill where they were surrounded by dozens of prostitutes, the organizers of the festivities. The ladies of each of Suzhou's pleasure houses had set up long tables, where they feted anyone who made a basic donation—a concession to the recent scarcity; traditionally, the food was free. With their delectable viands and potent spirits, the matrons and their beauties were soliciting future business though not transacting it on the spot, for the Lao Lang Festival was an occasion for them to advertise but not to ply their trade. Daosheng found it amusing that the women would use food to sell themselves, as though it were as strong a recommendation as their more common, prurient forms of appeal.

"I simply must have Little Butterfly," she quipped, "for her luscious…mushu pork."

"I don't know, Wife," returned Nanyu. "Jade Girl's eggplant with garlic sauce has got me thinking that maybe it is time to take a concubine after all."

The Ouyangs visited several tables, until they were as stuffed as they'd ever been. The sun set, and the myriad candles along the walkway up the hillside sparkled intoxicatingly, even though they had steered clear of alcohol. Rising sky-lanterns made them crane their necks to watch, and soon they sat down on the ground, to enjoy a more comfortable view of the ascension. No one heeded them, and they passed a good hour in contented forgetfulness. After a time, a group of four boys emerged from the crowd, carrying a seated wooden figure of Lao Lang on poles. Followed by a train of madams and other local dignitaries, they turned up an angled pathway and disappeared into a small temple.

"Who is Lao Lang, anyway?" asked Nanyu.

"Some say he's a deified prime minister from ancient times," answered Daosheng. "I think it quite fitting that the legacy of an official would be commemorated by prostitutes."

Nanyu contorted his mouth.

"He also doubles as the god of opera," Daosheng continued.

Indeed, not long after she spoke, about fifteen men and

women in theatrical costume, accompanied by others more plainly dressed and carrying musical instruments, moved past them and entered the little temple, where their patron deity was now guest of honor. Nanyu and Daosheng listened to what was going on inside and heard first a fuss and then a prayer. Then, in a fanfare of drums and cymbals, an opera began. Male and female singers joined in a series of arias. Daosheng recognized some of the tunes, but neither she nor Nanyu could hear any of the lyrics clearly.

Suddenly, however, the music paused, and they could make out a female character's spoken lines:

> "The princess has attained woman's estate, so it's time to select a royal son in law. His majesty has made it clear that if we limit our choice to our own race, we might not be able to find a man with both the administrative and military talents needed for the prosperity of our country. Therefore, we are going to pick a human being."

"What could that be about?" wondered Nanyu.

"It's from a play called *A Dream Under the Southern Bough*," said Daosheng, "by the same person who wrote *The Peony Pavilion*. It's about a man who marries into a kingdom of ants. His wife, the princess, helps him through his career, but then she dies, and he loses everything. At the end of the play, it turns out it was all a dream."

A costumed young lady who was carrying a tray of food to the temple heard Daosheng's remarks and looked down at the still-seated couple. "Excuse me, Miss," she smiled, "but are you familiar with *Southern Bough*?"

"A little bit," replied Daosheng. "I can play a few of the tunes on the *pipa* tolerably well."

"What great luck!" exclaimed the actress. "It just so happens that one of our accompanists is ill with fever. That's why we sound a little off, as you may have noticed. Would you like to fill in, for tomorrow's performance? We're just going to do a few of the popular scenes. It will be in Master's garden, just a private party for some of his friends, so you won't have to be nervous."

"'Won't have to be nervous'?" repeated Daosheng. "I'm sure that 'Master' and his friends will be a very discerning audience — hard to please and unsparing with criticism."

"Well," said the performer, "I suppose you're right. We will have to be on our toes, as we generally do; but Master takes good care of us. I'm sure he would appreciate your helping us out."

"Who is your master?" Nanyu broke in.

"My master is the honorable Zou Diguang. He is the owner and director of the troupe."

"Is he a scholar?" Nanyu pursued.

"Yes, he holds the metropolitan degree, though he's had no official post for some time."

Nanyu looked at Daosheng.

"I see no reason why we should refuse him," he said.

"So it's settled then!" said the actress. "Please come to Dragon Hill Villa — Master's house — on Bell Tower Street, at midmorning."

Nanyu started at the mention of Bell Tower Street, Daosheng at the mention of Dragon Hill, the location of the princess's tomb in *A Dream Under the Southern Bough*.

"And what is your name, sister?" asked Daosheng.

"Just call me Ah-Hui," the young woman replied, using a diminutive. "And now I really must go. Everyone's waiting for these dumplings. See you tomorrow!"

She hurried off in the direction of the temple. Nanyu and

Daosheng rose, collected their things, and trudged off in search of a carpenter's workshop.

ロ𝅘ロ𝅘ロ𝅘

Dragon Hill Villa was rather small for a mansion, with a limited number of rooms. But it was surrounded by an extensive garden of rare plants and curious rocks that suggested famous or legendary mountain landscapes, similar to but much larger than the tabletop displays Nanyu had seen on Three Mountain Street back home. Covered walkways enclosed and traversed the space, which was so carefully designed that no matter which way a visitor looked, he was treated, as it seemed, to a perfectly composed painting, with foreground, mid-ground, and background proportioned neatly in thirds and internally framed by landscape elements and by the pillars and lattices that adorned the sides of the walkway itself. The garden's main feature was an expansive pond, with islands of miniature mountains, surrounded by lotuses, but otherwise open enough to resemble a large lake. A walkway terminated in a spacious pavilion at its edge where the performance of selected scenes from *A Dream Under the Southern Bough* was to take place. A square red rug in the middle of the pavilion served as the stage.

Ah-Hui, in stage makeup, greeted Daosheng and conducted her to the musicians' area at the side of the rug. The other accompanists handed Daosheng a *pipa* and treated her in a sisterly fashion, making sure she was comfortably seated, pretending, out of pity, not to notice her oversized feet, and familiarizing her with the list of the day's tunes. As for Nanyu, he felt out of place, for he had not really been invited and he fit into none of the recognizable groups that were present. There was no way for him to pass as actor or musician, lacking as he did the training and the culture; and he had no desire to fraternize with the servants, assuming they were not too busy to be kind to him. That left the host, Zou Diguang, and his three friends, who were sitting in a row along the balustrade, facing the red rug and chatting. Nanyu was reluctant to trespass upon their company. He waited for Zou to welcome or at least to acknowledge him, but he waited in vain.

In the meantime, the performance began. The first chosen scene depicted the wedding of the hero—a man named Chunyu Fen, whom Nanyu judged to be something of a lout—and the enchanting ant princess. Nanyu caught the references to flute-playing and "clouds and rain" that were distributed throughout the libretto. He appreciated even more all the ways in which the ant princess was shown to support her husband: Barely is their marriage consummated before she reconnects him to his estranged father and secures him a post as prefect of Southern Bough, to which she accompanies him and helps him to govern wisely.

Nanyu lowered his eyebrows a few scenes later, at the turning point of the play, in which the princess's health begins to deteriorate, her decline occasioned by the successful, rather than the unsuccessful, experience of bearing and raising children. Accustomed to think of children as being essential to a story's happy unfolding, Nanyu was shocked to hear such lines as "Bearing so many babies simply ruins one's health" and "It's they who call me Mother that have eroded my youthful looks." He glanced to the side at Daosheng, but she continued to play, unfazed.

Nanyu returned his attention to the remaining scenes:

The princess retires alone to a remote estate to nurse her health but is soon attacked there by a hostile chieftain, who hopes to carry her off.

"Until now, war has been a distant thought [she sings
    to her son],
and its eruption frightens me to death.
No other general can save me
except that your father in person leads the troops."

In the event, though, she rallies both her personal strength
and the populace, including the women, for

"If any foe should come in sight,
The women are the first to fight."

She climbs the battlements and dons a suit of armor, singing,

"Let me first remove my embroidered socks and bow-
    arched shoes
to pull on a tight pair of pointed leather boots.
Giving the tassel one more shake,
I raise my arms for the rerebrace.
Tug in my silken blouse.
Over it comes the coat of mail
and the silvery breastplate of a half-moon shape;
the hem of my scarlet skirt streams out from beneath.
Like a heavenly warrior I appear to be,
above the endless rows of abates.
Like an expert archer I draw my bow
and notch an arrow from a gilded hold.
Like the mastermind of the other sex
my orders are issued on slabs of gold.
What a sight!
Give me a rousing cheer.

See the lion belt around my tiny waist.
A fair general waves the signal flag.
A flaming cloud, I mount the tower to take command.
Let him in blank amazement gawk."

The chieftain, however, more enraged than amazed, shoots an arrow that grazes her cheek. Fortunately, Chunyu Fen arrives in the nick of time, to drive the enemy back, for, as he sings:

"No motive better justifies a fight
Than saving the life of one's loving wife."

After her husband saves the day, the princess is grateful and self-reproachful. Alas, her life is preserved for only a brief time, for her health finally gives out, and Chunyu inters her on Dragon Hill.

The last few scenes, in which Chunyu's fortunes decline after her passing – and in which he debauches himself with other women – were omitted from the day's showcase, and Nanyu was left with no idea as to how the play was supposed to end. As much as he enjoyed the singing and the combat segments, Nanyu tried to keep his ears open to the comments of the connoisseurs for whose benefit the play had been staged. Although Nanyu had been most impressed by the princess's martial appearance, the three learned guests instead praised the lead actress for capturing her sickly state.

"How tender, how beautiful, her dancing was," one of them said. "Her frailty was very touching."

"Indeed," continued another. "'Her songs linger in the air, above the lonely and sad river.'"

Zou Diguang beamed. Nanyu looked at the ground, wondering what he would say if invited into the conversation, which he was not.

Presently, he was joined by Daosheng, escorted by Ah-Hui.

"Thank you for the loan of your wife," said the actress. "She certainly helped us recover our full sound. No doubt our Master is very pleased. In fact," she lowered her voice, "I would be happy to ask him on your behalf: Perhaps he would take you in."

"Take us in...to the company?" asked Nanyu.

"Why not? Big sister is clearly skilled enough. Even though she's, uh, not the best suited for the red rug, she could continue with the *pipa*. Master himself doesn't train the musicians, but he recognizes talent when he sees it. So what if she's been trained elsewhere? All the better, if we can 'reap what others have sown.' Master won't mind if she's a little older than most are when they join us. The contract would be unconventional, but I'm sure something could be arranged."

"Contract?" asked Nanyu, noting that Daosheng had stiffened at the word.

"Of course," said Ah-Hui. "That's how it's done. My old father sold me to Master when I was seven, and fortunately I took to the singing and dancing, so I could stay on. Master even found a husband for me."

"As you can see," whispered Daosheng, "I've already found a husband for myself."

"Oh, that's all right," said Ah-Hui, trying to be helpful. "Master can find a use for him; or perhaps," she now addressed Nanyu, "you could arrive at some sort of settlement."

Nanyu realized that Zou Diguang was now looking over at Daosheng. He felt something twitch in the side of his face.

Daosheng said, "Thank you just the same, sister, but it's time for my husband and me to be on our way. I was honored to be a part of your troupe, even for just a few hours."

They gathered their belongings and departed before the

luncheon was served, continuing their journey east.

卍卍卍

It was another several days later that Nanyu and Daosheng arrived at Taicang. They had been walking in silence, but as they drew closer to the magistrate's yamen, they found themselves in the midst of an uproar. A knot of agitated men was hounding someone in its midst whom Nanyu and Daosheng could not see, bombarding him with curses such as "Shame!" and "Traitor!" After discharging a fair amount of this abuse, the mob parted and sent its victim on his way with a few kicks to the rump, and only then did the Ouyangs notice that he was dressed in the fine (though now disheveled) robes of a merchant or gentleman and that he had shaved his scalp, leaving only a short pigtail in the rear. Someone who appeared to be the magistrate, also with only a pigtail, shouted into the crowd from the top of the yamen steps, "You can keep your hair or your head but not both!" The four shaved and pigtailed pikemen accompanying him descended into the riot to arrest its instigators, but the crowd scattered.

"What's happening?" Nanyu asked a man who was brushing by.

"What's happening is that we're to be shaved like criminals. The Manchus have given us ten days to adopt their barbarous hairstyle, or else…" He drew his finger across his throat. "Of course, the new magistrate and all the rich folks in town have shaved themselves already. Fuck the lot of them!" He stomped off.

Nanyu called after him, "Does *everybody* have to shave?" But the man was already gone, and Nanyu and Daosheng also hurried away from the yamen. After zigzagging for a few blocks, they ran again into the malcontents, who had regrouped at the base of a hill. One of them leaped to the top of a rock, his full mane of hair flying all around his head with a poignant bellicosity.

"Chinese men have Chinese customs!" he harangued the gathering. "But now the barbarians want us to shave our foreheads and wear a 'coin-sized rat tail' behind!" As curses nearly drowned him out, he roared at the sky, "I say no! We Chinese must not be turned into beasts!"

Amid the chorus of indignation, Nanyu heard a man shriek, "Are they going to brand us, too?" and someone else said, in a more restrained but deeper voice, "If we cut our hair, we'll lose our wives."

Nanyu remembered Daosheng pressed against him in the throng and roused himself to extricate her. He put his arm around her shoulder and led her out of the restless mass, finding an escape route along a side street. Soon he and his wife were catching their breath in a quiet space in front of a little temple. Daosheng checked to make sure that they still had all their possessions, and she was relieved to find on her person the two silver ingots that remained to them. Perhaps they were the same pair for which they had exchanged their first earnings and upon which they had gazed on that hot day in their tearoom. It was now one summer later, and Daosheng tried to commune with the ingots again, grasping them tightly. As for Nanyu, he could think only of his hair. He struggled to fathom the degradation that was now mandated for him, and the fact that he had to shave his pate himself, to render himself so inhumanly ugly, was especially galling. Even more oppressive was the notion that it wasn't his own body he was required to despoil but the corporal inheritance of his father. He nearly cried at the thought of his father's disappointment, and then he gagged at the realization that Ouyang Gen would be subject to the haircutting order too. The vision of his father with a "coin-sized rat tail" was the most appalling aspect of the new situation, and Nanyu took a step back in the direction of the angry mob. In the next instant, however, the sight of Daosheng once again dispelled all other concerns.

She noticed his hesitation. "How conflicted you must be, Husband, with your spirit torn in so many ways," she smiled, "yet at the end of your agonizing, you remain here with me, my hero."

"True enough, Wife," said Nanyu, "but how can I continue as your hero, if I'm to be a slave?"

"Very easily, as long as you're *my* slave."

"Now is not the time for joking, Wife. The whole world is being forced to choose between humiliation and death."

"You mean half the world, Husband: the male half. The female half is confronted with such a choice daily and has been since time began."

"What do you mean, Wife? Have you ever been sheared like a sheep?"

"You know that I have, Husband, or perhaps you've forgotten what I looked like when we first met?"

Nanyu checked his self-pity.

"You'll recall also," Daosheng continued, "that I was being transported into a kind of slavery on that same occasion; and please consider, too, how my 'natural' feet have rendered me something of a pariah, although I admit that the case of footbinding presents women with different modes of coercion, pain, and humiliation from what you men are experiencing now."

Nanyu exhaled.

"Yes, my hair has grown back and my men's feet have lately proven quite useful, but that is because I have been lucky. And the most important stroke of luck, as I've said before, was meeting you."

Although she was not smiling, the mandorla effect, the radiance about her, was becoming visible to Nanyu's eyes.

"Somehow, Husband—when sufficiently challenged, that is—you revert to your basic liberality. No one else would have accepted a woman with no hair and big feet who was, incidentally, another man's concubine. So if you think that I will reject you just because of a little shaving, then you are mistaken."

Daosheng jingled the two silver ingots in her hand. "Let's count our lucky stars, Husband. I count two. We'll manage."

Nanyu focused on Daosheng's face and calmed down. "Yes, Wife, we have been in tight spots before. Since you, once again, are keeping your head, perhaps I'll be able to keep mine."

"Interesting turn of phrase, Husband. No doubt your literary education is paying off...but yes, let's consider the situation: The haircutting order, I suppose, is a loyalty test, and it might backfire in the Manchus' faces. They have incited great anger and turned much of the populace against them. If you are resolved to keep your hair, you would have a lot of righteous company. Perhaps you could make a contribution—either your carpenter's strength or your scholar's smarts—to the resistance."

Nanyu again looked back toward the riot, but Daosheng held his arm.

"Taicang, however, may not be the best place to wage the battle." She looked into his eyes. "You saw, and heard, that the magistrate and local gentility have cut their hair and thus cast their lot with the Manchus. You can be sure they've already sent for the army, and you know what's likely to happen when it gets here. Remember Yangzhou, Husband?"

Nanyu thought for a moment and then began nodding, not just his head but his entire upper body. He started looking around, seeking the best exit from town.

"Yes, Husband," said Daosheng. "Let's try somewhere else,

where the defenders of our customs present more of a united front."

She replaced the silver ingots in the folds of her robe, and she and Nanyu took up their bundles. They struck out again for the east, away from the setting sun.

🌀🌀🌀🌀🌀

The countryside did in fact prove, for the time being, safer for travelers than the larger towns, for the people who lived outside city walls, not sharing the concern for law and order that preoccupied urbanites, were less likely to have conformed to the haircutting decree and to molest Nanyu for his unshaved scalp. It turned out that the Ouyangs were fortunate to have escaped Taicang, for, as they heard from excited villagers, the gentry maintained its grip on the town and enforced the haircutting order. An unshaven rural militia laid siege but was soon brushed aside by the Manchu army.

A few days later, as Nanyu and Daosheng entered the environs of Jiading, they beheld large numbers of armed, full-haired men heading into town. Apparently, Jiading's newly-installed magistrate had been evicted, and the local gentry, led by a scholar named Hou Tongzeng, had declared themselves for the restoration of the old regime. Hou contributed his family's fortune to the supply of nearby militias, and nearly every village in the region answered by sending troops. It was in the midst of these eager recruits that Nanyu and Daosheng now found themselves.

"It looks like Jiading can boast some leadership and that the people are responding to it," said Nanyu. "Why don't we try our luck here?"

He and Daosheng joined the influx of men moving through

the city gate and began searching for a suitable commander. They were, however, strangers, and nobody, with or without any authority, would trust or even talk with them. It proved impossible to obtain an introduction to Hou Tongzeng himself, which Nanyu much regretted, since he had absorbed a great deal of Mencius by now and felt certain that he could impress that gentleman with his understanding. While access to the top echelon was denied him, Nanyu still hoped that destiny would lead him into the orbit of some other captain, similar in quality if not in rank; yet after questing all afternoon for such a man, he grew discouraged. As sweat rolled off his forehead, he began thinking out loud and hit upon the desperate expedient of taking his and Daosheng's last two ounces of silver and simply buying a commission in the militia or perhaps using it to bribe his way into Hou Tongzeng's presence. After all, Nanyu expounded, hadn't the learned Hou himself likewise used money in lieu of sagely inspiration to marshal Jiading's righteous braves? Daosheng heard him muttering and vetoed the idea.

The Ouyangs circulated through town for two more days, spending the night at Enlightenment Temple, where they slept on the steps of a minor altar. Despite their efforts to join the resistance, however, they were denied entry to it, owing to the distrustful nature of its leadership and its rank and file. Worse, not only were the different militias reluctant to recruit outsiders, but they soon took to squaring off against each other, setting up their own checkpoints and toll barriers and squabbling over turf. Having come into Jiading only because the gentry promised to support them, furthermore, many militias began to shake the gentry down. With the situation in the streets turning anarchistic, Nanyu was finally permitted to enroll in the "monk militia" at the temple, but the invitation seemed to be extended chiefly for the equipment fee he was expected to provide. In formation, the monk militia struck Daosheng as a shabby lot, and she wondered in an aside to her husband how valiantly a bunch of baldies could be expected to fight for the right to keep one's hair. Nanyu ended up sharing Daosheng's poor appraisal of the prospects for successful restoration in Jiading, and the two of them quit the city one day at dawn. Outside the eastern gate, they saw pigtailed soldiers assembling, and they ran away as fast as they could.

In a few days (as they later heard), the Manchus' siege artillery arrived, and the stage was set for the final assault. The pigtails swarmed into the city, accosting everyone with long hair and demanding, "Southern barbarian, hand over your valuables!" When the citizens had nothing left to be extorted, their throats were cut, their women crucified and raped. The soldiers used long poles to poke under houses, looking for people who might be hiding. Waterways were clogged with corpses, and about twenty thousand were killed overall. Hou Tongzeng drowned himself, along with his sons and servants.

ⱳ ⱳ ⱳ ⱳ ⱳ

Refugees once more, Nanyu and Daosheng tried to keep to smaller, less-traveled thoroughfares, avoiding the towns, which no longer offered hope of safety. The countryside was completely convulsed and people were killing each other as though scything grain. The men of neighboring hamlets went to war against each other, with the shaved-scalped murdering the full-haired, and vice-versa. Nanyu and Daosheng remained vulnerable, no matter what Nanyu decided to do with his hair, and they fled even from their own shadows. One evening, they were suddenly overtaken by a group of armed men, and they were terrified. But fortunately the bravos were wearing long hair and were too absorbed in discussing their options to take any interest in troubling wayfarers.

"Jiangyin is still holding out," one of them said. "Let's try there."

"Jiangyin is too far upstream," said another. "We'd be attacked by the rat-tails before we got near there."

"So what? Bring them on!"

The discussion became heated. Nanyu worried that the militias of all the nearby counties would converge on them, for all the noise they were making, and sure enough, another group of soldiers soon arrived via a tree-lined lane. The newcomers, however, also sported full heads of hair, and Nanyu heard men from the different groups greet each other as "loyalists," the term which now applied to those who resisted the Manchu government, and its haircutting decree, in the name of the old regime. It occurred to Nanyu that the bulk of these "loyalists" were bondservants and poor people whose revolt the previous year had been suppressed by the old regime. As he pondered this reality, Nanyu gathered that consensus among the bravos was shifting toward a march to the east.

"Why?" someone asked, slow to be convinced. "What's going on there?"

"In Xinchang, a provincial civil service degree holder named Zhu Xiangsun organized a brotherhood called the Society for Cherishing Loyalty, to fight for the old dynasty. He'll need men like us." The speaker was a burly man wielding a halberd, and the combined body of loyalists decided without further delay to join the Society at Xinchang.

Nanyu and Daosheng exchanged glances. If a reunion with Zhu Xiangsun in Xinchang had been their objective all along, it was by now unlikely that the two of them could get there by stealth. A good three or four days of travel yet remained, and the intervening country was in a state of turmoil. Assuming that they could avoid getting bushwhacked in the open, they would remain at the mercy of locals for hiding places and for boat transport across the copious rivers and canals that lay athwart their path (bridges, with their checkpoints, were out of the question). Betrayal would be only a matter of time. Now, fate had provided them with a potential escort, but one that still needed to be won over.

Nanyu pulled himself up to his full height and proclaimed, "I know Zhu Xiangsun. Take us to him, and he will make you his personal bodyguard."

"And who might you be?" demanded the man with the halberd.

"A friend of his," said Nanyu. He did not give his name, realizing that status was more important. "In fact, he is my senior in study."

Nanyu's language implied more than shared academic interests; it left open the possibility that he had actually passed the provincial examination sometime after Zhu had. He was not only exaggerating his academic stature but also gambling that the men's attitude toward the elite had yet to turn from the reverential to the murderous.

The halberd-bearer was taller than Nanyu, and he wore a thick, black beard, somewhat resembling Wei Su's but making him look more like a bandit in an opera. Nanyu thought of the chieftain in *Southern Bough* and took a step closer to Daosheng.

The bearded man, however, seemed to be debating within himself. His eyes darted around for a while before narrowing in a squint. "If he's your 'senior in study,' what are you doing out here, dressed like a bumpkin?"

"Madame and I are traveling from Nanjing."

There was an imperial academy in Nanjing, a fact not lost

on the halberd man and his darting eyes. The other militiamen began fidgeting.

Nanyu pressed on. "As for the way we are dressed, 'A scholar who loves finery is not worthy of the name.' Besides, how else, besides by dressing plainly, should good people expect to pass through chaos, unnoticed by ruffians?"

The halberd-bearer hesitated as to how to respond to "ruffians." Nanyu removed his edition of Mencius from his bag.

"These are the works of Mencius," he said, "presented to me by provincial examination graduate Zhu Xiangsun."

"I'm supposed to kowtow to this little blue box?"

"Aren't you the one who just decided to march one hundred and twenty *li* to join provincial examination graduate Zhu Xiangsun and his Society for Cherishing Loyalty? Are you going to walk all that way, just to be in the luminous presence of a peddler or carpenter, or are you joining him because he's a *gentleman*? You know that what makes him a gentleman is in this little blue box."

"He gave that to you?"

"He did."

"Did he write something in it for you, like scholars do?"

"Yes," said Nanyu. He opened the first page of the first folio, to reveal some notes that Zhu Xiangsun had written concerning the edition, though Zhu had not in fact inscribed the book to him. The desperado squinted at the writing and nodded his acceptance, conceding the argument.

"What is your name, little brother?" asked Nanyu, putting the Mencius away.

"This insignificant person is surnamed Zhang, 'bow-long' Zhang," the man said, naming the components of one of the only two characters he could read and write. "My given name is Yue, as in 'jump,'" he said, conveying the meaning of the other.

By way of further illustration, he mimed the action of an archer drawing his bow and then jumped forward.

"Let's go, then, Zhang Yue," said Nanyu, "and let's teach the rat-tails a thing or two!"

His words elicited a rousing shout, and then the company, now numbering forty-two, moved out.

8

AUGUST TO SEPTEMBER, 1645

NANYU'S BAND FORCED a bridge over the Wusong River, scattering its pigtailed guards, and crossed into Shanghai County. They climbed a hill, slept in shifts, and started again the next day at dawn, bypassing the small county seat, really little more than a fishing village, and heading straight for Xinchang, to the southeast. After spending all the next night tramping through a marsh, they were by the following morning merely hours from their goal, and they closed the distance determinedly.

Xinchang was situated, as it were, in the center square of a tic-tac-toe board (or the Chinese character for "well"), demarcated by crisscrossing rivers and canals. The region's fields, circumscribed by brackish waterways, were heavily saline, and were used for the production of salt. ("Xinchang" means "New Field," in this case, "New Salt Field.") Nanyu observed a few farmers raking up piles of salt from rock-lined evaporating pools, although most of the men he could see were armed with spears and not with rakes. Evidently, others besides Zhang Yue had heard of Zhu Xiangsun and his Society for Cherishing Loyalty. Men of all descriptions came from far and near to join. Nanyu reckoned that the large, long-haired cohort, making good use of the rivers and canals for defense and for mobility, would be able to mount a tenacious stand.

Daosheng, for her part, was more impressed by the numerous commemorative arches that seemed to span every road. One that particularly caught her eye was the "Archway of Widow Chastity," which commemorated the purity of local widows who chose to kill themselves rather than to remarry. She also noticed an "Archway of the Scholars" and several similar memorials celebrating exemplary performances on the civil service examinations. Many of the scholarly and other achievements recorded in stone seemed to belong to men surnamed Zhu.

The town itself was cramped and crowded, when Nanyu's troop arrived there at mid-morning. Both Nanyu and Daosheng recalled Three Mountain Street in Nanjing, but the various residences, restaurants, and other establishments of Xinchang seemed to be more densely packed. The narrow streets were filled with armed men, and although restaurants were doing a brisk business, most of the other concerns, such as the curio shops and booksellers, were boarded up and a few of them appeared to have been looted. Nanyu's men were foraging widely up and down a street known for its delicate crabmeat snacks—its eateries had now switched to simpler fare such as barley porridge—when a voice called out, "Brother Ouyang!" and Nanyu turned to behold the grinning Zhu Ningxin. The two men rushed together and seemed about to embrace before resorting to comradely back-slapping instead. Zhu Ningxin was accompanied by the three housemen, Zhang, Fang, and Qiao, whom Nanyu remembered from the retreat from Beijing.

"What wind has carried you here?" asked Zhu Ningxin.

"The wind of war," replied Nanyu. "It seems not quite to have died down, since our last meeting."

"Indeed not," said Zhu Ningxin. "In fact, if memory serves, the guns began speaking on the very hour that you and I became acquainted. Perhaps you are a harbinger of ill fortune!" He guffawed, slapping Nanyu on the back again.

"We escaped Nanjing after the barbarians entered, and then we passed through both Taicang and Jiading, just ahead of...certain death," recounted Nanyu with a pause, as though realizing the danger for the first time.

"Where is your honorable father?" asked Zhu Ningxin.

"Still in Nanjing," answered Nanyu, as he looked around to ensure that neither Zhang Yue nor any of his recently-acquired retinue was standing close by. "He wanted me to get my sister out of town for a while, not knowing how the barbarians would behave. Of course, we both pleaded to stay with him, but he insisted."

Zhu Ningxin gave Daosheng a silent acknowledgement, and then he looked back at Nanyu. "So may I presume that you and your *meimei* have come to Xinchang to visit our humble home?"

Nanyu cleared his throat. "We have longed to thank you and your brothers more properly for the gracious assistance you extended to us last year, and," Nanyu opened his bag to reveal the blue box of Mencius, "I am naturally most eager to receive more of His Honor Zhu Xiangsun's illuminating tutelage."

Zhu Ningxin nodded. "I can think of nothing that would please Second Brother more. Of course, you are most welcome!" he said. He dipped his head once more, and then his smile turned almost sheepish. "I doubt, though, that we will be able to recreate the 'tranquility in the tempest' that we enjoyed on that little bridge in Beijing. This time, it would seem that we are at the very center of the storm."

"Yes," said Nanyu. "We have heard about His Honor's righteous enterprise." He saw out of the corner of his eye that Zhang Yue was striding over, curious to see to whom he was talking. "In the best of times," he went on, "it would be wrong for my sister and me to impose upon your hospitality without bringing a gift, and now, in this…strife…we would especially hate to be a burden. Fortunately, we have not come empty-handed but bring something that we hope will prove useful: forty men, armed and equipped. This is Zhang Yue, the leader."

Zhang Yue recognized Zhu Ningxin as a man of importance and bowed. "Is this the His Honor who started the Society?"

"No, this is his younger brother."

Zhang Yue bowed again. Zhu Ningxin stood ambivalent. He was shocked that his artist friend had presented him with a brigand, although the latter's expressions of respect mollified him. He said nothing.

"Most of the righteous braves you see on this street are mine," continued Nanyu. "They wish to serve as His Honor's bodyguard."

A smile returned to Zhu Ningxin's face, albeit an ironic one. "Perhaps they can protect Second Brother from all his other bodyguards," he said.

Nanyu and Zhang Yue fell silent. Zhu Ningxin's attention roamed up and down the street before returning to his friend and his friend's man.

"Second Brother sent me into town to plumb the depths of the people's feelings," he said. "Now he won't have to rely merely on my observations. We'll bring Little Zhang home for questioning, and Second Brother can hear for himself how things are." He gestured at the milling crowd in the street. "The rest of your men will have to stay in this area. I recommend they take up their posts on the Bridge of Eternal Prosperity."

Nanyu assured Zhang Yue that he wasn't going to be interrogated under torture, and after directing his followers to the nearby Bridge of Eternal Prosperity (which, according to Zhu Ningxin, had been financed by one of his ancestors), accompanied the young scion up a twisting alleyway with Daosheng, Zhang

Yue, and the three housemen in tow.

௸௸௸

The sun was just reaching its zenith, heralding another sweltering late-summer day, and Nanyu was pleased to be nearing the end of his quest. Zhu Ningxin continued to point out local landmarks — a school, a bridge — that had been constructed under the sponsorship of his family, and the narrowness of the alley and the closeness of the frontages created a sense of intimacy, quiet, and calm. When Zhu Ningxin wasn't enthusing about something, the only sounds that could be heard were those of the party's footsteps and the swishing of their pantaloons. Occasionally, they passed sturdy women washing dishes in the street or heard families eating their lunches inside their houses. Once, Nanyu harkened to the rhythmic clanging of an unseen little brother or sister whipping up a meal in a wok, and he savored the aroma of garlic and chili as he moved past. By the time the group arrived at the portal of the Zhu family's mansion, Nanyu was so overcome by sensations of comfort and domesticity that he failed to remark on the door being closed, even in the daytime.

Zhu Ningxin called out, and the gate swung open. When a servant ran out to greet him, Zhu Ningxin sent the man off to request the presence of his brothers, and then he welcomed everyone inside.

The Zhu family compound was a two-courtyard mansion, with the southern courtyard, in which the newcomers now stood, dedicated to the preparation and serving of meals, the entertaining of guests, and the discussion of business; the northern courtyard was reserved for the living quarters of the brothers and their families. Presently, Zhu Jinqing and Zhu

Zaixin emerged from a doorway leading to the second courtyard. When they saw Nanyu and Daosheng, they smiled and strode over. Joined by Zhu Ningxin, they ranged themselves in birth order, with Jinqing in the lead, bowing and raising their inward-turned hands in the scholars' salute.

"What wind…?"

"The wind of war."

Zhu Jinqing ordered a light lunch and bade Nanyu to sit at a rectangular table, shaded by an oak tree. He took care to place himself at the head, followed by his brothers Zaixin and Ningxin, and with Nanyu at the foot. Daosheng and Zhang Yue were led off to the kitchen, from which four teenage girls were already issuing, all carrying plates of marinated eggplant, which they placed on the table for the three hosts and their guest. Another girl poured tea.

"Please excuse the absence of Second Brother," apologized Zhu Jinqing, "but he is in conference with Master Fang and Master Yan, two of Shanghai County's most promising stipendiaries."

"Are they talking about the Society for Cherishing Loyalty?" asked Nanyu.

"Indeed they are."

"Excellent! His Honor will be happy to know that word of his great undertaking has spread halfway up the Yangtze valley," said Nanyu, exaggerating a bit. "The 'black-haired people' are inspired and excited. They know that it offers them the best chance to keep their black hair." Nanyu had tried a little play on words. "Black-haired people" referred to the common people.

Zhu Jinqing smiled. "Yes, the members of the Society for Cherishing Loyalty revere nothing more than the old dynasty and its customs."

"Perhaps Zhu Ningxin has already told you that I brought forty stalwart loyalists with me. I gladly place them at the

Society's disposal."

"Many thanks."

"In fact, I hope that I can be of service to the Society myself. I have been studying His Honor's edition of Mencius, as he recommended. I believe its insights will prove as efficacious in our current situation as they were last year, on the Canal."

Zhu Jinqing said nothing, leaving Nanyu to concentrate on his eggplant, which he dispatched in short order. He expected his plate to be replenished, but it was not.

A somewhat awkward half hour passed before a door opened on the north side of the courtyard and the sounds of formal leave-taking spilled out. Zhu Xiangsun appeared in the doorway, along with two other gentlemen. As they continued bowing and wishing each other well, Zhu Jinqing rose and called for the head servant to "Escort Master Fang and Master Yan to the door." Nanyu heard Zhu Xiangsun say, "Please forgive my not seeing you off. My friend Mr Ouyang is here, bringing word of the situation in the villages. Take care! Take care!" Nanyu stood up at the mention of his name, but it took a few minutes more for the two to depart, and he remained standing throughout, grinding his teeth whenever Zhu Xiangsun repeated, "Don't be so quick to leave," as was the formality on such occasions.

Finally, the stipendiaries were gone. Zhu Xiangsun advanced half the distance to where Nanyu was standing.

"What wind...?"

"The wind of war." Nanyu raised his arms in the scholars' salute, and Zhu Xiangsun reciprocated.

"I hear that you've had quite a journey," said Zhu Xiangsun. "I also hear that you managed to attract a following along the way. I should like to discuss these matters with you, if you have a moment now."

Nanyu nodded, bowed also to the other brothers with an

"Excuse me," and trotted over to Zhu Xiangsun. The latter called to Zhu Jinqing, "Send in his man, too," and then he turned and led Nanyu back into the south-facing room, which functioned as his office.

While they waited for Zhang Yue, Zhu Xiangsun asked, "How is your honorable father?"

"He is healthy, although of course I am worried about him," replied Nanyu. "He wished to remain at home, instructing me to keep Little Sister away from the barbarians."

"Ah, your *meimei*," said Zhu Xiangsun, "I take it that she has 'come down from the mountain'? Fourth Brother tells me that she has grown her hair."

"Ah, yes," Nanyu said. "Father preferred that she help earn some income, under the circumstances."

"Quite understandable," said Zhu Xiangsun. "And what work did your honorable father give her?"

"We ran a tea shop."

"'We'? You and your *meimei* together?"

"In fact, she did such a fine job that I was at leisure to read Mencius."

"Ah," Zhu Xiangsun smiled. "So while she was laboring with her muscles, you were laboring with your mind."

"Yes, Your Honor, you might say that."

Footsteps approached, and there stood Zhang Yue, escorted by Qiao Yin, one of the housemen. Qiao was armed and Zhang was not, and Nanyu thought that the loyalist looked useless without his halberd. Zhu Xiangsun dismissed Qiao Yin and addressed Zhang Yue. "Come in, close the door, and sit down."

Zhang obeyed before remembering to bow, which he did from his seat. Then he asked, "Is it true that I am to be in Your Honor's bodyguard?"

"We shall see," said Zhu Xiangsun. He turned back to Nanyu.

"Where did you encounter this man?"

"On a stretch of road, this side of Jiading," answered Nanyu. "It was most fortuitous."

"Fortuitous? How so?"

"Well, in the first place, Ouyang Daosheng and I needed protection from the rat tails. In the second place, it was from Little Zhang here that we learned of the Society for Cherishing Loyalty. You might say, then, that he is doubly responsible for our safe arrival here."

"How many other men were with Little Zhang, when you met up with him?"

"There were two groups of twenty, which joined into a single company, as soon as we determined to come here."

"Were they organized as a militia, under a reliable captain?"

"No, but they seemed to be getting along well enough without one."

"Indeed! Did you know anything of their past activities, whether or not they had always behaved in an orderly fashion?"

"No."

"Then why would you keep company with such men?"

"As I said, we were greatly in need of *some* company, and under the circumstances, Your Honor, the only credential I needed to see was their long hair."

"'Under the circumstances,' to borrow your phrase, it is all the more essential to know men's characters, starting with this man's right here." He gestured toward Zhang Yue. "Tell me, Little Zhang, to whom are you bound?"

"To no one, Your Honor."

"I see. To whom *were* you bound, say, last year?"

Zhang Yue hesitated, but at a nod from Nanyu, he answered, "To Mr Gu, of Songjiang, and I stuck with him last year."

"So when did you turn renegade?"

"Just a week or so ago. I didn't want to, but Master left me no choice."

"Indeed!"

"You see, Your Honor, he cut his hair and ordered me and all his people to do the same. So I just ran away and was on my way to Jiading, where Mr Hou said the people wouldn't have to cut their hair, but then the barbarians took Jiading and a bunch of us were wandering around, until we heard about Your Honor and the Society for Cherishing Loyalty, and then we met Mr Ouyang, who said he knew you and that we could be your bodyguard." Zhang Yue smiled.

"So you 'just ran away' from your master, Mr Gu? You didn't murder him or threaten to?"

Zhang's smile vanished. His lips twitched, and then he looked at the floor. Zhu Xiangsun's stern expression turned wrathful. He was about to slam his fist on the table, when Nanyu spoke up.

"What of it, Big Brother?" he said. "Gu was a traitor, so Little Zhang whacked him, and you're a loyalist, so he's come to join you. If everyone did as Little Zhang did, we'd be able to drive the barbarians out in a few days. We'd win. Isn't that what the Society for Cherishing Loyalty is all about?"

"*If everyone did as Little Zhang did…!*" Zhu Xiangsun exploded. "Do you really want more Jiadings? You saw what happens when the riffraff gets involved." He took one more look at Zhang Yue, who sat petrified, as the two gentlemen argued over him. "Qiao!" he called to his houseman, who appeared instantly. "Show Little Zhang out! Get Zhang Hui and Fang Long and wait with Little Zhang in the courtyard. I'll be done with Mr Ouyang momentarily, and then I'll have additional instructions."

Zhang Yue rose and left with Qiao Yin, too frazzled to remember to take his leave of either Nanyu or Zhu Xiangsun. In the few seconds' interval, Nanyu cast about for a new tack.

"As to Jiading," he said, "perhaps Mr Hou was not an enlightened leader of men. Perhaps Your Honor could do better."

"I wouldn't presume," said Zhu Xiangsun.

"Don't be modest, Teacher. I've seen you manage under pressure," said Nanyu. "On the Canal, last year, you awed Captain Ni's militia with your elucidation of Mencius. 'The gentleman's virtue is like the wind; the virtue of the common people is like grass. Let the wind sweep over the grass, and the grass is sure to bend.' Even as you recited it, you proved it. Your virtue swept over the common people, and they bent. What worked at the Zaolin Lock last year could work here in Xinchang now."

Zhu Xiangsun permitted himself a smile, yet he remained immune to Nanyu's enthusiasm. "Yes, I suppose that, in spite of the terrible events of last spring, I was able to do my part to ensure that the common people would continue to show their betters due deference. However, as the year unfolded, the Way did not prevail, and chaos reigned. It infected the common people, who became unresponsive to virtue and who instead took to imitating—nay, even surpassing—the bad elements in their depravity. Until the Way prevails again, I'm afraid that my meagre virtue—which you, sir, quite exaggerate—can be wielded to little effect."

"But it is the Manchu barbarians, Teacher," essayed Nanyu, "who have trampled on the Way. Their haircutting decree prevents all of us—both high and low—from honoring the bodies inherited from our parents. The common people are angry at this insult to our customs, and righteously so. In righteousness, cannot the gentlemen find common cause with the 'black-haired people'—regardless of their...prior status as bondservants? Isn't righteousness itself a virtue?"

Nanyu believed that he had made a strong argument for

recruiting former bondsmen, and he went on to make several more, both philosophical and practical. Zhu Xiangsun, however, was concerned only with maintaining the rigid distinction between masters and servants. He absolutely refused to allow bondsmen to join the Society.

"Brother Ouyang, perchance you are insufficiently informed about what transpired last summer," he said. "After our emperor was persuaded by his villainous advisors to promulgate that infamous edict about 'giving the people a new beginning,' we witnessed an unprecedented catastrophe. It was not merely that gentlemen and commoners became indistinguishable—we had already sunk to that state long ago. It was, rather, that gentlemen and commoners had exchanged places. Servants were issuing orders to masters, just like sons issuing orders to fathers! You have mentioned righteousness, and righteousness is indeed one of the Eight Virtues, but it is only when the righteousness of the son remains under the control of the father that order prevails. When the honor of the father becomes subject to the righteousness of the son, then chaos prevails. We were fortunate to have survived last year with our honor intact.

"When the haircutting order became known," he continued, "we were indeed profoundly outraged, but at the same time, we were apprehensive of a repetition of last year's horrors, and alas, the initial response to the haircutting order was not encouraging. Again, the ringleaders took advantage of the discontent to incite their gangs. You may think that we can turn this rabble against the invaders, but barbarism cannot be enlisted to combat barbarism. The gentleman does not make 'common cause' with rebels and murderers. Instead, he must strive at all hazards to maintain control of the righteousness of those below. As it is said in *The Book of Changes*, 'The gentleman, by making a clear distinction between above and below, sets limits to the people's ambition.' When no clear distinction is made between above and below, how can ambition be controlled?"

"The gentleman..." Nanyu put his hand on the table that lay between him and Zhu Xiangsun, as though supporting himself. He collected his strength and his thoughts before proceeding. "Actually, Teacher, I've been fascinated by the power of the gentleman, ever since your dialogue with Captain Ni at the Zaolin Lock. I've studied the matter in Mencius, and I've longed to seek your advice in person. Who could have known that the matter would have taken on such a practical, uh, urgency by the time I found you."

Zhu Xiangsun nodded. "You are right, Little Brother. The principles contained in Mencius are especially pertinent today. Though my understanding of them is far from perfect, I will provide what guidance I can."

"Well," began Nanyu, "I don't know anything about 'making a clear distinction between above and below.' I've never read *The Book of Changes*. In Mencius, though, it seems that what the gentleman does is *to set the example*."

"Quite right," said Zhu Xiangsun. "The gentleman does indeed set the example. 'When someone above shows a preference for anything, there is certain to be someone below who will outdo him.'"

"Well, it seems to me," continued Nanyu, "that the next question is: What is the 'anything'? If the common man — or 'someone below' — will follow the gentleman's example in anything, then...well...the gentleman can make the common man *do* anything."

"That's a crude way of putting it, Little Brother."

"Later in the book you gave me, Mencius says, 'The gentleman draws the bow but does not release the arrow; he just gives a little jump.' It seems to me that all we have to do...all *you* have to do...

is to draw the bow and give a little jump, and then thousands of common men will launch their thousands of arrows into the hearts of the barbarians and traitors. They're waiting for your signal, as we speak."

Now it was Zhu Xiangsun's turn to gather himself, with his hand on the table. "All the more reason to be careful," he said. "Mencius's rather regrettable warlike image seems to have confused you. Remember, the gentleman is the guardian of the Way of the sages, which teaches that human nature is good. He must always, therefore, be an example of goodness, so as to induce the common people to revert to their intrinsically good nature. Inciting them to lawlessness, as you propose, would be an act of perversity."

He let the lesson sink in, and then he proceeded. "It would also be, as I have already said, suicidal. If I were to encourage bondservants to revolt, then I would be encouraging disobedience, like a general commanding his troops to mutiny. How long could I expect to maintain authority over the disobedient and mutinous?"

"But I thought that was the whole point," said Nanyu. "You are a gentleman. Your authority over the common people is natural."

"Therefore, you will permit me to wield it in a natural way," said Zhu Xiangsun, "as was taught by the sage king Yao:

"Encourage them in their toil,
Put them on the right path,
Aid them and help them,
Make them happy in their station,
And by bountiful acts further relieve them of
hardship."

Zhu Xiangsun reached over the table and clapped Nanyu on the shoulder.

"And that brings us back to Little Zhang," he said. "I want you to take my men, Zhang, Fang, and Qiao, and to escort Little Zhang back to the Bridge of Eternal Prosperity, to rejoin the other runaways. Then you must prevail upon them to disband and to resume peaceful occupations. You seem to have some influence over them; here's your chance to use it for the good. Give them one ounce of silver apiece—my chamberlain will provide it—and encourage them to establish simple trades. Urge them also, should they fail in their trades and have no choice but to indenture themselves to new masters, to serve them faithfully and contentedly."

Zhu Xiangsun smiled. "You'll see. People like Little Zhang are brawny, but they are simpletons. It's actually quite easy to induce a simpleton to revert to his basic docility—as easy as teaching a monkey to climb a tree."

Nanyu said nothing. Zhu Xiangsun's smile grew conspiratorial. He glanced left and right, and then he said, "When you are finished with Little Zhang, we'll have another matter to discuss. It relates to your *meimei*."

"Oh?"

"Yes. Has your honorable father made any arrangements for her, as far as you know?"

"Ah…no. You see, she may return to the nunnery after all."

"Truly? She seems most unlike a contemplative. I've yet to notice her reciting sutras."

"Well, lately we seem always to be running, with no leisure for study."

"Perhaps if another prospect were to open up, she could settle down, with no need to return to the nunnery after all."

"Another prospect?"

"Yes. My brother Ningxin."

"Ningxin…"

"The two of you are very close anyway. Why not become brothers-in-law?"

"Oh. Well, that's…Of course, I'm quite honored."

"Nonsense. You're a talented young man, with a desire for learning. It's not as though the distance between our families is insurmountable."

"But what of her…oddity? That can't be acceptable, can it?"

"It would be acceptable to Ningxin. He's not the eldest sibling, so it doesn't really matter. Furthermore, once married, your *meimei* won't be gallivanting about, anyway. She will take her place in the inner quarters. No gossip's eyes will ever glimpse her peasants' feet."

"No, I suppose not."

"Please do consider it, then, on you father's behalf."

"Teacher, you're aware that he's a carpenter, yes?"

Zhu Xiangsun paused, and his eyebrows leaped almost imperceptibly. After the briefest hesitation, he said, "Then he's not likely to object, is he?"

Nanyu rocked back and forth. His head passed through a ray of blazing afternoon sun, streaming through a gap in the shutters, and he was intermittently blinded. "Why us?" he said. "I mean, why Daosheng?"

"I think you know the answer to that," grinned Zhu Xiangsun. "Didn't you just tell me that she was able to manage your tea shop singlehandedly, giving you all the time you needed to study Mencius? A clever girl like your *meimei* would be a fine asset for Ningxin, who is also inclined toward learning. Not to mention," Zhu rose from his seat, "we could always use another talented young man in this family—and in the Society, don't forget."

He helped Nanyu to his feet, put his arm around his shoulders, and walked him to the door. "I know you'll say the right things to Little Zhang and the others and that your words will have the best effect. My housemen will be doing some provisioning in town afterward, so you'll have to return alone. Will you remember the way?"

Nanyu nodded and made a scholars' salute.

"I won't see you off, then."

Emerging from his office, he caught sight of Qiao Yin, who was keeping Little Zhang company with the other two housemen, and waved him over. He also called for his chamberlain.

"Wait a minute," said Nanyu, as he stood in the doorway. "Aren't we going to need a go-between, for the...affair we discussed?"

Zhu Xiangsun chuckled. "I had no idea you were such a stickler for the formalities, Little Brother. Don't you know the *Book of Songs*?

"Here is a lady I have met in love;
Here are the wedding dishes, all in a row."

Qiao Yin and the chamberlain arrived. Zhu Xiangsun issued them their instructions and then retreated back into his office. Qiao went to mobilize the others in the courtyard, and the chamberlain trotted off to fetch a bag of silver, which he discreetly handed to Nanyu. Little Zhang asked for his halberd, but the housemen would not restore it to him, and he belatedly perceived that he was being ejected from the premises under guard. He was about to protest when Nanyu passed him the sack of silver, with a look in his eyes that persuaded him to desist. The five men trooped silently through the courtyard and out the main gate, Nanyu straining for a glimpse of Daosheng. He spotted her in the kitchen, chopping vegetables.

They traversed the quaint neighborhood through which they had arrived earlier, with Nanyu now oblivious to its charms. He was at least as distracted when he returned alone at twilight.

꿰꿰 꿰꿰 꿰꿰

At dinner, Nanyu was seated among the brothers. He estimated that he should have been ranked, according to age, between Zaixin and Ningxin, but he found himself promoted one space, to sit just below Xiangsun. The latter was keen to know how Nanyu had handled his mission.

"Did Little Zhang and his crew give you any trouble?" he asked.

"No, Big Brother," replied Nanyu. "They were putty in my hands, just as you said they would be."

"Splendid! You have learned enough of the Way from Mencius to have achieved some sway over the common people. No doubt the task of leadership will grow even easier for you, especially if you are given more wholesome followers. On that score, you should know that my friends Fang and Yan are selecting reliable people from among their families and neighbors. They'll make fine additions to our Society."

Nanyu could only smile.

"For now, though, we shall speak no more of that," Zhu Xiangsun added. "We've killed a pig and a few chickens for this meal, so let's enjoy it. Your *meimei*, by the way, has already proven most helpful in the kitchen. A few of these dishes are hers. She certainly is clever."

Nanyu savored the spinach and turnip dishes that were unmistakably his wife's. It had been some time since he'd tasted them, and the flavors took him back to a previous incarnation. Already intoxicated with longing, he began drinking to the endless series of toasts offered by all four of the brothers, and he soon felt very warm in the heart and fuzzy in the limbs. He lolled his head back and bathed his face in moonlight. All around him faded into dark and strange shapes. He returned every toast, every few minutes or so—"Teacher, to your health!" "Ningxin, Brother, long life and happiness!" He picked at unhusked shrimp and finely chopped crabs, hoping to extract meat from shell. Futile. Now my hands are slimy. Can I lick my fingers clean? Would it be…proper? No, please don't refill my cup. A whirl of activity: They refilled my cup. Oh, why couldn't you just listen to me?—I mean, Thank you, thank you; it's quite tasty. Another flask? I hate sitting on stools. My back is getting tired. When we were at home, in the tea room, I could lean back against the wall and be attached to something. Now, I'm swaying on this fucking stool, with nothing to hold me up. Everything's spinning. They killed a pig. And a few chickens. The chicken meat is already between my teeth, but where's the pig? I guess he takes longer to cook. Oh, here he is. Yes, let's all clap our hands for the dead pig. He doesn't look very happy. They're cutting him up. They're giving me his choicest meat. What an honor.

"Where is Daosheng?"

The evening air had cooled, and a breeze caressed Nanyu's cheeks. For a long time, he couldn't make out his wife, among the shifting mass of shapes. Suddenly, he saw her talking to Zhu Ningxin, who was forcing a *pipa* upon her. Daosheng was demurring; the others were calling and clapping. She took the instrument, rose, and crossed the courtyard to sit on a low bench, from which she could see the entire table, though Nanyu's vision was too blurred to tell where her gaze fell. She began to play a tune he recognized, and she sang:

"You and I
Have so much love
That it burns…like…fire

"In the fire we bake a lump of clay
And we mold a figure of you
And we mold a figure of me

"Then we take both of them
And break them into pieces
And mix the pieces with water

"And mold again a figure of you
And a figure of me

"I am in your clay
You are in my clay

"In life we share a single quilt
In death we'll share one coffin."

Everyone in the courtyard had fallen silent, and all that could be heard was the trampling of feet and shouting in the street outside, which seemed louder than it should have been. Finally, Zhu Ningxin rose above the slumping feasters with a broad grin and gestured toward Daosheng.

"Excellent, Little Sister!" he said. "What touching frailty, like a jade bracelet turning or a phoenix singing. Who is the author of that lyric?"

"I am," said Daosheng.

Zhu Ningxin's lips formed a circle, as he looked left and right. "And what do you call it?" he asked.

"I call it," said Daosheng, "'For My Husband.'"

There was a tremendous impact upon the front gate. Then came a second attack and a third and finally, with a splintering crash, the door flew open, and a wedge of howling men swarmed over the threshold, polearms leveled. Women screamed; male residents shouted in surprised and yet anticipated indignation. Nanyu leapt up, grabbed Daosheng, and carried her to the kitchen.

It seemed later to Nanyu that the entire proceeding consisted of three distinct phases. The first phase was the initial rush into the courtyard, in which the men of the Zhu family, together with everyone else who happened to be gathered around their table, were slaughtered. Jinqing and Zaixin managed to get to their feet but didn't make it three paces before they were impaled by spears. Ningxin had already been standing to praise Daosheng's singing; he had just enough time to turn toward the advancing assailants, only to be brained by a halberd blow delivered by one of them. Though killed instantly, he kept standing for a while, with Nanyu watching, until he fell. Zhu Xiangsun, the would-be leader of the rebels now come to murder him, refused to rise. Remaining defiantly seated, he ignored the mob that surrounded him and begrudged no acknowledgement of the torrent of halberds, cudgels, swords, knives, and fists that rained upon him. In the end, almost nothing was left of him, and his blood mingled with that of his brothers and the more nondescript bystanders of the courtyard. This first phase of the action lasted less than a minute.

The second phase consumed about ten minutes and was devoted to the search for hidden survivors. Most of them were women or younger men, who were easily discovered under beds or in wardrobes and then dragged to the slaughter pile in the courtyard. They were stripped and searched for concealed jewelry, and some of the women disappeared within jeering huddles of savagery, which left them naked, used, and dead in the pooling blood on the tiles. There were others who escaped humiliation, yet none—besides Nanyu, Daosheng, and the few sculleries cowering in the kitchen—escaped death.

When the frenzied killing was over, a more deliberate looting began—the third phase of the action—and continued indeterminately. The frustrated loyalists swarmed locust-like through the residence, seizing everything from inlaid chopsticks and lacquered boxes to writing desks and chairs. A stash of silver ingots was informally divided into something like shares, with each desperado taking as much as he could without incurring jealousy. Some of the pillagers began smashing up the larger furniture that could not be carried; but most of them, once laden with spoils, simply decamped, leaving their weapons behind.

Nanyu struggled to take it all in from a corner of the kitchen, as Zhang Yue guarded the doorway. Nanyu was still clutching Daosheng, from having carried her in, but as the drink and the blood of the dinner feast overwhelmed him, he sank to the floor, where he clung to Daosheng's legs. Closing his eyes did nothing to stop the vision of carnage; covering his ears did nothing to stop the sound of screaming. He remained dizzy, silent, and barely breathing, for what seemed a lifetime, buffeted by the concussions of breaking furniture.

Finally, there came the sound of approaching footsteps. "Ah, here's the promising young artist with his *meimei*. See how he protects her." It was Qiao Yin, one of the Zhu family's housemen, who had brought his associates, Zhang Hui and Fang Long, in tow. All three had retained their halberds and seemed rather intent on Nanyu.

"No one touches him," said Zhang Yue, filling the doorway.

"Wouldn't dream of it," said Qiao. "As long as he keeps

making himself useful, anyway."

In the meantime, Daosheng had reached down and pulled Nanyu up by the arm. She continued to steady him, with her hands on his shoulders.

"My, they're looking sweeter and sweeter," Qiao drawled. "I wish I had a *meimei* like that."

It was not uncommon for lovers to address each other as *gege* (older brother) and *meimei* (younger sister). Zhang Yue, simple soul, assumed that such terms of endearment could apply also within a marriage and thus failed to grasp, then or later, Qiao's sarcasm. He could not have missed, however, the general menace in Qiao's voice, and he snarled, "No one touches Madame Ouyang, either."

The housemen cackled, and then Qiao said, "Fine. We'll leave Madame *meimei* alone for a while, too. As a matter of fact," he continued, "she'll do for our purposes, especially considering the state her *gege* is in. Just let us in, man. We want to ask her something."

Qiao, Fang, and Zhang Hui leaned their halberds against the wall and made conciliatory gestures. Zhang Yue stood aside, and the three big men filed in. They each carried fistfulls of paper that they had snatched from some desk or strongbox, and they thrust them at Daosheng. It was apparent to her that this archive constituted the chief part of their plunder for, besides a few ingots of silver, their pockets were empty.

"It is true that Mr Ouyang is indisposed for the moment," said Daosheng, leaning her husband carefully against the wall before releasing his shoulders, "though I'm sure I can answer for him. Let me see what you've got there." She collected the papers from the three of them, like an examination proctor.

One by one, Daosheng smoothed the documents out and summarized their contents. "This is a land deed...This is a compact for a village school...This is a eulogy for a relative."

Upon rendering each classification, she returned the paper in question to Qiao Yin, who conveyed it disappointedly onto the floor. Before long, though, Daosheng reported, "Ah, here's a set of tenancy contracts. We may be getting closer to what you're looking for."

The housemen waited.

"Your names are Qiao, Fang, and Zhang, yes?" Daosheng cleared her throat. "Qiao Yin. Both your parents were lost in an epidemic. An uncle indentured you to Zhu Jinqing. Fang Long. Your father had gambling debts. It was either sell you or become a eunuch. Zhang Hui. Your father was a tenant who couldn't pay the rent. All of you are indentured for life."

"Not anymore," said Fang Long, and as each of the bondsmen, in turn, retrieved his contract from Daosheng, he tore it up and threw the confetti heavenward. In each case, some of it rained back down upon his head, compelling him to brush it off, his first act as a free man.

"Well," said Daosheng, "What now? Are you going to try to find your families?"

"What families?" said Fang Long. "Assuming they're still alive, they're the bastards who sold us."

"Maybe it's not too good an idea to hang around here, either," said Zhang Hui, eying the mountain of corpses in the courtyard.

Qiao Yin was looking in the same direction. "Pretty fucking funny," he said. "That *wang ba dan* Zhu Xiangsun was the best chance we had to keep our hair. Now that we're free of him, we have to get sheared like livestock. How pathetic." The others, including Zhang Yue, also cursed.

Daosheng waited for a pause in their grumbling and then said, "I suppose we should consider the situation: Hundreds of fighting men have come here to Xinchang, hoping to join the Society for Cherishing Loyalty. I gather, however, that Zhu Xiangsun spurned most of them while he was alive, and he can't lead any of them now that he is dead. In fact," she continued slowly, "the only result of his leadership has been mutiny, which may be growing general, even as we speak. Mr Fang and Mr Yan might still be active on the Society's behalf, but if they're operating under Zhu's instructions — or his philosophy — they're sure to be as ambivalent and ineffective as he was, not even considering their lower rank. The fundamental problem," she concluded, "is one of command: Who can wield authority over, ah, the Society?" She'd almost said "the mob."

All of them were now pondering the reeking courtyard, when Zhang Yue said, "How about Mr Ouyang?"

None of the others replied at first, pending some measurement of general opinion. Nanyu himself seemed oblivious to the suggestion.

After looking into her husband's eyes, Daosheng said, "Although Mr Ouyang led you safely here from Jiading, it's doubtful that he would be able to fill Zhu Xiangsun's shoes, as leader of a larger movement."

"But I heard him talking to His Honor," Zhang Yue protested. "He had the right idea, to stick together against the barbarians and traitors."

"Yes, Little Zhang, we're all agreed that uniting the Society is the right idea. But the question, as I just said, is who can turn the idea into a reality." Daosheng ventured another glance into Nanyu's eyes.

"Mr Ouyang seems pretty well used up," said Qiao Yin. "The only reality he's fit to make is a puddle of puke on the ground."

"Now, now, Brother Qiao," said Daosheng, "Mr Ouyang is indisposed, as I said."

"Well, then, how about you, Big Sister?"

"How about me for what?" said Daosheng, noting her promotion from "little sister" (*meimei*).

"How about you for our leader? At least until Mr Ouyang shakes off whatever it is he drank."

Daosheng took yet another look at her husband and then turned toward her new devotee.

"I'm flattered, Brother Qiao, but pray tell: Why do you need someone like me to be your leader? You're a strong and clever man, not unlike the humble founder of our valiant dynasty. Why not just take over the Society yourself?"

"Oh, no, Big Sister!" Qiao Yin blanched. "The Great Ancestor was the prince of light…a true sage…maybe even the Maitreya. Me, I'm just a bumpkin…a no-account…." His voice trailed off.

"All right," exhaled Daosheng. "So you don't feel up to it, and neither do any of you boys, I guess." Nobody even bothered to speak, and she went on. "You still haven't said why I'm qualified, why you would follow me."

But there wasn't any answer to that question, either, or if there was, it wasn't verbal but apparent in the black-haired men's demeanor, which had evolved from the resentment shown toward supposed betters in general to the deference shown toward them in particular. Perhaps, in the course of their little council in the kitchen, Daosheng had graduated from an unknown to a known quantity — one that was educated — and the change in the former servants' regard had proceeded apace. They were now quite devoted to her, and her influence over them seemed magical.

Nevertheless, Daosheng, for one, did not believe in magic, and she knew better than to let any fantastic notions go to her head.

"Brothers," she said, "It seems to me that things in Xinchang are falling apart, not coming together. Even the few men I might have been able to count on — Mr Ouyang's band of loyalists from outside Jiading — have mostly absconded."

They all saw that it was true. Only a small number of scavengers remained in the Zhu family compound.

"Perhaps they're satisfied by the amount of plunder in their hands," she continued, "or perhaps they're ashamed of the blood on their hands. In any case, they're gone. The rest of the Society, assuming it still exists, doesn't know me from the Moon Rabbit."

"You could still win it over," Fang Long broke in.

"Not under current conditions," said Daosheng. "It would be like trying to gather sand in the wind."

"Is that it, then?" said Qiao Yin. "We're just going to give up?"

"I think it would be prudent to get out of here, no matter what," said Daosheng. "This place is ill-fated. Do any of you really want to stick around?"

No one did.

Zhang Hui said, "But where should we go?"

"Let's try Hangzhou," said Daosheng. "It was the capital of the south once, and there's an imperial prince there, so rumor has it."

The men assented and at once addressed themselves to securing all the foodstuffs in the pantry, which they divided among four framed packsacks and shouldered themselves. Daosheng hadn't ever removed the silver and important papers from her robe, so she was already packed. Nanyu had set his bundle down in the courtyard and still felt unready to go looking for it. But when Daosheng made to undertake the search on his behalf, he came to himself and held her back. He moved ahead of her, out through the doorway and into the fatal space. He trod lightly through the lake of blood, trying to minimize the splashing sound, until he found his possessions at the edge of the ooze. The bag was pretty well tainted, which appeared to have rendered it unattractive to the looters, for it was otherwise intact. Nanyu pulled it open and found that his album and Four Treasures were miraculously preserved, for they had been propped up by the box of Mencius, when he had set everything down. The Mencius itself, however, was permeated with blood. Nanyu grabbed it and shook a few red drops off of it and was pleased to note that it was not actually soaked. He removed the folios and began sponging everything off with a brigand's dropped head-wrap and was still engaged in this labor when the others emerged from the kitchen area, prepared to leave.

Daosheng apprehended what her husband was about and doubled back to retrieve an extra carrying sack, which she threw, perhaps to him, perhaps at him, as she passed. Nanyu finally got his accoutrements repacked, took one last, sober look at the carnage, and hurried off in pursuit of his following, leaving crimson footprints in his wake.

〇〇 〇〇 〇〇

The small band of loyalists got away from Xinchang, which was, as Daosheng had predicted, in a state of tumult, and headed southwest. The six of them were just numerous—and armed— enough to avoid trouble, though they decided to keep their own company and to refrain from approaching any other group, even if its members wore long hair. The fact that there was still long hair to be observed attested to the uncertain governance in the country through which they moved, but there was no heroic resistance to the new regime in evidence, either. Everyone seemed to be keeping clear of everyone else, waiting. These conditions suited the travelers, and they passed out of Nanjing Province in a few days, entering Jiaxing Prefecture in Zhejiang Province. Hangzhou lay just beyond.

As they proceeded through Jiaxing, the truth about restorationist activity in the area emerged from rumor. An imperial prince had indeed established a "regency" at Hangzhou earlier in the summer, but it had almost immediately capitulated, and now the city was held by the Manchus. However, the surrounding countryside remained unoccupied, with resistance to the haircutting order nearly unanimous; and a second remnant prince had set himself up at Shaoxing, right across Hangzhou Bay. The situation seemed hopeful, at least compared to the chaos of the lower Yangtze Valley.

The Ouyang troop of six pressed on, circling westward around Hangzhou, en route to Shaoxing. Arriving one night in Yuhang County, the wayfarers, accustomed to seeking higher ground as a safety precaution, camped out on Yellow Crane Mountain, a small, craggy rise in a complex of incongruous peaks, which dominated an otherwise featureless plain. There, they discovered abandoned huts once used by wood-gatherers, and they availed themselves of the lodgings. Waking refreshed the following morning, no one was particularly eager to move on, for the place seemed congenial enough to warrant a few days' additional rest. Accordingly, the four freedmen began scouting and soon found a plentiful spring, and Nanyu and Daosheng tidied up the little hermitage, organizing the laundry and commissary.

It was the first time husband and wife had been alone together, in a peaceful setting, in quite a while; the sense of calm seeped inward, and poisonous thoughts turned charitable. The silence in which they prepared their new homestead was no longer solitary but shared, and by the time they were finished, they were smiling. They moved off together to a little overlook and stood side by side as they admired the way the lowlands shone in the midmorning sun, with the scattered shadows of clouds moving slowly across the fields. They had still yet to converse, and Nanyu sought some means of breaking the ice. He decided that a softly chanted song would do the trick but resolved against reprising any of the ditties from their Qinhuai days, which he feared Daosheng would interpret as a plea simply to set back the clock and thus avoid dealing with more recent experiences as paired souls. Therefore, he whispered:

> "Then we take both of them
> And break them into pieces
> And mix the pieces with water
>
> "And mold again a figure of you
> And a figure of me
>
> "I am in your clay
> You are in my clay"

He delivered the lyrics with neither melodrama, pathos, nor romance. Daosheng looked across the plain and began humming the tune.

Nine days passed.

On the tenth day, finding themselves running low on food, all members of the little company descended from Yellow Crane Mountain, intending to provision themselves at the Yuhang market before continuing to Shaoxing. After a street-side breakfast of roasted sweet potatoes, the refugees were discussing how to pool their funds and prioritize purchases, when they caught sight of a knickknack man, peddling his wares in front of a little temple. According to passers-by, the bald peddler was able to slip in and out of Hangzhou, bringing to the people of Yuhang and other counties the miscellaneous merchandise more commonly available in larger cities. He was, indeed, a walking emporium, with everything from rattan sandals to cricket cages, children's toys, cooking pots, and musical instruments, hanging off his back-borne travel-box or some other part of his body. He was also hawking handbills, bearing the latest intelligence from Hangzhou and beyond, including news of the Manchu government in Beijing. At first content simply to listen to the man's blaring of the headlines, Nanyu and Daosheng were startled to hear him shout, "Wei Su promoted, despite indictment!"

They both hurried over to the man and exchanged a few coppers for a hand-copied gazette bulletin, similar to the one bought by Ouyang Gen near the Drum Tower in Nanjing nearly sixteen months ago, when they had also sought news of Wei Su. The Ouyangs brought it back to their little table at the potato vendor's and, while the others waited, read the following:

At the close of the seventh month, Grand Secretary Li Jiantai nominated Wei Su, of Nanjing, then serving in the Ministry of Revenue, to be promoted to Vice Minister of Personnel. While His Majesty considered the appointment, Grand Secretary Ning Wanwo impeached Wei Su, calling him a 'thrice-serving minister' and accusing him of 'ten heinous crimes,' as follows:

'Item: Wei Su's father and uncles, forming an evil faction, have "borrowed the tiger's authority," extorting from and terrorizing the gentry and common people of Nanjing. They have appropriated the garden of a prince of the defunct dynasty. Said garden was supposed to have been designated the official property of Our Dynasty and is worth one hundred thousand gold; but the evil faction obtained it by means of a bribe of three thousand ounces of silver, as well as by protecting a local official from charges of rape, in exchange for his cooperation. The evil Wei faction parades about Nanjing in sedan chairs and employs footmen who beat pedestrians—both Manchu and Chinese—until they bleed. They circulate bribes to conceal their misdeeds. The gentry and common people uniformly despise them!

'Item: Wei Su sent henchmen onto Manchu land enclosures, where they divided territory amongst themselves and began illegally collecting rent. Some 842 acres of land and 6730 ounces of silver are involved.

'Item: Wei Su occupied farmland reserved for the army and paid no taxes on the produce. When questioned by administrating officials, he set his housemen upon them. The housemen made spurious counteraccusations against the officials and kidnapped and beat the father of one of them, until a settlement of one hundred ounces of silver and two oxen was paid.

'Item: Wei Su failed to remit lawful taxes on his ancestral land in Liyang County, Nanjing Province. When pressed by the Liyang Country tax captain, a man named Chen Denggao, he sent his henchman, surnamed Cui, and ten others to the Liyang County seat, where they murdered Chen's son.

'Item: Wei Su coerced a Liyang County landowner named Wang Fengxian into commending him his land, in order to place it within Wei's tax exemption privileges. For this supposed favor, Wang agreed, under detention and beating, to deliver two hundred ounces of silver and two horses, and Wei took over five buildings belonging to Wang.

'Item: Wei Su initiated a false lawsuit against two Liyang men surnamed Tang. His henchmen, including the aforementioned Cui, tied the Tangs up, broke their legs, and force-fed them dog dung, until they agreed to pay two hundred ounces of silver.

'Item: Wei Su, via his henchman Cui, extorted one hundred ounces of silver from a Nanjing carpenter, surnamed Ouyang, falsely alleging that Ouyang had sold him defective furniture.

'Item: Wei Su denied wages to two laborers at his Beijing residence, a married couple surnamed Lin. When Mr Lin requested payment, Wei had him flogged thirty strokes and accused him of stealing fifty ounces of silver. Lin's relative, surnamed Chen, was incarcerated at the local yamen, until fifty ounces of restitution was made to Wei.

'Item: Wei Su's father and uncles refused to allow two Nanjing butchers to conduct business until they agreed to pay cash tribute and to provide free pork every month.

'Item: Wei Su employed the aforesaid Cui to harass a Nanjing courtesan, also surnamed Ouyang, who hanged herself.' —

Nanyu and Daosheng had both groaned when they read the news of Nanyu's father, and now they gasped. Daosheng panted through gritted teeth, "Wei Su got impatient, or maybe Mother just couldn't stand it anymore."

Grief soon got the better of her, and she began exclaiming, "We never had the chance to see her one last time…We should have been there!" Presently she was distraught, wailing, pounding the table, and falling out of her seat. The men were alarmed, and Nanyu, acting on instinct, ordered a return to Yellow Crane Mountain. All five of them half-led, half-carried Daosheng out of the marketplace and back along the dusty road toward their recent refuge. As soon as he was able to think, Nanyu directed the two Zhangs to circle back to the market and finish their provisioning. He tossed them a bundle of coins, with a "Meet us back at camp."

As he supported Daosheng by the arm, Nanyu read to the end of the handbill, which reported the Manchu emperor's ruling on the accusations against Wei Su:

His Majesty rescripted: 'The Empire is not yet fully pacified, and the people remain trapped in the "fire and water" of war. All talent must be harnessed to rescue the people from their plight. The petty bickering of the type that destroyed the previous dynasty must promptly cease. In the case of Wei Su, not a single witness has stepped forward to confirm the veracity of these embellished claims. All officials, north and south, must unite in the service of the Empire. We implore you!'

As a result [the handbill concluded], His Majesty dismissed the charges and approved Wei Su's promotion to Vice Minister of Personnel.

Absorbing the import of what he had read, Nanyu briefed Qiao and Fang.

"Our enemy from Nanjing has cheated my father and driven Madame's mother to kill herself," he said. "Let's just try to keep Madame comfortable, and then...well...this may affect our plans."

They soon arrived back on Yellow Crane Mountain and Nanyu resituated Daosheng in her hut where she alternated between hysteria and catatonia. By the time the two Zhangs returned, Qiao and Fang had got the fire going, and Nanyu managed to prepare a squash soup, which he served to his wife. He sat on the ground next to her pallet, holding her hand and running his fingers through her hair. She dozed off and slept for the rest of the afternoon, but she awoke after a few hours, and the ensuing night was sleepless for them both, as she tossed and flailed her arms before finally drifting off again just before dawn. Nanyu did the same.

It was the husband who regained consciousness first, however, as the sun rose in its insistent way, commanding all mankind to rise with it, to resume life's struggles. Nanyu tiptoed out of the hut, nodded to Fang Long, who was alone on guard, rekindled the fire, and cooked a batch of rice porridge. He took a bowl of it with him and ascended to Yellow Crane's summit, where he ate while surveying the country below. To the east, the sun continued to climb above where he knew Hangzhou to be, and the farmland in that direction glowed rosy, with thousands of breakfast fires sending up curling wisps of silver smoke. In and around the town of Yuhang, Nanyu detected isolated signs of bustle, as he noticed carts and donkeys moving along their routes between the fields. Sometimes the wind would gust, and Nanyu could see its invisible wave, sweeping across the paddies. He set down his empty rice bowl and turned in all directions, trying to visualize where lay Nanjing, Beijing, Shaoxing, and then Beijing again. A breeze now blew in from the north, rippling his hair and chilling his face. Did it contain the first hint of cooler weather, the end of the summer? Nanyu blinked away the dust, bent to retrieve his bowl, and descended again to the camp.

He stole into the master hut, where Daosheng still lay sleeping, and unpacked his Four Treasures and four-leaf album, which he brought with him again outside. Spilling a bit of spring water from a jug prepared by his men, he mixed a modest range of colors and then sat down on a rock a short distance away. Taking up his brush, Nanyu began delineating, on the final leaf of the album, his fellowship's mountain camp, although he reduced the number of thatched cottages to one. To accord with the logic of the album, furthermore, he transformed the season from late summer to deep winter; and once he had altered the setting, his original boldness reasserted itself. He exaggerated the topography, remolding it into a convulsion of serpentine ridges and crags, overgrown with gnarly brushwood and incised with streams. Upon the inhospitable landscape, he superimposed a howling sleet storm, which warped the pines, frothed the waters, and incited swirling masses of dead leaves. The result was that the mountain hut stood out at as an island of tranquility in a nightmare of chaos. It was the most powerful painting Ouyang Nanyu—or anyone of his generation—ever executed. Biting his lip in concentration, Nanyu applied the finishing touches: drawn shutters over the cottage's window and two pairs of shoes outside the door—a well-known suggestive trope, bordering on the pornographic. He inscribed the scene "Thatched Cottage in the Winter Mountains," including no additional poetry, and then finally, on the left edge of the leaf, he appended a colophon for the entire collection: "These four depictions have been faithfully created for our illustrious patron, His Excellency Wei Su, by Ouyang Nanyu and Ouyang Daosheng, on Yellow Crane Mountain in Yuhang County, in the eighth month of the year *yi you.*"

When the ink had sufficiently dried, Nanyu carried the album to the master hut, where he found Daosheng awake but inert. He showed her his work, and she studied it expressionlessly, spending the most time in consideration of the colophon. Then, she nodded once and returned to her contemplation of empty space.

Accompanied by Zhang Yue, Nanyu brought the album into town and handed it to the knickknack man, whom they found in his accustomed place, suggesting that he share, in any proportion he saw fit, whatever proceeds he might realize from its sale. The knickknack man did in fact exchange the album for four ounces of silver at a Hangzhou art shop, where trade continued to thrive despite the wars. He passed a few coppers to Nanyu, the next time he saw him.

9

SEPTEMBER 1645 TO NOVEMBER 1646
AND AFTERWARD

ONE YEAR PASSED. During the brisk autumn, a strange boiling sound was heard in the skies above northeastern Zhejiang, which the people interpreted as a sign of Heaven's anxiety. Misty rain fell from cloudless skies before ceasing altogether, and the region slipped into drought. The winter lingered, cold and dry, with spring bringing no relief. One morning, before dawn, two stars appeared to be orbiting each other, swinging each other around, before one of them shot toward the south. Sometime later, there was a general meteor shower, and a few days after that, Heaven seemed to be calling like a lonely bird.

To the north, the new rulers wrung full measures of revenue from war-ravaged farms. To the south, the old regime, likewise, struggled to keep its armies supplied. When summer came again, the conquerors' army surged out from Hangzhou, fording the drought-shallowed Qiantang River, which cradled the city. The loyalists fell back.

In Nanjing, Wei Su's father died, and Wei was compelled to take leave of his ministerial post and begin a three-year mourning period. Returned to his home, he found solace in the direct oversight of his local interests, in consultation with his chamberlain, Cui, and his other henchmen. One day in late summer, he dispatched Cui on an errand, and the young man set out for Hangzhou, with ten armed tenants.

They traveled by river, sailing down the Yangtze on a hired boat. Cui wore his accustomed horsehair hat, but it now sat lower on his head, for he had shorn off his hair. It would have fallen halfway down his nose, were it not for the "coin-sized rat tail," which propped it up in the back. Cui's men were all hatless, and their shaved scalps shone in the sun like lizard skins. Their vessel turned into the Grand Canal on the south bank, skirted Lake Tai, continued along the Canal, and tied up at the wharf in Hangzhou. They spent the night in a tavern with rooms for lodgers, dropping Wei Su's name liberally to lower the price, and in the morning conscripted a Yuhang County peasant to serve as a guide.

"Do you know how to get to a place called Yellow Crane Mountain?" Cui asked him, and they set out westward.

They traveled on foot, Cui having overruled his men's request to hire or commandeer carts, which were beneath his dignity. He would have liked to borrow a sedan chair or at least a horse from the Hangzhou prefectural yamen, but Wei Su had often warned him against putting on airs and "borrowing the tiger's authority." Besides, the ten swordsmen were imposing enough. They parted crowds as they trooped into Yuhang, where they quartered, free of charge, for the evening. The next morning, they sharpened their swords and advanced toward the hills. With the morning sun behind them, they cast long shadows in front, Cui's horsehair hat casting the longest. The sun also shone on the lackeys' shaven heads, making Cui feel as though he were at the center of a constellation of stars.

Cui called to the guide, whose surname was Wang. "Little brother, which one is Yellow Crane Mountain?"

"Right in front is Jump-Over Mountain. Yellow Crane is next to it."

"Is there anyone living on Yellow Crane Mountain now?"

"There's a few who showed up last year."

"Long-hairs, fleeing the north?"

Wang hesitated.

"Yes, you people were all long-hairs until recently," Cui admonished, "but never mind that. Our concern is only with those folks on the mountain. One of them is some kind of artist, right?"

"I don't know about any artists, sir. The only people living up there are a scholar, his wife, and –"

"A scholar and his wife?" Cui said. "No, we're not looking for some old bookworm. The guy we want is barely twenty."

"The one on the mountain is around twenty."

"Well, what's his name, for Heaven's sake?"

"I don't remember, sir. It's a two-character name…pretty unusual…"

"Is it Ouyang?"

"Yes! Ouyang. Master Ouyang. And his wife is called Madame Ouyang."

"Of course she is, blockhead!" Cui barked. "Well, well. Master and Madame Ouyang! As it turns out, Little Wang, we've got a bit of unfinished business with Master and Madame Ouyang. Take us up there now. We'll see who's putting on airs."

Cui's posse advanced past the Temple of the Buddha Sun, at the base of Yellow Crane Mountain. Outside the main gate, twenty spearmen stood assembled, their pigtails hanging down from under conical hats.

"Ah, militia!" Cui called. "I am the chamberlain of His Excellency Wei Su, Vice Minister of Personnel. My men are here to serve an arrest warrant. Who is your sergeant on duty?"

One of the militiamen stepped forward, a quizzical expression on his face.

"I deputize you and your troop," Cui proclaimed. "Fan out and form a second line, behind my men. Move!"

The bearded, halberd-wielding sergeant seemed about to giggle. Then, he nodded at his soldiers, and they obeyed Cui's instructions to the letter, so that two of them followed each of Cui's men close behind. At Cui's order to "Level weapons!" they did so, covering one shoulder blade per spear.

As the combined force began ascending the slope, Cui continued to mutter, "Master and Madame Ouyang. Who do they think they are?" After a while, he called back at the militia sergeant, "We'll make quick work of them. They won't give us any trouble."

"No sir, no trouble."

"What's your name, anyway, sergeant?"

"You can call me Little Zhang."

The terrain was leveling off, though all the men were panting from the climb.

"You from around here?"

"Oh, near enough."

"You don't sound like it." Cui twisted his head around and studied Little Zhang with narrowed eyes.

"Well, I'm one of the Captain's personal retainers, you might say, kind of like his bodyguard."

"'The Captain'? You mean the captain of this militia?"

"Yes, sir." They had reached the clearing where the cottages were. The men halted in formation, and Cui held out his arms, framing each hut with his thumbs and forefingers, as though recreating an album leaf painting.

"Well, then" he said, as he verified every detail, "what's his name, this captain of yours?"

"Ouyang Nanyu," said Zhang Yue, just as the man himself emerged from the master hut, to stand in the center of Cui's composition.

"You!" Cui shrieked. His hands flew apart and became fists, which he began flailing about at the sides of his head.

Nanyu made a slight movement, a barely perceptible twitch, and his militiamen formalized the capture of Cui's posse, with very little prodding. As Cui's men threw down their swords, Zhang Hui, Fang Long, and Qiao Yin dashed out of their huts to collect them. Then, the militiamen used their spears to force Cui's men down by the shoulders. Zhang Yue turned Cui around and took his short sword, and he also searched him for smaller blades and written intelligence but found nothing. Cui was permitted to keep the several ounces of silver and the copper coins he was carrying, and he was not forced to sit or kneel. Nonetheless, he ground his teeth as he regarded his quarry turned captor.

Nanyu was wearing a round Manchu cap with upturned brim, made of rattan, which sat well on his shaved head and left plenty of room for his pigtail. His robe was of the high-collared Manchu style now mandated for all men, fastened at the right shoulder, with tight belt and tapered sleeves. He glared at Cui for a few seconds, as the latter continued to mutter and curse. Finally, he asked, in a voice no louder than a whisper, "What did you say your name was, again?"

"You know damn well it's Cui, you dog's head!"

"Why have you invaded Yuhang County with ten armed thugs, Cui?"

"To serve an arrest warrant."

"Very well. Produce the warrant."

Zhang Yue broke in. "He wasn't carrying any warrant, Captain."

"Oh, fuck that!" Cui stomped his foot. "Quit playing games. The real question is how you got to be a militia captain, *Captain*."

"I'll have you know," Nanyu raised his voice, "that my militia captaincy is ex officio of my concurrent posting as Confucian Drill Instructor of Yuhang County, which appointment I received by virtue of my status as tributary civil service degree holder, effective this past spring." The tributary status that Nanyu claimed placed him on the third tier of the elite hierarchy, below Wei Su and Zhu Xiangsun but still prestigious enough to qualify him for some local offices.

"Bully for you," Cui said. "Wait a minute. Yuhang hadn't submitted until a month or so ago, after the spring."

"I went into Hangzhou to take the qualifying exam, although I gave my native place as Yuhang. The prefect of Hangzhou made me a tributary, to help with the pacification here, when the time came."

"I guess that's when you cut your hair, when you crossed the lines to get into Hangzhou?"

"Yes. Little Zhang's halberd is as sharp as a razor."

"Pretty eager to change sides, though, huh? How unseemly."

"Not quite as eager as your boss, and nowhere near as unseemly."

"Where did you get these four goons of yours? They're not militia."

"They're my personal retainers, acquired during my travels. The prefect let me appoint them as my staff."

"Husband, should the prisoner be the one asking the questions?"

It was Daosheng. She advanced slowly but steadily from the master hut to stand beside Nanyu, never taking her eyes off Cui, who sneered at her every step.

"Indeed not, Wife," said Nanyu. "It just seemed that he should be made to understand whom he was dealing with."

At Nanyu's words, Cui guffawed and returned the focus of his contempt from the wife to the husband, his expression luminous with mockery.

"Ah, so that's the way of it!" he brayed. "The vixen's got you under her spell, little brother. That explains Beijing. That explains everything. What a riot!" He shot his eyes back at Daosheng. "So the dirty nun is now Madame Ouyang. Long time no see, Madame. You've got hair growing up there too, now, huh? Didn't hubby know at the time that you were damaged goods, or was the carpenter's boy not particular?"

Qiao Yin, Fang Long, and Zhang Hui fell upon him as a man, knocked him down, and began kicking him.

Daosheng called them off. "Thank you, brothers. That's enough," she said.

Cui checked for broken bones and wiped the blood off his nose but didn't try to get up. When he next returned his attention to the Ouyangs, it remained fixed on Daosheng, with his earlier disdain replaced by a fuller-bodied hatred. From the ground, he sputtered, "You think you're clever, but His Excellency will never forget how you stole from him. He'll have his revenge, in the end. If you kill me, he'll only send someone else, or maybe he'll just ask the new magistrate to have you arrested. Either way, there's no escape for you."

Daosheng said, "You're in no position to make threats, and, from what I hear, neither is your master. I admit we underestimated him before, but time is running against him now. With more talented men such as my husband stepping forward to serve His Majesty, your master is becoming less indispensable and more of a liability, as evidence of his crimes continues to mount."

She walked closer to where Cui lay.

"In fact," she said, "I think it's high time we turn our discussion to the subject of his crimes — and yours — and dismiss the question of whatever injury he thinks he received from us.

You have used the word 'revenge.' It seems to me that we are far more entitled to it than he is."

"Apropos of that," Nanyu added, "you also mentioned something about our killing you."

Cui's jaw tightened.

"Yes, I caught that too, Husband. Let's keep to the procedure, though, and ascertain the facts first, if not for his sake then for ours."

She cleared her throat and addressed Cui: "We are primarily interested in the injuries you dealt to us; however, whatever past crimes you committed in the service of your master may be relevant, too, for they shed light on your character. I'm talking about the allegations contained in Ning Wanwo's indictment."

"Huh?" Cui belched.

"Did you murder the tax captain's son in Liyang and bully the Tangs, who were part of that bogus lawsuit?"

"The Tangs...was that the one with the dog shit?"

Daosheng twisted her mouth. "Yes, it was. You know about it?"

"Know about it? It was my idea."

"You don't deny it?"

Cui shrugged. "What's the point of denying it? You've got twenty men, and I've only got ten."

"So that's what it all boils down to, for you, brute force?"

Cui got his feet under the rest of him and stood back up. He probed the bruises on his face and spat blood on the ground.

"No, Madame Ouyang, not just for me. Brute force is what it all boils down to for the whole fucking world. Take a look around and try to tell me any different."

He squinted at Nanyu. "Hubby here knows what I'm talking about—*Master* Ouyang: tributary degree holder, Confucian Drill Instructor, Captain of Militia. Why else would you bother reading all those books, taking all those tests, and collecting all those fancy titles," he hissed, "unless it was to get your hands on four retainers, twenty militiamen, and a fuckable nun?"

Qiao, Fang, and both Zhangs were about to knock Cui down again, but Daosheng held up her hand.

"Actually, the fuckable nun came first," she said, discomfiting her defenders and all the other burly men in the clearing, "and all else followed accordingly; but regardless of the precise order in which Master Ouyang acquired his advantages, you're quite right: He got his hands on them one after the other, so that now you have fallen into our hands as well. And that brings us to how you have wronged us and what we intend — and are fully able — to do about it. We'll start with your bullying of my honorable father-in-law."

"What bullying? The old man sold His Excellency a bed he couldn't use, so the merchandise was returned, fair and square."

"Why couldn't His Excellency use the bed? Could he not sleep in it?"

"The bed wasn't for sleeping. His Excellency bought it with the understanding that a new wife was coming with it. When Master Ouyang took His Excellency's wife away, the bed became useless to him, and so he returned it to the original seller, for a refund."

"But the refund was more than the original price," said Nanyu. "You paid eighty-four for it and demanded a hundred back."

"Call the extra sixteen a handling fee. His Excellency did, after all, ship it up and down the Grand Canal."

"That's on his account, not ours."

"Well, then, the extra silver is just compensation for your injury to him — kidnapping his wife, I mean."

"Liberating his wife, you mean," said Daosheng. "His

Excellency wasn't injured, just because he wasn't able to keep what he stole."

As he sensed that the point was lost, Cui tried another tack. "Well, it doesn't matter," he said. "The old man didn't even have fifty ounces on him."

"So what did you do?" asked Daosheng.

"Well, you might say that I put him under a kind of bond," Cui said, "until he works off what he owes."

Nanyu stiffened. "You mean you've got my father working for nothing?"

"Rubbish. He's working for His Excellency. He should count himself lucky to be alive."

One woman and thirty-six men stopped breathing. It suddenly seemed very dark, although no clouds had passed before the sun. Daosheng, so overcome by anger that it had long ago ceased to be anger, stood rooted to the ground like a piece of seaweed on the bottom of the ocean, swaying, waving, in an eddying emptiness of stupendous density and volume. She could barely work her jaw, but the words escaped her like the last bubbles to rise from the mouth of one who has drowned:

"You killed my mother."

"No I didn't. She killed herself."

"You drove her to it. Wei Su sent you to plague her, until she couldn't take it anymore."

"As a matter of fact, His Excellency washed his hands of her. He said he didn't care who had her anymore, so I figured it might as well be me. Why shouldn't the loyal servant get a slice of fancy meat, once in a while?"

"The bastard doesn't want to live!" The chorus sounded, and the entire Yuhang contingent was astir. However, the executioners required a conventional sign of victimization from Daosheng before they acted. Perhaps if she had rushed hysterically at Cui or fainted to the ground, then they would have dealt Cui the death he was asking for. Instead, Daosheng rubbed her face and forehead and said, "That's enough."

"Damn right it is," said Cui. "Like I said, you had me a long time ago. Do whatever you're going to do, if you dare, and quit boring me with all this talk."

Daosheng massaged her temples one last time, and then she spoke to the retainers and militia. "Thank you, brothers. I know you would punish him for me, but that service falls to my husband, Master Ouyang, to perform."

She turned to Nanyu.

"Husband," she said, "this man has wronged your father, my mother, you, and me. Revenge would be righteous and justified. I know what you're capable of. I know what you've already done for me. I know that you'd still do anything for me. The moment is now. Our enemy is in your power. What do you choose to do?"

Nanyu looked for the thousandth time at his wife. Where once was the radiant halo, her hair now lay lifeless and dull. Where once beamed mirthful spirit, her eyes now sank in their sockets. Of course, he too had changed since becoming her husband. He removed his Manchu cap and ran his fingers along his shaved scalp; when they reached the back of his head, they naturally grabbed at his pigtail. "Merciful Buddha," he said.

He released his pigtail and replaced his cap. He walked up to Little Zhang and grabbed Cui's short sword. Then, he stomped back to where the prisoner stood and delivered a kick to the back of the legs that dropped him to his knees.

Standing behind Cui, he swung the short sword like a scythe, and the onlookers gasped to see something flying into the trees, but it was only the horsehair hat—Nanyu had kept the flat of the sword facing forward. Before anyone know what to expect next, Nanyu leaned down, seized Cui's pigtail, and lopped it off with a single uppercut.

He threw the sheared braid in Cui's face. "Congratulations," he said, "you're a rebel now. Run along south, if you want to keep your head."

Nanyu turned and gestured toward the posse. "You bastards have a choice," he said. "Cut off your queues and try your luck with Cui, or go crawling back to your master."

No one so much as looked at Cui.

"Fine. Now all of you get the fuck out of here."

Cui was too shocked to say anything, nasty or otherwise. He grimaced with resentment in a way that Nanyu found almost pitiable, and then he turned and began trotting down the slope. He separated himself from his former confederates, before any of them realized that they could capture him for a reward, and, as Nanyu watched, made off toward the south.

Nanyu gave Little Wang, Cui's reluctant guide, a string of coppers and told him to forget what he had seen and heard. The two Zhangs, Fang, Qiao, and the twenty spearmen escorted him as far as the Temple of the Buddha Sun; and then he walked home, telling his family that he'd been delayed by a request to carry firewood, which had, fortunately, paid well.

电电电电电

Meanwhile, after Nanyu had seen everybody off, he returned to the clearing, where Daosheng still stood, staring at Cui's late pigtail on the ground.

"Thank you, Husband," she said.

"You're welcome," Nanyu replied, and then he added, "It was the least I could do."

"I know what you mean," Daosheng nodded, "but it was sufficient. No former contemplative could have hoped for more."

"I'm glad you think so," said Nanyu, trying to sound as upbeat as possible, "but this business isn't over, you know."

"Yes, Husband, I do know. But even if you had executed them all, we would still be in the same position. We've never been in control of the situation. All we can do is to try to anticipate Wei Su's next move and plan accordingly."

"All right, then. Let's plan."

"Very well," Daosheng said. She looked downslope, in the direction their enemies had just retreated. "In about a week," she began, "he will know everything that happened here. Either his ten lackeys will tell him, or Cui himself will find some way to rejoin him and make his own report. If he were more secure, he'd let us twist in the wind for a while, but I don't think he wants the story of today's defeat to spread. No, he'll try to finish us off as soon as possible, especially now that he's confirmed where we are."

"I'm not running again," said Nanyu.

"No, we're not." Daosheng shook her head. "No more scurrying away. Our position here is as strong as any we're likely to find. In fact, our strength determines Wei Su's next move: Since his thugs can't beat us on this mountain, he has no choice but to attack us through the law."

"You make it sound like it's something he doesn't want to do."

"It is something he doesn't want to do, or else he would have done it first. Operating through the magistrate's office will require him to commit himself openly; also, it's a process he can't control as reliably as that of sending in his cutthroats."

Nanyu furrowed his brow. "A powerful man *is* the law, Wife. He has the confidence of the Emperor. Surely he can have his way in a court case. We're underestimating him again."

Daosheng almost smiled. "He's underestimating *you* again,

Husband. You just bested his henchman in the field. You can best him in court."

"How?" blurted Nanyu, his voice breaking.

"By means of the status you've worked so hard to attain," Daosheng said. "You're a tributary degree holder, immune to physical punishment. You can't be beaten or tortured in court. He can't bully you the way he bullies commoners, and the magistrate or whoever tries the case is bound to accord you respect. You'll have a chance to defeat his arguments."

"All right," said Nanyu, nodding. "Let's talk about his arguments."

"Well," said Daosheng, "First we have to consider what he'll charge you with. He'll probably allege that your treatment of Cui was improper, perhaps even rebellious, since it was by your act that the dynasty's hair order was violated."

Nanyu looked at the ground.

"You'll have to argue on the basis of motive," Daosheng thought out loud. "Explain that your intention wasn't to encourage rebellion but to render a just sentence of exile. Then, you'll have changed the subject from your criminality to Cui's, and you'll be on firmer ground. Cui did, after all, incriminate himself in this clearing today. He admitted his role in the mistreatment of the Tangs in Liyang, as well as the unlawful coercion of your father and...my mother. There were witnesses. Once Cui is shown to have wronged our parents, then your treatment of him falls under the category of righteous revenge and becomes perfectly legal, even if exile is a rather unorthodox form of revenge. Furthermore, since the allegations concerning Cui were recently made in Ning Wanwo's indictment of Wei Su himself, then, by substantiating them, you can turn the tables on him, accuse the accuser. More complaints will be raised against Wei Su, and His Majesty may decide to give him up, sooner rather than later."

Nanyu bit his lip, thinking.

"Wei Su may claim that you kidnapped me in Beijing," Daosheng went on, "and he may produce that forged contract — remember, the one he supposedly bought out, from my mother — as proof that I was bound to him." She almost smiled again. "I really hope he does. If it has his seal on it, just show the magistrate this, which bears his seal, too, and he won't be able to dispute the authenticity." She pulled out from her sleeve Wei Su's letter to Niu Jinxing, implicating Wei in the betrayal of Beijing. "This is something that can ruin him, as we've already discussed. I wonder if he's guessed that we have it, though it won't help him, if he has."

She handed the document to Nanyu, who secured it in his robe.

"He may accuse us of incest," she said, "but all you'll need to do is to reveal who my father was, and that's even more dirt that will stick to him." She looked out across the plain. "I really think we've got him."

Nanyu forced a smile but found himself shaking his head at the same time. "Wife," he said, "you're placing too much faith in...justice."

"No, Husband," Daosheng said, turning to face him. "I'm placing my faith in you, as I always have."

🐉🐉🐉

The Ouyangs, Qiao, Fang, and the two Zhangs settled back into their routine. All six continued to live on Yellow Crane Mountain. Every morning, the men hiked into Yuhang, where Nanyu assisted the education intendent in the instruction and management of students at the county school, and his retainers trained with the militia and acted as auxiliary constables.

Daosheng spent her days alone on the mountain, where she occupied her time with painting—nothing but sparse bamboos, in monochrome ink, devoid of human figures or even birds. Occasionally she visited the Temple of the Buddha Sun, to read sutras or to offer prayers. In the evenings, the men would return, and Daosheng would retreat into the master hut.

Late one autumn afternoon, Nanyu dismissed his students early and came back home. He found Daosheng sitting on a rock near the summit, catching the last rays of the sun. She was rubbing her hands on her legs, to keep them warm in the falling chill. Nanyu sat next to her, putting his arm around her shoulder. He stroked her hair, caressed the smooth surface of her cheek, cooled autumn red, and rocked her gently. Neither husband nor wife said anything.

A loose gathering of puffy clouds floated above the western horizon, extending across the blue sky the thinnest tendrils of wispy white. When the sun began to set, the clouds became tinged with pink and purple, and the strands of ribbon stretching across Heaven turned crimson. Even as the hues deepened, they never grew lurid, and Nanyu and Daosheng felt comforted by the softness. The sun sank lower, into a final orange ember in the west. Then, it was Heaven's color that changed most affectingly, to deeper and deeper shades of blue, until all above seemed to have settled down to rest. The dull clouds now hung silently in the translucent space of dusk, and a single bright planet became visible. It seemed to demand the Ouyangs' attention, like care itself, and the feeling of comfort was gone.

Even after the stars came out, even after the other men returned for the night, that one planet blared most brightly. It almost hurt the eyes.

Early the next morning, Daosheng was arrested and charged with witchcraft.

The detachment of officers had come all the way from Nanjing. They bound Daosheng's hands, led her down the mountain, and placed her in a wooden cage on wheels. Nanyu, Qiao Yin, Fang Long, Zhang Hui, and Zhang Yue were arrested too, as possible accomplices and witnesses. The four retainers were tied up and made to ride in an open cart. Nanyu, with his tributary status, was entitled to ride on a horse, which, by now, he was able to do. The arrest conformed to all the legal formalities, and the Yuhang County magistrate had been informed of it. He accompanied the arresting officers as an observer and wished the prisoners well when they were led away. Nanyu and Daosheng separately guessed that Wei Su had filed his lawsuit directly with the provincial governor in Nanjing, thus avoiding the Hangzhou and Yuhang courts, which were friendly toward the defendants. Nanyu was only loosely guarded, but he was forbidden to approach Daosheng's cart, and so the two of them never spoke, nor were they ever afforded so much as a glimpse at each other's faces.

Transportation to Nanjing took several days, and the party passed through the same country that Nanyu and Daosheng had crossed the previous year. Everywhere, head-shaven farmers and shopkeepers were struggling to recover. Occasionally, Nanyu would recognize a temple or town, and his sense of tragedy and defeat deepened. The procession overnighted at county yamen offices, with the prisoners placed in cells and the constabulary enjoying guest rooms. Nanyu, with his privilege, was included with the latter group, and it occurred to him that the amenities were the finest he had known.

They reached Nanjing, and Nanyu found the familiarity, particularly the smells, nearly unbearable. Brought straight to the governor's yamen, he was again given a guest room, while the others were clapped in the dungeon. Nanyu's hosts instructed him not to leave or to meet anyone. They treated him to an evening meal—Nanjing pressed duck—and a few local tributaries presented themselves and tried to engage him in conversation, but he was not up for a chat and only picked at his food. That night, he vomited what little he had eaten and barely slept. Next day was the trial.

It was held in the governor's main chamber. Nanyu was led in and beheld an imposing dais at one end of it, on which had been placed a rosewood chair with dragons carved into the handles and back. In front of the chair was a large writing desk, empty, save for a single wooden block. A placard demanding "AWE AND SILENCE" was posted alongside the desk. Two guards armed with halberds flanked the chair, and seated in it was Governor Hong Chengchou, a withered man with sunken eyes who nonetheless seemed to complement the carved dragons. Hong Chengchou was the highest-ranking officer of the old regime to have joined the Manchus. He had not, strictly speaking, defected to them but had become their prisoner in an early battle north of the Great Wall. After the fall of Beijing to Li Zicheng and the suicide of the emperor Chongzhen, Hong had agreed to help his captors punish the rebels and form a new dynasty. He was trusted by the young Manchu emperor, Shunzhi, and had probably, Nanyu reckoned, been a party to His Majesty's expedient exoneration of Wei Su the previous year. His full title was Pacificator of the Lands South of the Yangtze River.

Nanyu was the first of the involved persons to be admitted. He approached the dais and knelt. Governor Hong waved him to his feet but provided him no chair, directing him to stand a bit back from the platform. As soon as he reached his designated spot, a door opened to the right, and the other prisoners were brought in, beginning with Daosheng. Nanyu saw life only in her eyes and, he imagined, behind her third eye, in her inner soul; otherwise, her hair was matted and her robe filthy. His heart pounded as, still handcuffed, she was forced to the floor by a sergeant and made to continue kneeling, directly before the dais. Qiao, Fang, and the two Zhangs were thrown down to one side, in a line between two pillars, and their guards remained standing over them. Then a door opened on the left, and in walked Wei Su.

He advanced to the dais as Nanyu had done, knelt, and then retreated, stepping around Daosheng, to stand beside Nanyu. He was less flamboyantly dressed than during the long-ago Lantern Festival, the only other time Nanyu had seen him, and, of course, his head was now shaved and a queue hung down from underneath his round, Manchu hat; yet his beard was still a bristly black, and he seemed even fatter than before. Nanyu could not see Daosheng's face but noticed her shaking her head.

Wei Su was the first to speak. His intonation was gregarious, but it broke the silence like a crossbow bolt. "Good morning, Governor," he said. "I trust your honorable father remains in good health. And how is your eyesight today?"

"My father clings to life, and I'm half blind, as I'm sure you already know," said Hong. "What matter do you presume to impose upon my attention, Vice Minister?"

"Why, a grievous evil, Governor," said Wei, "one that has wrought great calamity wherever it has visited. Thanks to me, it kneels before you now, awaiting justice, in the form of the faithless whore called Ouyang Daosheng."

"Who are the others?" asked the Governor.

"Standing beside me," Wei replied, "is a deluded young man named Ouyang Nanyu, and those brutes are his equally befuddled followers."

"Ouyang Nanyu," said Hong, pointing at him. "Account for yourself."

"Governor," said Nanyu, "I am native to this city but was recently awarded the tributary degree in Hangzhou and am now Confucian Drill Instructor and Captain of Militia in Yuhang County." He swallowed once. "I appreciate the courtesy the Governor has extended to me by allowing me to stand and respectfully request that the accused, Ouyang Daosheng, be permitted to stand as well, for she is my wife."

"Aha!" said Wei Su. "You see how muddled the Young Master is, Governor? In fact, the accused is *my* wife."

Governor Hong took a moment to cultivate a frown. Then, he turned to Wei Su. "Vice Minister, do you really think that among all the urgent tasks attendant to the pacification of the Empire, your squabble with a schoolboy over a woman should take priority?"

"Ah, why no, Governor. I wouldn't dream of such a thing," said Wei Su. "The last thing on my mind would be to intrude my insignificant personal business into your overflowing travails. That is why I initially sought to resolve the matter privately. As soon as I learned where my wayward wench had got to, I dispatched my chamberlain and a number of reliable servants thither, with instructions to fetch her back. Little could I have expected that my loyal men would run afoul of this young whelp's so-called retainers and rag-tag militia and receive the most villainous treatment at their hands."

"As I said," growled Hong, "a squabble with a schoolboy over a woman."

"Patience, please, Governor!" bowed Wei, "and listen to what Master Ouyang did to my faithful chamberlain: After bleating to him for some time, concerning various trivialities, he suddenly flew into a rage and cut off my man's queue! Then, he sent him south to join the rebels!"

Hong Chengchou ceased glowering at Wei Su and turned to Nanyu. "That was most ill-considered, Young Master," he said. "Since no violations of Our Dynasty's Holy Edicts are to be tolerated, neither, then, are they to be caused. Sending the Vice Minister's man into the ranks of the rebellion, needless to say, compounded your crime."

Nanyu breathed in, and his nose whistled. "Your servant will not try to evade responsibility, Governor," he said. "I admit my fault. I ask only that you judge my actions in the light of human nature, filial piety, and righteous anger, for the man I dealt with, the Vice Minister's chamberlain, was the same man, surnamed Cui, who has been identified in connection with a variety of crimes –"

"The allegations to which you allude," Hong broke in, "His Majesty has already reviewed and judged to be embellishments."

"But Cui cheated my father and killed my wife's mother!"

Governor Hong raised the wooden block from the desk and slammed it down three times, slowly, with great effect.

Wei Su waited a moment and then gestured with both hands at Nanyu. "As you can see, Governor," he said, "the Young Master has been entirely stripped of his senses. This rash outburst of his proves it. In fact, I divined that there was something wrong with him as soon as I heard, from my surviving men, what had transpired on Yellow Crane Mountain in Yuhang, where the vicious ambush took place. The lawless punishment he meted out to my poor Cui was indeed a monstrosity. It could only have issued from a depraved, nay, as you shall see, a tortured mind. Nothing but deviltry can explain it; indeed, nothing but deviltry can explain how he managed to capture my keen chamberlain and intrepid housemen in the first place. The Young Master could not have brought it about by his own talent. Look at him,

Governor, and you cannot fail to notice: He is but 'half a bottle of vinegar.' No, he has certainly been under a powerful influence, something too diabolical for me alone to contend with — yes, something that threatens the peace of Our Dynasty. And that is why, Governor, I have brought this case before your court. I beg for leniency for the boy; he is merely a victim. Instead, we must subject his bewitcher, who I feel certain is this woman, my demon wife, to the most stringent investigation."

"Exactly what sort of witchery are you expecting to uncover, Vice Minister?" the Governor asked.

"I believe the correct legal term, Governor, is *erotic entrancement.*"

"Erotic entrancement was considered a crime in ages past, but today it is not."

"Indeed, you are right, Governor. Yet if something is vexing the people in even the smallest county, then the magistrate is bound to look into it, if just to calm the little people's fears. In the present instance, as I have already mentioned, disobedience, rebellion, and chaos have raised their heads wherever this slut has passed. It is not only reasonable but, I daresay, mandatory for the Governor to inquire into such a strange phenomenon."

Governor Hong squinted at his folded hands on the table. He turned in the direction of the group of sergeants who were guarding Nanyu's men. "Did anyone who went on the Yuhang expedition find any dolls or figures of people, with human hair and clothing, in the search of the accused's home?"

"No, Governor," the senior sergeant answered.

"Any prohibited or occult books or charts?"

"No, Governor."

Hong thought for almost a full minute. Finally, he said, "Those four men are the only witnesses, beside the Young Master, to the accused's behavior on Yellow Crane Mountain and perhaps elsewhere. Take them and interrogate them."

"Yes, Governor," and Qiao, Fang, and the two Zhangs were conducted out of the room.

"Vice Minister," Hong continued, "I'll assume that your man, Cui, has not dared to make his way back here. As for your other men, you're satisfied that their accounts are complete?"

"Indubitably, Governor. There is no reason for them to be questioned further."

"Well, then, all that remains is…" Hong turned and whispered something to one of his attendants, who bowed and left the room.

The man returned, carrying an elongated block of wood with screw-operated vises mounted on the ends. The inner surfaces of the presses were ridged. Nanyu almost whimpered when he saw it, but Daosheng only shook her head again. The guard shoved the kneeling Daosheng sideways, and she fell on her shoulder, with her wrists still tied behind her. He grabbed her right leg, pulled it straight, and forced it down, until the ankle was positioned at the center of the right-side vise. He tightened the screw until it was snug, and then he did the left leg.

Nanyu remembered something.

"Governor…Isn't it customary for women to be subjected only to the finger press, while the ankle press is reserved for men?"

Wei Su chewed on his tongue for a bit. Then he put on a wide smile.

"Brilliant!" he said. "Governor — Pacificator — I marvel afresh at your sagacity. You have threatened to apply a harsh mode of questioning, in order speedily to perceive whether I or the Young Master love the accused the more. Lo and behold! Master Ouyang is indeed nearly in a swoon, and a desperate apprehension inflames his brow! And yet the demonstration merely confirms what I have just now argued: The lad is unnaturally smitten.

Honestly, Governor, have you ever known any husband to evince such a sentimental attachment to his own wife?"

Hong Chengchou said nothing, while studying Nanyu.

"Yes, you see it too, Governor—quite suspicious indeed! Let us press our advantage and put a few questions to the charmer. Not only will we swiftly wring a confession from her, but we will also be able to gauge the extent of her power over the Young Master. It would be a case of 'one exertion, two benefits.'"

"I beg leave to repeat, Governor," quavered Nanyu, "that the ankle screw is for men."

Wei Su chuckled. "Manly feet deserve manly treatment," he said. By this time, the sounds of the other prisoners' interrogation—the shouting of questions, the blows of iron rods, and the screaming—were becoming audible.

Hong considered for one final beat and then nodded to the sergeant, who began tightening the screws at Daosheng's ankles. She clenched her teeth, at first, determined not to shout out. After the longest few instants Nanyu had ever experienced, she began groaning and finally burst forth with a wrenching howl that slammed Nanyu in the chest before slowly fading away. Hong held up his hand, and the sergeant paused and stood at attention.

"What is your name, woman?" the Governor asked.

"Ouyang Daosheng." She was gasping.

"Do you have a husband?"

"Yes."

"Who is he?"

"The Young Master."

"You are aware—both of you," Hong added, glancing at Nanyu, "that your marriage is unlawful?"

"Governor, my original surname is Wang, after my father, Wang Yin, a native of Liyang County. I go by the surname

Ouyang, out of respect for my mother, Ouyang Zhenli, who raised me. Both my father and my mother were driven to death by Wei Su."

"Ah," remarked the Vice Minister, "Now 'the sea recedes and the rocks emerge.' Here is the girl's confused motive. And her testimony isn't even all true, for she was raised not by her mother but by the wicked nuns at Cock-Crow Temple."

"You should know!" choked Daosheng. "That's where you sent Cui to kidnap me!"

"Vice Minister," Hong broke in, "are you, or were you, indeed acquainted with the accused's parents?"

"Only vaguely," answered Wei, "and merely in the context of business relationships, although I wish I had taken more care to avoid getting tied up with them. Wang Yin was an upstart pig thief and Ouyang Zhenli a proud whore. Both were given to shifty dealings while still unmet, and their perfidiousness increased, once they merged their crooked interests into a single criminal enterprise. Naturally, Wang Yin soon overextended himself and was duly punished by the magistrate. Ouyang Zhenli then washed her hands of their ill-spawned daughter—one almost feels sorry for her—and deposited her with the nuns, to continue plying her lascivious trade unencumbered. No doubt, the whore-child grew up on a diet of rumors and distortions, linking me to her parents, and so she developed a baseless resentment against me. But of that, I would learn only later."

Daosheng shrieked, "You pig-fucking bastard from hell!"

"Ah, well," said Wei Su, "that might as well count as the she-fiend's confession. Our work is done here."

Nanyu, stooped over and holding his breath, raised his eyes toward Governor Hong, awaiting the fatal sentence.

Instead, Hong Chengchou pointed at Wei. "So, it is a squabble over a woman, after all," he said, "with a couple of pigs thrown in. Vice Minister, I warned you twice about bringing your shenanigans before my court!"

Wei Su opened his mouth to protest, but at that moment, one of the sergeants came in from the side room, where dreadful outcries still echoed. "Governor," he reported, "we have discovered some shocking facts about the others."

"Tell."

"They are all bondservants who murdered their masters," the sergeant said. "One of them killed a Mr Gu of Songjiang last year; and the other three betrayed the family of Zhu Xiangsun, in an even bloodier affair."

"Zhu Xiangsun?" asked Hong, "The provincial degree holder who tried to set up that Society for...what was it?"

"The Society for Cherishing Loyalty," supplied the sergeant.

"Where was this, again?"

"In Xinchang, Governor. The three of them, Zhang Hui, Fang Long, and Qiao Yin, were Zhu Xiangsun's housemen. They were at the center of the conspiracy."

Hong lowered his eyebrows. "What conspiracy do you mean?" he asked. "The Society itself was a conspiracy."

"Actually, that was the problem, Governor," the sergeant said. "Zhu Xiangsun wouldn't let any bondservants join, so they ended up murdering him."

"And Zhang, Fang, and Qiao, three of Zhu Xiangsun's own favored housemen, joined in, rather than defending their master?"

"Yes, Governor, only they didn't just join in. It sounds like they led the charge, and they were merciless. They burst in on Zhu Xiangsun's family and killed them all."

"How many, all told?"

"Six died in addition to Xiangsun himself, including his three brothers, Ningxin, Jinqing, and Zaixin. Jinqing was Xiangsun's oldest brother. His fate was especially cruel, for he died with his three sons, Lianguan, Fuguan, and Jiaguan."

"Pity," Hong said. "Though they were rebels, they were upright men. One never wishes to hear of upright men suffering such treachery."

The Governor took a look around the chamber, apparently distracted. Then, he readdressed himself to the sergeant. "Were you able to determine the extent of the accused's involvement in the affair?"

"It is difficult to assess the testimony, Governor," the sergeant said, as another chorus of agony spilled in through the side doorway, "but the three men in question seem unusually loyal to the woman; they speak of her reverently, as the one who set them free."

Wei Su began nodding ostentatiously. He waited, while Hong Chengchou instructed the sergeant to concentrate the questioning on Fang, Qiao, and Zhang Hui and dismissed him. Then he said, "Puppets, mere puppets. How regrettable, though, that we should learn of the tigress's capacity for mischief only from her cat's-paws. I humbly suggest, Governor, that we renew our examination of the accused herself, taking care to treat with great skepticism anything she might say."

"Yes, Vice Minister," said Hong, exhaling, "I suppose you are right."

"I believe she was on the verge of cracking already," said Wei, "at the close of our last round of questions; but just to ensure that we obtain an unequivocal confession, I urge that the screws be tightened and that the accused be stripped."

There was a moment of non-comprehension, and then Daosheng snarled, "You'd like that, you pervert!"

At almost the same time, Nanyu said, "Governor, I am a tributary degree holder, this woman is my wife, and I forbid that she be stripped."

Wei Su said, "Governor, I am a metropolitan degree holder, this woman is *my* wife, and I demand that she be stripped."

"I'm surprised at you, Vice Minister," said Governor Hong. "If, as you insist, the accused is your wife, then it is most indecorous for you to move that she be exposed in court."

"Please pardon the interruption, Governor," said Nanyu, before Wei Su could retort, "but I humbly presume to ask when the Vice Minister shall be required to prove his assertion that Ouyang Daosheng is his wife. As for my own claim to be her husband, more than twenty Nanjing residents were witness to our wedding, and scores more patronized the Qinhuai tea shop that we ran as husband and wife, two years ago. These witnesses can be brought before this court to testify, Governor. I doubt the Vice Minister can produce witnesses of his own, though he is, of course, welcome to try."

"Well said, Young Master," beamed Wei, "but you've failed to consider that a sorceress bent on seducing you would naturally hide behind the trappings of a conventional wedding and would fool you into thinking that the marriage was your idea and that you were happy with her—nay, even that you loved her. The sinister art of erotic entrancement conforms precisely to this pattern. I say again, Young Master: You have been tricked."

Governor Hong remained silent, and Wei Su felt compelled to continue.

"Very well," he said. "I will be quite happy to validate my claim that I am the accused's true husband, and I daresay my narrative will also shed light on how the Young Master became the harlot's serviceable tool. However, first I must insist that, if we are to be deprived of the benefit of seeing the vixen directly exposed, then we might at least cause the screws to be tightened. Her unaffected reactions to my revelation of the truth would be most instructive."

Governor Hong half nodded and half shrugged, and his attendant descended from the dais and tightened the vises. Daosheng began screaming without pause, and her wailing became the accompaniment to Wei Su's ensuing recitation.

"Even after leaving her obscene child with the nuns of Cock-Crow Temple," Wei began, "Ouyang Zhenli kept her under contract, the same kind of contract that binds singing girls to their madams; for the vile mother was no doubt planning to employ her own ill-starred daughter in the capacity of common bed-wench."

"Nonsense!" Daosheng called out.

"As soon as I gathered that such an unscrupulous scheme was afoot—for Ouyang Zhenli was as indiscreet as she was inhumane—I resolved to rescue the waif and to gift her with a respectable life as mistress of my inner chambers. I made a very generous settlement with the avaricious Ouyang Zhenli and bought out her daughter's contract. The transaction occurred just after my attainment of the metropolitan degree and first posting to the capital. I journeyed to Beijing via the Grand Canal to take up my responsibilities," Wei continued, omitting the name of the emperor who had entrusted him with those responsibilities, "and made arrangements for my betrothed to follow in a subsequent boat."

"The only thing you arranged was for Cui to kidnap me, you bastard!"

"Unfortunately," Wei went on, "I made the mistake of offering passage on the same vessel to the Young Master, then a struggling artist, to whom I had condescended to become patron. It is easy to reconstruct what followed: The minx exploited the close proximity to ensnare the Young Master in an erotic entrancement. Whether she inherited the talent from her wanton mother or learned it from the heterodox nuns who raised her, it was formidable enough to make the Young Master her willing minion by the time of their arrival in the capital, where I, out of the goodness of my heart, had already prepared her happy home. Barely were our nuptials concluded—and I can produce plenty of respectable witnesses of my own, to attest that they were—when the inhuman bitch, in spite of all I'd done for her, called in her lewd favor, and her creature, the Young Master, took the bit in his mouth and absconded with her. Plainly, he has been under her thrall in all the days since, and he remains so today. Heaven knows the extent of what he—or his retainers, apparently—would do for her sake."

He paused and then concluded:

"And so, of the two men standing before you now, Governor, one is the accused's husband, the other, her slave."

No one spoke. The only sounds to be heard were those of torture.

Nanyu took a deep breath, and the air rushed in, past his parched throat.

"Governor," he said, "the Vice Minister has alluded to a certain contract, supposedly binding the accused to her late mother, which he claims to have transferred to himself. Might not the Vice Minister be asked to show the contract at this time, for the sake of good procedure?"

Governor Hong looked at Wei. "Yes, Vice Minister. Let's see it."

Wei grinned sheepishly. "Alas, Governor, I'm afraid the contract has been lost, owing to the recent instability."

"Indeed?" Hong squinted. "Surely you would not have failed to secure such an important document, Vice Minister. It would appear to carry some weight as evidence in this prosecution, which you yourself have initiated."

"Governor," said Nanyu again, before Wei could open his mouth, "your servant believes that the Vice Minister is reluctant to produce the alleged contract for two reasons: first, that it is a forgery; and second, that he does not wish his personal seal, which he affixed to the forgery, to be submitted as evidence, for fear of other incriminating papers, bearing the same seal, coming to light."

Wei Su stiffened his chin.

Hong, however, leapt to his feet and shook his finger at Nanyu. "This is your last warning!" he shouted. "His Majesty has cleared the Vice Minister of all wrongdoing, and he is not on trial now!"

"He betrayed Beijing to Li Zicheng," whispered Nanyu.

"He did what?"

In lieu of answering, Nanyu took out Wei Su's letter to Niu Jinxing. He walked up the steps of the dais and, with both hands and a slight nod, handed the letter to Hong Chengchou, before returning to his place.

With a stern expression, Hong perused the letter. "I recognize your seal, Vice Minister, and I even recognize Niu Jinxing's handwriting, in the so-called rescript. Heaven knows I had occasion to view many samples of it, in captured rebel correspondence, over the years."

Hong Chengchou had fought against the Dashing Prince under two dynasties, and he now looked upon Wei Su, who had served three dynasties, including that of the Dashing Prince.

"Blank artillery rounds. I heard about that."

Wei looked neither at Hong nor at Nanyu. "Governor, I have never betrayed Our Dynasty."

"Not yet."

Wei smoothed back the nonexistent hair at his temples. The beatings in the side room had ceased (for Zhang Hui, Fang Long, and Qiao Yin were dead), and the only sounds now to be heard were those of Daosheng's labored breathing. Wei turned to pass a final, savoring gaze over his one-time concubine's broken body, and his habitual smirk returned. He slowly extended his arm, to point at the prostrate woman, and raised his eyes once more to Governor Hong.

"But don't you see, Governor," he said, "the bewitcher had infiltrated my household by then. It could have been no mere coincidence that she arrived at the capital a scant few days before the renegade Li. Naturally, this female embodiment of willfulness would seek a place beside her male counterpart, the so-called Dashing Prince, hoping perhaps to become his chaotic queen. Having opened my heart to the urchin, I failed to guard myself against her—oh, curse my innocence! It was but quick work for her to employ her favored tactic of erotic enchantment, and— woe is me!—I became the unwitting medium for her treasonable traffic with the enemy, which resulted, a few fateful days later, in the loss of our Holy Dynasty—I mean, the defunct dynasty… Ah, in short, Governor, the accused is no ordinary intriguer. Her demonic machinations have had their doleful effect, not only on the foolish Young Master and myself, but upon All Under Heaven. I rest my case."

Nanyu said, "Merciful Buddha! Is there nothing that cannot be blamed on a woman?"

Daosheng laughed through her agony. "You shall have your answer directly, Husband."

Governor Hong waved his hand. "Enough of this. I find Ouyang Daosheng guilty of casting erotic entrancements. She is to be returned to Cock-Crow Temple and denied all contact with men. Vice Minister, now that you are free from the witch's influence, I expect you to be a paragon of probity from now on. I will be watching you. The same goes for you, Young Master.

Take two days to visit family in Nanjing—excepting, mind you, your former wife, with whom you are altogether forbidden to communicate—and then my runners will escort you back to Yuhang County, where you will resume your service to Our Dynasty. Respect this verdict! Dismissed!"

Two guards emerged from the side and removed Daosheng's feet from the presses. Then, they dragged her out. Both her ankles were shattered and bruised purple, and the ridges of the vises had cut into her skin, leaving parallel gashes, oozing blood. She and Nanyu locked their eyes together and held on until she disappeared over the threshold. Wei, Hong, and everyone else in the chamber cleared out, but Nanyu didn't notice. He was left standing alone with two crimson trails on the floor.

ロ۔ロロロロ

On the morning after the trial, Nanyu requested a horse from the Governor's yamen (where he continued to lodge) and rode to Shakyamuni Street, to visit his father, whom he found wringing laundry in front of his house. "Son!" Ouyang Gen exulted. "So you have 'returned home in glory!'"

Nanyu dismounted from his horse and attempted to kneel, but his father wouldn't let him, holding him up under his arm.

"None of that, Son," he said, throwing his pigtail back over his shoulder. "You're a star in Heaven now, and stars in Heaven don't kneel."

Ouyang Gen whisked Nanyu inside and seated him on the only stool in the kitchen. "Please excuse the shabby condition of my humble shack," he said, "and join me in a bowl of bitter melon soup—if you can still tolerate such rustic fare!" He kept smiling at his son, as he ladled out the soup. Then he backed off, to give Nanyu room to eat.

249

"I heard you were back in town," he lowered his voice, "for the trial. The Vice Minister turned out to be a tough customer, eh? Not tough enough, though. You took care of him—just like you took care of his do-boy down south. That'll teach them to mess with us!" He nodded, from his shoulders on up. "I was sorry to hear about your losing the girl, though. She was clever. Oh, well. You'll be able to take your pick of brides now!"

He refilled Nanyu's bowl. "I also heard what happened to that Zhu Xiangsun. He was the scholar who brought you back from Beijing, right? Merciful Buddha, what a mess. Turns out it was his own men who did him in—people he trusted. I guess most of them got away with it, too. The attackers numbered more than forty, but only five or six were ever tried and executed, including Zhang Hui, Fang Long, and Qiao Yin. They came here with you, didn't they?"

Nanyu had had enough soup. Without answering his father, he rose and stepped through the sitting and storage room, where the sleeping loft had never been replaced; and then he reached the workshop, where his eyes fell upon the four-poster bed with the inlaid mandarin ducks. It sat in a corner, though it was by far the biggest and most striking object in the room.

"I guess you heard about that," said the carpenter. "The thing must be cursed. First I get swindled out of a hundred ounces of silver on it; now it's impossible to sell at any price."

Nanyu touched his father on the arm, exited to the street, and returned with his saddlebag. Opening it, he counted out one hundred ounces of silver and expressed his wish to buy the bed. Ouyang Gen resisted briefly but soon accepted.

"Where did you get all that money?" he gushed. "What did you say? 'Fees'? Well, I guess a captain of militia has plenty of opportunities to collect them!"

Nanyu laid out another ounce or two, and his proud father

promised to have the bed shipped all the way to Yuhang.

"Now that everyone knows you're a tributary, we can be sure it'll get there without a scratch." He giggled. "We've really come up in the world, haven't we?"

Nanyu then took his leave, after pledging to send his father more money from time to time (which he did). He looked across at the Temple at the Edge of Heaven but decided against visiting. The Entrance to the Practice of the Benevolent World appeared to be closed.

◪◫ ◪◫ ◪◫

The next day, his last in the city, he wandered about aimlessly. He passed near the Drum Tower, where the beating of the hour hurt his ears. He took a turn around Cooling Hill, which was deserted. He walked along Three Mountain Street, but the mood there was subdued. Finally, toward evening, he found himself on Agarwood Street. He looked up and saw the front portal of the House of the Entrancing Fragrance, which seemed to have been sold and re-occupied. Rather than approaching the front door, he went up the adjacent side street until he stood on the footbridge across the Qinhuai. Then, he turned around and looked at the back of the house. Someone was running a tea shop on the first floor, although no women played the *pipa*. Indeed, among the staff and few patrons, there were only men, shaved-scalped and pigtailed, thin, silent strangers. On the second floor, in the bedroom, a faint candle cast flickering shadows on the walls, but nothing else showed of the dark interior.

◪◫ ◪◫ ◪◫

Over the next several years, the new government would continue to press the loyalists farther south. The last prince of the old regime would be captured in Burma and strangled.

Wei Su would rise to become Grand Secretary, though he remained notoriously corrupt. After a few more years, accusations against him finally stuck, Shunzhi having determined that he had outlived his usefulness. At his trial, he mounted a glib self-defense, was found guilty, and was likewise strangled.

His chamberlain, Cui, never rejoined him in Nanjing or elsewhere, though it was not from lack of trying. Immediately upon his southward banishment by Nanyu, he had doubled back and tried to return north, disguised as a monk. A suspicious military officer in still-restive Jiading took him into custody, quizzed him on the sutras, and then, finding him a fraud and ignoring his invocation of Wei Su, summarily beheaded him.

Zhang Yue survived his beating, despite losing copious flesh and muscle from his rear and the backs of his legs. He accompanied Nanyu back to Yuhang, borne there on a litter, and served him steadfastly ever after.

The Ouyangs' four-leaf album remained in Wei Su's possession until his execution, when, together with the rest of his estate, it was seized and sold by the government. It changed hands among wealthy connoisseurs for several generations. A full description of the album was included in a catalogue published during the reign of one of Shunzhi's successors, but it appears to have been lost soon after that.

Several of Daosheng's bamboo studies survive today, in private collections, although nobody knows who painted them.

Ouyang Nanyu maintained his tributary status and continued to serve in minor official positions in the lower Yangtze valley. At one point, he was named education intendant of Xinchang and in that capacity contributed a biography of Zhu Xiangsun to the official county history. The 284-character essay would be his sole literary legacy (see Appendix). During this time, he performed his official tasks diligently and slept alone each night in the four-poster marriage bed.

Toward the end of Shunzhi's reign, Nanyu was promoted to education intendent and militia captain in Zhenjiang County, just as the merchant prince Zheng Chenggong (also known as Coxinga), ostensibly on behalf of the old regime, invaded upriver. Nanyu was last seen on Zhenjiang's battlements, leading the defense against Zheng's marines. His fate in the action is unknown, and he is lost to history thereafter.

There are two ways to imagine what happened to Nanyu. The first supposition is that he died a martyr to the young Manchu dynasty, while making a valiant stand at Zhenjiang. A cannon shot or mutilation at the hands of Zheng's rebels would explain why his body was never found.

The second possible scenario is that Nanyu defected to Zheng Chenggong at the height of the battle. According to this version, Nanyu sheared off his pigtail and marched with Zheng's army as it advanced from Zhenjiang, right to the gates of Nanjing. He gazed with longing at the Baozhi Pagoda, rising in the distance above Cock-Crow Temple, in the city that seemed so ripe for liberation. Then, alas, he wept bitterly when the Manchus reinforced Nanjing at the last minute and Zheng's forces had to retreat. In this eventuality, Ouyang Nanyu, with no options remaining, accompanied Zheng Chenggong as he re-embarked with his navy, sailed back down the Yangtze and on out to sea, and captured the island of Taiwan, which became his kingdom of consolation.

In the aftermath of Zheng's incursion, One-Eyed Jingang, with one assistant, called on Baichi Shi'ai at the Temple at the Edge of Heaven, to ask if he had any tea for sale. The abbot could only apologize. Disruptions to the markets, he explained, had left him with only a small supply of Rain Flower on hand. Jingang, however, expressed satisfaction with the local variety, and was happy to obtain a modest amount at a nominal price.

At the conclusion of the transaction, Jingang's assistant hobbled off to offer prayers at the Altar of the Iron Buddha. Watching her go, the abbess asked, "Were we wrong to have encouraged them?"

"I think not," answered Baichi Shi'ai. "They were only following their natural inclinations. For us to oppose them would have been to act contrary to nature."

"But our teaching is a discipline," Jingang said, "a discipline of liberation from attachments. I thought that it made sense to nurture their sagely tendencies — particularly the girl's, even after she'd 'come down from the mountain.' As a dutiful wife, she would have been accumulating good karma, practicing the one discipline available to her as a layperson. As she progressed in her discipline, there was always the chance that her sagehood would spread to her husband, with liberation from worldly attachments as the reward. In the event, though..." she shook her head, "their marriage only further immured them in the world. They remained in the nature of two piteous passion-clinging bugs. The result cannot be called happy."

Baichi Shi'ai nodded. "Sagehood and discipline both failed when they were turned against the forces of nature. Their hope of transcending the world died when they sought to prevail against the world, when they — especially the boy — grasped at power and hoped to wield it against their enemies. As a general rule, whenever the world is in turmoil, the only hope is flight. Any act of resolution, any attempt to resist, will always lead to great harm. Posterity should take the case of Ouyang Nanyu as an object lesson."

Appendix

From *The History of Xinchang*, "Biography of Zhu Xiangsun," by OUYANG NANYU, his protégé and witness to his death.

IT WAS THE SEVENTEENTH year of the Chongzhen Emperor's reign. Li Zicheng occupied the Sacred Capital.

The Hongguang Emperor ascended the throne in Nanjing. His proclamation contained the phrase "Our wish is to give the people a new beginning." Bondservants passed the word amongst themselves that they no longer had to serve their masters. In several villages in Songjiang Prefecture, thousands of bondsmen began seizing their contracts of indenture from their masters at swordpoint. The prefect mobilized the militia and captured and executed them. Order was restored for a time.

The Manchus moved southwards. The Hongguang Emperor was made a prisoner. The countryside was completely convulsed and people were killing each other as though scything grain.

In Xinchang, a provincial civil service degree holder named Zhu Xiangsun organized a brotherhood called the Society for Cherishing Loyalty, to fight for the old dynasty. Men of all descriptions came from far and near to join. Zhu Xiangsun, however, was concerned only with maintaining the rigid distinction between masters and servants. He absolutely refused to allow bondsmen to join the Society. Again, the ringleaders took advantage of the discontent to incite their gangs. They burst in on Zhu Xiangsun's family and killed them all. Six died in addition to Xiangsun himself, including his three brothers, Ningxin, Jinqing, and Zaixin. Jinqing was Xiangsun's oldest brother. His fate was especially cruel, for he died with his three sons, Lianguan, Fuguan, and Jiaguan. The attackers numbered more than forty, but only five or six were ever tried and executed, including Zhang Hui, Fang Long, and Qiao Yin. As a general rule, whenever the world is in turmoil, the only hope is flight. Any act of resolution, any attempt to resist, will always lead to great harm. Posterity should take the case of Zhu Xiangsun as an object lesson.

Notes

Chapter One

The seventeenth year of the Chongzhen Emperor's reign. The reign of the Chongzhen Emperor was the last of China's Ming dynasty (1368-1644). The seventeenth year of his reign corresponds to 1644 on the Christian calendar. **Cock-Crow Temple** (*Ji ming si*) is still a working nunnery and tourist attraction. The **Drum Tower** (*Gu lou*) also still exists; **Three Mountain Street** does not, but a subway stop near its former location now bears its name. The **Qinhuai River** entertainment district has been reconstructed for tourists. The general descriptions of **Nanjing** are based on Louis Gallagher (tr.), *China in the Sixteenth Century: The Journals of Matthew Ricci, 1583-1610* (New York: Random House, 1953), pp. 268-270 and Wu Ching-Tzu, *The Scholars* (Beijing: Foreign Languages Press, 2000), p. 270. **Peng bird**. Burton Watson (tr.), *Zhuangzi: Basic Writings* (New York: Columbia University Press, 2003), pp. 23-24. **Kingly air.** See Barry Till and Paula Swart, *In Search of Old Nanking* (Hong Kong: Joint Publishing Co., 1984), pp. 6-7 and Ye Chucang (ed.), *Shoudu zhi* (Nanjing: Zhengzhong shu ju, 1935), p. 4. **Treasure Gate** (*Ju bao men*) was the southernmost gate of the Nanjing city wall. It is now called China Gate (*Zhonghua men*). **One-Eyed Jingang** is a historical person, though from an earlier time. See Beata Grant, *Daughters of Emptiness: Poems of Chinese Buddhist Nuns* (Somerville: Wisdom Publications, 2003), p. 54. The **Temple at the Edge of Heaven** (*Tian jie si*) was located south of Nanjing and no longer exists, although ruins and reconstructed buildings can supposedly be found at a kindergarten that stands where the temple once did.

See   http://www.chinanews.com/cul/2012/02-13/3662774.
shtml. **Mahayana Pavilion**. All of the scenes in this book that
take place at the Temple at the Edge of Heaven follow the map of
the temple grounds that is included in *Shoudu zhi*. **Baichi Shi'ai**
is a fictional character. **Ouyang Nanyu** is a fictional character.
Ouyang Gen is a fictional character, although his given name is
that of the upstart philosopher Wang Gen (1483-1541). **There's
nothing that can't be learned** approximates a realization made
by the character Wang Mian in *The Scholars*, p. 3. **On display
among the merchandise there**. See Ina Asim and Garron Hale,
"Colorful Lanterns at Shangyuan" (interactive CD-ROM, 2004),
which depicts a Nanjing street scene during the Lantern Festival
in the seventeenth century, although it is not Three Mountain
Street. Throughout this scene, I have imagined the Ouyangs to
be in the painting that this CD-ROM explores, except that I have
moved the storyteller's gallery to be a little closer to where the
bed is displayed. **The filial son does not alter his father's way for
three years after he has passed** is from the *Analects* of Confucius,
4:20. See Arthur Waley (tr.), *The Analects of Confucius* (New York:
Vintage Books, 1938), p. 106. **Fly away on the back of a crane**.
A Daoist named Wang Ziqiao (575-545 BCE) supposedly exited
society in this fashion to become an immortal. **Never, under
any circumstances, sit for the civil service examinations and
become an official**. Wang Gen's injunction follows that of Wang
Mian's mother in *The Scholars*, p. 11. **Breaker of families** also
approximates *The Scholars*, p. 7. **The stolen mansion is naught but
the cage of anxiety** is an invented trope, though the latter phrase
can be found in Harry Miller, *State versus Gentry in Early Qing
Dynasty China, 1644-1699* (New York: Palgrave Macmillan, 2013),
p. 122. **The sage recognizes a 'this'**… See *Zhuangzi*, p. 35. **Cui** is
a fictional character, loosely based on Bailiff Chai, who appears
in the first chapter of *The Scholars*. **Wei Su** borrows the name of a

big-shot scholar-official in the same source, although his physical description resembles that of Ruan Dacheng (1587-1646), a despised scholar-official from history who became the villain of the drama *The Peach Blossom Fan*; and his career is patterned after that of Chen Mingxia (c. 1601-1654), yet another scholar-official. The **metropolitan examination** was the superlative civil service examination. **Ouyang is an unusual name**. Two-character surnames are indeed rare in China, but Ouyang, perhaps, is the most common among them. **Clients**. Wei Su's use of favors to organize a faction of students (and potential officials) at the Temple at the Edge of Heaven is suggested by the historical Tang Binyin (b. 1569), who built such a network, using the temple as his base. See Harry Miller, "Opposition to the Donglin Faction in the Late Ming Dynasty: The Case of Tang Binyin, *Late Imperial China* 27.2 (January 2006), p. 40. **Shakyamuni Street** is invented, although there seems (from the aforementioned map) to have been a smaller Shakyamuni Temple, in front of the Temple at the Edge of Heaven, on the site where I am imagining the Ouyangs to have lived. **His Excellency Wei Su has noticed your work** follows *The Scholars*, pp. 5-6. Nanyu's promised commission of **four ounces of silver**, at one ounce per album leaf, also follows *The Scholars*, p. 6, in which Wang Mian is supposed to be paid twenty-four ounces for a set of twenty-four paintings. **Such an unlucky number**. The number four is inauspicious is China, because the word for "four" sounds like the word for "death" in Chinese. **The Dashing Prince / Li Zicheng** is historically authentic. He lived from 1606 to 1645. **Grand Secretary Li Jiantai** (d. 1649) is likewise historical, and the military campaign anticipated here by Cui would likely have been well known. See Kenneth M. Swope, *The Military Collapse of China's Ming Dynasty, 1618-1644* (New York: Routledge, 2014), p. 193.

Chapter Two

Grand Secretary Li Jiantai's army left Beijing for the front and immediately began disintegrating. See *The Military Collapse of China's Ming Dynasty*, pp. 193-194. **Sixty strokes of the bamboo** was the penalty for same-surname marriage, which was legally considered to be incestuous. See Ann Waltner, *Getting an Heir: Adoption and the Construction of Kinship in Late Imperial China* (Honolulu: University of Hawaii Press, 1990), p. 62, which suggests that the legal prohibition may have become downgraded to a social taboo but that violations did continue to occur. **Grand Canal**. For routes and approximate transit times, I have referred to Timothy Brook, *The Confusions of Pleasure: Commerce and Culture in Ming China* (Berkeley: University of California Press, 1998), pp. 41-56 and Jane Kate Leonard, *Controlling From Afar: The Daoguang Emperor's Management of the Grand Canal Crisis, 1824-1826* (Ann Arbor: Center for Chinese Studies, The University of Michigan, 1996), esp. pp. xix-xxi. The best aid for visualizing the Ouyangs' trip is the set of beautiful color maps in *Qing dai da yun he quan tu* (Hangzhou: Zhejiang guji chubanshe, 2013). **Women would shower him with kerchiefs of fruit wherever he went**. See K'ung Shang-jen, *The Peach Blossom Fan* (New York: New York Review Books, 2015), pp. 23, 40, 41-42. **Ouyang Daosheng** is a fictional character based on Guan Daosheng (1262-1319), wife of the artist Zhao Mengfu (1254-1322) and painter and poet in her own right. **Ouyang Zhenli** is a fictional character, whose given name is borrowed from the foster mother of the heroine of *The Peach Blossom Fan*. **His Excellency buys friends from your temple and karma from mine**. The use of temples as bases for building political factions has already been discussed. Making donations to temples was a means to enhance social (and political) status. See Timothy Brook, *Praying for Power: Buddhism and the Formation of Gentry Society in Late-Ming China*

(Cambridge: Harvard University Asia Center, 1994). **While he 'combs my hair' in the next room**. See *The Peach Blossom Fan*, p. 16. **I hear that one of his generals is a woman – former generals, actually, because she ran off with another man**. See *The Military Collapse of China's Ming Dynasty*, p. 122. **You have unbound feet!** Daosheng would have been more historically authentic with bound feet. In fact, according to Dorothy Ko, *Teachers of the Inner Chambers: Women and Culture in Seventeenth-Century China* (Stanford: Stanford University Press, 1994), pp. 147-151, 169-171, she probably would have been proud of her "three-inch golden lotuses," had she been given them. Dr. Beata Grant, in personal correspondence, accepts the outside chance that a cloistered upbringing might have spared Daosheng the ordeal (or the honor) of having bound feet, as is described in this book. Nanyu's reaction to Daosheng's unbound feet can only be imagined. Although men wrote conventionally, and approvingly, of tiny feet, footbinding was women's business, and men had comparatively little to say about it. **In dharma, there is no male or female** approximates statements that appear in Beata Grant, "Da Zhangfu: The Gendered Rhetoric of Heroism and Equality in Seventeenth-Century Chan Buddhist Discourse Records" *Nan Nü* 10 (2008), p. 181. **'Real men' and 'real women' – Why split hairs?**...is attributed to the historical One-Eyed Jingang. See *Daughters of Emptiness*, p. 55, although I have modified the translation. **Bell Tower Street** is the character Wei Su's Beijing address in *The Scholars*, p. 3. **The mansion's three courtyards**. For visualizing Wei's mansion, see https://depts.washington.edu/chinaciv/3intrhme.htm. **The Dashing Prince had attacked Datong**. See *The Military Collapse of China's Ming Dynasty*, p. 197.

Chapter Three

Wang Yangming (a.k.a. Wang Shouren, 1472-1529) was the

foremost philosopher of his age. He developed the idea of intuitive knowledge, from which sprang the doctrine of living in the present. **Li Zicheng began attacking the Xizhi gate** and **Many of the defending artillerists, in cahoots with the rebels, were firing blanks**. See *The Military Collapse of China's Ming Dynasty*, p. 200. **Provincial degree holder**. The provincial degree was the penultimate civil service degree. **The brothers' occupations alternated between commerce and study**. This is similar to the generational scheme described in *The Confusions of Pleasure*, p. 215. **Zhang, Fang, and Qiao** are historical persons of unknown social origin (see Appendix), though I have made them housemen of the Zhu family. **Tongzhou, Tianjin**. The military vicissitudes in these cities, and in **Shandong Province**, a little later, are abstracted from Tan Qian, *Guo que* (Taipei: Dingwen shuju, 1978), pp. 6053-6055, 6067. The **Confucian Drill Instructor** was a local officer. See Harry Miller, *State versus Gentry in Late Ming Dynasty China* (New York: Palgrave Macmillan, 2009), pp. 152-153, which notes a Confucian drill instructor, surnamed Ni, acting as militia captain. **Chapter Three: Duke Wen of Teng.** The following symposium follows D.C. Lau (tr.), *Mencius* (London: Penguin Books, 2004), pp. 52-54, except for one sentence. **I have authority for what I do**. See D.C. Lau (tr.), *Mencius* (London: Penguin Books, 1970), p. 96. **Executed several of Li Zicheng's agents**. See *Guo que*, p. 6067. **Romantic setting of moonlit deck; bliss of wedding night; how to describe this joy?** See Tang Xianzu, *The Peony Pavilion* (Bloomington: Indiana University Press, 2002), p. 212. **Suqian**. In the chaotic military situation, the "lines" would not have been obvious, yet Suqian, a town on the Canal, seems to have remained in (Ming) government hands at this time. See *Guo que*, p. 6070. **Man and wife together, we have reached Nanjing… With little ado, we have become man and wife…the clouds and the rain…Now that Feng Yi the River Spirit comes to strike** his drum / I understand the flute-playing skill of the noble daughter of Qin…And when my dream reached the summit of delight / There came flower petals showering down. See *The Peony Pavilion*, pp. 220 (Daosheng has substituted Nanjing for Hangzhou), 221, 52/94, 193, 59, respectively. **Those who bore holes in the wall**… is from *Mencius*, III/B/3. See *Mencius* (1970), p. 108. **Holding hands**. In *The Scholars*, p. 365, Du Shaoqing holds hands with his wife, as they stroll about Cooling Hill (*Qing liang shan*) in Nanjing. **Apricot blossoms**. See *State versus Gentry in Early Qing Dynasty China*, p. 49 and *The Peony Pavilion*, pp. 57, 60, 69, 134, 203. **This nun is seventeen**… The stanza is based on Andrea S. Goldman, "The Nun Who Wouldn't Be: Representations of Female Desire in Two Performance Genres of 'Si Fan,'" *Late Imperial China* 22.1 (June 2001), p. 106. **I beg of you, Zhongzi**… See Arthur Waley (tr.), *The Book of Songs* (New York: Grove Press, Inc., 1960), p. 35. **Moral virtue is a form of karma** is an invented statement, yet the equation of Confucian virtue and Buddhist spirituality is discussed in "Da Zhangfu: The Gendered Rhetoric of Heroism and Equality," pp. 186-193. **Here is a lady I have met in love**… is modified from *The Book of Songs*, p. 68. **The news of the fall of Beijing reached here about ten days ago**. See Lynn Struve, *The Southern Ming, 1644-1662* (New Haven: Yale University Press, 1984), p. 16. **Fast-mouth**. See "The Shrew," in H.C. Chang, *Chinese Literature: Popular Fiction and Drama* (Edinburgh: Edinburgh University Press, 1973), pp. 23-55. **The House of the Entrancing Fragrance** is the home of the courtesan Li Xiangjun and her mother, Li Zhenli, in *The Peach Blossom Fan*. Li Xiangjun was a real person who lived from 1624 to 1654. In Nanjing today stands a House of the Entrancing Fragrance (*Mei xiang lou*), a tourist site, which is billed as the historical home of Li Xiangjun. However, the building actually dates from the late Qing dynasty (1644-1911), after Li Xiangjun's time, according to

https://zh.wikipedia.org/wiki/%E9%92%9E%E5%BA%93%E
8%A1%97%E6%B2%B3%E6%88%BF. Descriptions of the house
in this book generally follow the tourist attraction. For **Scrip
Street** and **Agarwood Street**, see http://baike.baidu.com/item
/%E9%92%9E%E5%BA%93%E8%A1%97. **Fasting...gentleman
of a woman...liberate other sentient beings**. See "Da Zhangfu:
The Gendered Rhetoric of Heroism and Equality," pp. 180, 181-
182, 184, 192. **Wang Yin** was the original name of Wang Gen
(the upstart philosopher). Yin means silver. **Stipendiary student**
was the lowest status in the hierarchy established by the civil
service examination system. A stipendiary was someone who
had passed a qualifying test. He drew a stipend and wielded
some privileges but held no formal degree and was ineligible for
office. If he desired to advance, he would generally seek either
a tributary degree (see below) or a provincial degree, with the
latter qualifying him to compete for the metropolitan degree.
He let a few pigs wander onto Wang Yin's farm. This method
of provoking a dispute resembles a scheme that appears in *The
Scholars*, pp. 47-48, 53. **Nanjing custom** concerning the mother
of the bride giving away her daughter and the bride's family
providing liquor is gleaned from *Shoudu zhi*, p. 1110. **I don't
want to go, Mother!** The bride's feigned reluctance to leave her
natal home conforms to modern Taiwanese custom, as does the
wedding feast that follows. **In the storeroom was the sleeping-
tree**... Daosheng has modified a poem from *The Book of Songs*, p.
21. **The Emperor is dead!** See *The Southern Ming*, p. 16, for details
on when this news reached Nanjing.

Chapter Four

The Hongguang Emperor ascended the throne in Nanjing.
See *The Southern Ming*, pp. 17-19. **Wu Sangui** was a historical
person, who lived from 1612 to 1678. **Hongguang...issued a**

rallying edict. See *The Southern Ming*, p. 19; Zhou Shiyong, *Xing chao zhi luë* (1644), esp. ch. 1, p. 9b. **If you don't know how, why pretend?**... See Kenneth Rexroth, *The Orchid Boat: Women Poets of China* (New York: McGraw Hill, 1972), p. 61. **You held my lotus blossom** is from the same source, p. 60. **This official wears no official sash**... This is a poem called "Making Fun of Myself on People Day" by Yuan Hongdao (1568-1610). See Jonathan Chaves, *Pilgrim of the Clouds: Poems and Essays from Ming Dynasty China* (New York: Weatherhill, 1978), p. 35. I have shortened and modified the translation. **As long as my parents are still alive, how can I have the freedom to do as I please?** See Ling Mengchu, *Chu ke pai an jing qi* (Changsha: Yuelu shushe, 2003), p. 53. I have altered the verb tense of the sentence. **Seeing through fixed types.** See "Da Zhangfu: The Gendered Rhetoric of Heroism and Equality," p. 204. I have re-attributed this sentiment to One-Eyed Jingang. **The sage embraces things**... See *Zhuangzi*, p. 39. **Rain Flower, Heaven's Pool, Dragon Well, Heaven's Eye, Water Sprite.** See http://baike.baidu.com/item/%E9%9B%A8%E8%8A%B1%E8%8C%B6; https://en.wikipedia.org/wiki/Chinese_tea; Victor Mair, *The True History of Tea* (New York: Thames & Hudson, 2009), p. 113. The three lyrics beginning **The Qinhuai lolls, On the many-curved Qinhuai,** and **Meandering, melancholy Qinhuai** are based on song lyrics in Song Jiaqi (ed.), *Jinling lüyou ci* (Nanjing: Jiangsu renmin chubanshe, 1987), pp. 208, 216-217, 220. **Daosheng devised numerous improvements...an ingenious method of flavoring the tea... lattices for the windows.** Daosheng is following the example of Chen Yun, the heroine of the memoir *Six Records of a Floating Life*. See Shen Fu, *Six Records of a Floating Life* (London: Penguin Books, 1983), pp. 67-68, 69, 63. **Daosheng invented new dishes.** These snacks were preferred by the literatus Jin Shengtan (1610?-1661). See Tie Qinlu, *Jin Shengtan chi du* (Taipei: Guangwen shuju,

1990), p. 67, although the sesame oil was added by the present writer. **Outgoes and income**. These estimates are extrapolated from Charles J. Dunn, *Everyday life in Traditional Japan* (North Clarendon: Tuttle Publishing, 1969), p. 87, where it is reported that one cup of tea sold for one copper in contemporary Japan. **The equivalent of about two ounces of silver**. See Richard von Glahn, *Fountain of Fortune: Money and Monetary Policy in China, 1000-1700* (Berkeley: University of California Press, 1996), pp. 106-109, 160. **Gong Xian** was a Nanjing-based eccentric painter, who lived from around 1618 to 1689. **I just sold a landscape painting for two ounces of silver...literati paintings...inkstone field...many of them come in person, in their tall, four-horse carriages, right to my rustic door**. See Jerome Silbergeld, "Kung Hsien: A Professional Chinese Artist and his Patronage," *The Burlington Magazine* 123.940 (July 1981), pp. 404-406. **That, then, is freedom**. Gong Xian's discourse on freedom actually follows the playwright Liao Yan (1644-1705). See Chun-shu Chang and Shelley Hsueh-lun Chang, *Crisis and Transformation in Seventeenth-Century China: Society, Culture, and Modernity in Li Yu's World* (Ann Arbor: The University of Michigan Press, 1992), p. 348; Liao Yan, "Xu su pipa juben," in Zheng Zhenduo, *Qing ren za ju er ji* (Hong Kong: Longmen shudian, 1969), p. 128. **Paintings by other artists are all of places where people have gone... The world has many wondrous and inaccessible places...** See Katharine P. Burnett, *Dimensions of Originality: Essays on Seventeenth-Century Chinese Art Theory and Criticism* (Hong Kong: The Chinese University Press, 2013), pp. 141-142. **Cooling Hill** (*Qing liang shan*) is where Gong Xian lived, though perhaps a bit after this time. **Phoenix**. See Richard E. Strassberg, *A Chinese Bestiary: Strange Creatures from the Guideways Through Mountains and Seas* (Berkeley: University of California Press, 2002), pp. 193-194. **There are those who labor with their minds and those** who labor with their muscles… is from *Mencius*, III/A/4. See *Mencius* (1970), p. 101. My version is slightly modified.

Chapter Five

The renegades pressed their advantage…Tavern lackeys and scullery boys rose in a riot…Masses of tenant farmers and other unfree people began chanting…Many wealthy families of the south were abandoning their country estates and seeking refuge in Nanjing. See Xie Guozhen, *Ming Qing zhi ji dang she yundong kao* (Taipei: Taiwan yinshuguan, 1968), pp. 280, 283; Frederic Wakeman, Jr., *The Great Enterprise: The Manchu Reconstruction of Imperial Order in Seventeenth-Century China* (Berkeley: University of California Press, 1985), p. 636. **A love without discrimination.** *Mencius* III/B/9. See *Mencius* (1970), p. 114. **'Reciprocity,' which, according to Confucius himself, is the one word that should guide us all our lives.** *Analects* 15:23. See Wm. Theodore de Bary and Irene Bloom (eds.), *Sources of Chinese Tradition*, Volume I (New York: Columbia University Press, 1999), pp. 59-60. **Between husband and wife, there should be differentiation.** *Mencius*, III/A/4. See *Mencius* (1970), p. 102 (modified). **Only if a husband has a remonstrating wife will he avoid falling into evil ways.** Daosheng is quoting from the *Classic of Filiality for Women*. See Richard Madsen, "Confucian Conceptions of Civil Society," in Daniel A. Bell (ed.), *Confucian Political Ethics* (Princeton: Princeton University Press, 2010), p. 8 (modified). **Because the government stored its population registers on islands in the lake…** See *Shoudu zhi*, p. 472. **A friendly two-copper fine…for any mention of taboo topics.** Again, Daosheng follows Chen Yun, in *Six Records of a Floating Life*, p. 65. **From Heaven's Peak the moon rises bright…** is a poem by Li Bai (701-762). See http://cn.hujiang.com/new/p533759/page4/. **The news about the Du family.** I have added the surname Du, but the anecdote follows *Ming Qing zhi ji dang she yundong kao*, p. 283. **Are we floating on Xuanwu Lake? How would we know?** is loosely based on *Jinling lüyou ci*, p. 90. **The most serious breach of filiality was to fail to produce a male heir.** *Mencius*, IV/A/26, in *Mencius* (1970), p. 127.

Chapter Six

In the first month, it has no form... The stanzas on the months of pregnancy and childbirth are modified from Wilt Idema and Beata Grant, *The Red Brush: Writing Women of Imperial China* (Cambridge: Harvard University Asia Center, 2004), pp. 558-559. **Southern military officials attempted to reestablish contact with Wu Sangui.** See *Guo que*, p. 6143. **The Classic of Filiality for Women says...** See *The Red Brush*, p. 59. **Shandong...Huai'an.** See *Guo que*, pp. 6150, 6155. **Suqian...violent hailstorm...Two of the defending generals near Suqian quarreled...** See *Guo que*, pp. 6157, 6164, 6166, 6173, 6175-6176; *The Great Enterprise*, pp. 510-511. **The ancients – a woman, in fact – advised putting baby girls under the bed...** The woman was Ban Zhao (45-c. 116 CE). See *The Red Brush*, pp. 36-42. **The Nanjing government ordered the wife of the general...The Nanjing court was shocked...The Manchu army was advancing.** See *Guo que*, p. 6183, 6190-6191, 6194, 6197; *The Great Enterprise*, p. 533. **With Manchu columns threatening to cut them off...Yangzhou...Nanjing.** See *Guo que*, pp. 6198, 6199, 6104, 6105; *The Great Enterprise*, pp. 556-578; *The Southern Ming*, pp. 55-57. **Nanyu was awakened by the sounds of the Manchu army entering the city.** See *The Great Enterprise*, pp. 579-580. **So much feeling might as well be none...The candle sheds a tear at dawn.** These are modified fragments of "On Parting" by Du Mu (803-852). See http://www.chinese-poems.com/dm1.html. **I know not where I'll come to die...** is suggested by the first of the "Seven Sorrows" poems by Wang Can

(177-217). See Stephen Owen, *An Anthology of Chinese Literature: Beginnings to 1911* (New York: W.W. Norton & Company, 1996), p. 252.

Chapter Seven

The Hongguang emperor was made a prisoner. See *The Great Enterprise*, pp. 580-581. **Former officials…were already rushing to offer their services to their conquerors**. See *State versus Gentry in Early Qing Dynasty China*, p. 24. **The surrendered ministers of the Nanjing government presented the Manchus with the names of some three hundred associates**. See *The Great Enterprise*, pp. 596-598. **Crimson Cloud Monastery** (*Qi xia shan*) still exists. Descriptions of it are based on the map included in *Shoudu zhi* and on personal visits. The abbot **Anshan** is fictional. **Lao Lang Festival**. This is probably a more modern Nanjing holiday, which I have transplanted to seventeenth-century Suzhou. See *Shoudu zhi*, p. 1151; Evy Wong (tr.), *Chinese Auspicious Culture* (Beijing: Foreign Language Press, 2002), p. 200. Daosheng is referring to Guan Zhong (c. 720-645 BCE) as the supposed **deified prime minister. The princess has attained woman's estate…** See Tang Xianzu, *A Dream Under the Southern Bough* (Beijing: Foreign Languages Press, 2003), p. 28. **Zou Diguang** was an opera troupe owner who lived from 1550 to 1626, and he was active in Wuxi, not Suzhou. **Dragon Hill Villa** is fictional, but Suzhou continues to be famous for its pleasure gardens. A **red rug** served as the acting area for opera. See Grant Shen, "Acting in the Private Theatre of the Ming Dynasty," *Asian Theatre Journal* 15.1 (Spring, 1998), p. 65. **Flute-playing… clouds and rain…Bearing so many babies simply ruins one's health…It's they who call me Mother that have eroded my younger looks**. See *A Dream Under the Southern Bough*, pp. 85, 86, 87, 154, 164. **Until now, war has been a distant thought…**

This passage, and the following three, are from *A Dream Under the Southern Bough*, pp. 166, 171, 180-181, 187. **How tender, how beautiful, her dancing was**, etc... **My old father sold me to Master when I was seven**. See "Acting in the Private Theatre of the Ming Dynasty," pp. 68, 70, 65. For the effect of the haircutting order in **Taicang**, see *The Great Enterprise*, pp. 651, 654. **We're to be shaved like criminals**. See Li Junying, "Qian xi Qing chu Han zu ren fan 'ti fa ling' de yuanyin," *Cang Sang* 2014.2, pp. 28-29. **Chinese men have Chinese customs!**, etc. is a slight anachronism, from the nineteenth century. See Li Wenhai and Liu Yangdong, *Taiping Tianguo shehui fengqing* (Taipei: Yunlong chubanshe, 1991), pp. 45-46. See also Lynn A. Struve, *Voices from the Ming-Qing Cataclysm: China in Tigers' Jaws* (New Haven: Yale University Press, 1998), pp. 64-65. **If we cut our hair, we'll lose our wives**. See *The Great Enterprise*, pp. 650-652. **The corporal inheritance of his father**. See *The Great Enterprise*, pp. 648-649; *The Southern Ming*, p. 61. **The people who lived outside city walls...were less likely to have conformed to the haircutting decree**. See *The Great Enterprise*, p. 651. **Jiading... Hou Tongzeng drowned himself with his sons and servants**. See *The Great Enterprise*, pp. 656-659 (The latter sentence is a direct quotation). See also Jerry Dennerline, *The Chia-ting Loyalists: Confucian Leadership and Social Change in Seventeenth-Century China* (New Haven: Yale University Press, 1981). **Enlightenment Temple** (*Yuantong jiang si*). See *Wanli Jiading xian zhi*, 18/1a, reprinted in *Siku quanshu cunmu congshu* (Jinan: Qi Lu shu she, 1996), vol. 209, p. 128. **Monk militia** was a contemporary institution, although I am not sure if one figured in the Jiading episode. See *State versus Gentry in Late Ming Dynasty China*, p. 151. **The men of neighboring hamlets went to war against each other, with the shaved-scalped murdering the long-haired, and vice-versa**. See *The Great Enterprise*, p. 651. **A scholar who loves finery is not** worthy of the name. Nanyu has misquoted the *Analects*, 14.3. See *The Analects of Confucius*, p. 180. **Zhang Yue** is fictional.

Chapter Eight

Xinchang was situated... See *Guangxu Nanhui xian zhi, shou*/1b-2a, 9b-10a, 1/12a-b, reprinted in *Zhongguo fangzhi congshu* (Taipei: Chengwen chubanshe, 1970), vol. 42, pp. 42-43, 58-59, 83-84. **Copious commemorative arches.** See http://xinchang. pudong.gov.cn/pdxcz_ssl/2015-01-08/Detail_601864.htm. **Bridge of Eternal Prosperity** (*Yong xing qiao*). See *Guangxu Nanhui xian zhi*, 2/63b, reprinted in *Zhongguo fangzhi congshu*, vol. 1, p. 222. **When the righteousness of the son remains under the control of the father**... See *State versus Gentry in Early Qing Dynasty China*, pp. 19-20. **As it is said in *The Book of Changes*...** See *State versus Gentry in Early Qing Dynasty China*, pp. 6-7. **The gentleman draws the bow but does not release the arrow**... This is from *Mencius*, VII/A/41. See *Mencius* (1970), pp. 191-192. See also Timothy Cheek, *Mao Zedong and China's Revolutions: A Brief History with Documents* (Boston: Bedford / St. Martin's, 2002), p. 65. **Encourage them in their toil**... This is from *Mencius*, III/A/4. See *Mencius* (1970), p. 102. **As easy as teaching a monkey to climb a tree.** See *State versus Gentry in Early Qing Dynasty China*, p. 6. **You and I / Have so much love / That it burns... like...fire**... This is a lyric by Guan Daosheng. I slightly modify Kenneth Rexroth's translation and title. See *The Orchid Boat*, p. 53. Andrew W.F. Wong, in http://chinesepoemsinenglish. blogspot.com/2013/08/guan-daosheng-i-and-you-song-clay. html, offers a different translation and repeats the legend that Guan wrote the poem to dissuade her husband, Zhao Mengfu, from finding a concubine, in which effort she was apparently successful. **The men of the Zhu family**... The episode narrated here is embellished but historical. See Zhang Huijian, *Ming Qing*

Jiangsu wenren nianbiao (Shanghai: Shanghai guji chubanshe, 1986), p. 601. **Humble founder of our valiant dynasty...** The Ming dynasty was founded by a commoner, Zhu Yuanzhang (1328-1398). **Restorationist activity in the area.** See *The Southern Ming*, pp. 59, 75-77, 89-90, 95. **Yellow Crane Mountain** was the hermitage of the painter Wang Meng (c. 1308-1385), the grandson of Zhao Mengfu and Guan Daosheng. **Grand Secretary Ning Wanwo impeached Wei Su.** This affair is based on Ning Wanwo's (d. 1665) impeachment of Chen Mingxia, which occurred a little later, in 1654. The details presented here are drawn from Ning's actual indictment and a separate list of charges against a less significant man named Zhao Yu. For the former, see *Ming Qing shi liao, bing bian* (Taipei: Academia Sinica, 1999), p. 350a. For the later, see *State versus Gentry in Early Qing Dynasty China*, pp. 74-75. **Hangzhou art shop, where trade continued to thrive.** See Holland Cotter, "After Conquest, Subtle Emblems of Protest, *New York Times*, September 9, 2011, C22.

Chapter Nine

A strange boiling sound... See Ye Mengzhu, *Yue shi bian* (Shanghai: Shanghai guji chubanshe, 1980), pp. 2-3. These phenomena were observed in Shanghai, some distance from northeastern Zhejiang. **The new rulers wrung full measures of revenue from war-ravaged farms.** See *State versus Gentry in Early Qing Dynasty China*, pp. 32-35. **The northerners surged out from Hangzhou, fording the drought-shallowed Qiantang River.** See *The Southern Ming*, pp. 95-96. **Right in front is Jump-Over Mountain. Yellow Crane is next to it...Temple of the Buddha-Sun.** *Yuhang xian zhi* (Hangzhou: Zhejiang renmin chubanshe, 1990), p. 734. **His robe was of the high-collared Manchu style now mandated for all men.** See *The Southern Ming*, p. 63. **The prefect of Hangzhou made me a tributary.** Nanyu's path to eminence might conceivably have taken this course. Ping-ti Ho, *The Ladder of Success in Imperial China: Aspects of Social Mobility, 1368-1911* (New York: Science Editions, 1964), pp. 27-29 suggests that tributary degrees were awarded more sparingly, but several local histories show many more being awarded. Nanyu's scheme of qualifying in Hangzhou and choosing to serve in Yuhang may be problematic, but the situation in the transition years might have made it possible. **Personal retainers** were not unknown. See *State versus Gentry in Early Qing Dynasty China*, p. 40. **Revenge would be righteous and justified**. See Michael Dalby, "Revenge and the Law in Traditional China," *The American Journal of Legal History* 25.4 (Oct., 1981), p. 295; Jiang Yonglin, *The Great Ming Code / Da Ming lü* (Seattle: University of Washington Press, 2005), p. 190. **You're a rebel now**. See Philip A. Kuhn, *Soulstealers: The Chinese Sorcery Scare of 1768* (Cambridge: Harvard University Press, 1990), p. 59. **Immune to physical punishment**. See *The Ladder of Success in Imperial China*, p. 18. **Hong Chengchou** is historical and lived from 1593 to 1665. See Arthur Hummel (ed.), *Eminent Chinese of the Ch'ing Period* (Taipei: Ch'eng Wen, 1972), p. 359; Chen-main Wang, *The Life and Career of Hung Ch'eng-ch'ou (1593-1665)* (Ann Arbor: Association for Asian Studies, 1999). **Erotic entrancement**. See Xiaohuan Zhao, "Sorcery Crimes, Laws, and Judicial Practice in Traditional China," *Australian Journal of Asian Law* 17.1. (2016), p. 9. **Isn't it customary for women to be subjected only to the finger press, while the ankle press is reserved for men?...Manly feet deserve manly treatment**. See Timothy Brook, *et al.*, *Death by a Thousand Cuts* (Cambridge: Harvard University Press, 2008), p. 43, which suggests that Wei Su would not have been able to modify the procedure. I have also changed the description of the apparatus, for easier narration. **You're a star in Heaven now**. See *The Scholars*, p. 35. **The last prince of the old regime** (i.e. the Yongli Emperor, 1623-1662) and **Zheng Chenggong** (a.k.a. Coxinga, 1624-1662) are historical. **Two piteous passion-clinging bugs**. See *The Peach Blossom Fan*, p. 296.

Appendix

The **Biography of Zhu Xiangsun** appears in *Guangxu Nanhui xian zhi*, 22/52b-53a, reprinted in *Zhongguo fangzhi congshu* (Taipei: Chengwen chubanshe, 1970), vol. 42, pp. 1574-1575. I have supplemented the text with Zeng Yuwang, *Yiyou biji*, paragraph 15. The latter source is apparently a never-published manuscript, available online at http://ctext.org/wiki.pl?if=gb&chapter=545540.

ACKNOWLEDGMENTS

Thanks to Alice Poon, Graham Earnshaw, Wu Jen-shu, Christian de Pee, Peter Chen-main Wang, Robert Hegel, Jane Kate Leonard, Beata Grant, Ann Waltner, Grant Shen, Donald Harper, Mara Kozelsky, Sandra Stenson, Denise Huddle, Helen Johnson, Judith Lie, Julia Barclay-Morton, Ben Robertson, Satomi Kamei, Debbie Cobb, Rebecca Young, Clarence Mohr, and all of my colleagues and students at the University of South Alabama.

ABOUT THE AUTHOR

HARRY MILLER was born and raised in Baltimore, Maryland and received his college education at Wesleyan University. He first visited China in 1986, spending most of his time in Nanjing, where afterimages of the Ming and Qing dynasties became lifelong fascinations. From 1988 to 1992, he lived in Taiwan and achieved near-fluency in Mandarin Chinese while working for a container liner company. Obtaining his doctorate from Columbia University, he settled in Mobile, Alabama, where he teaches history at the University of South Alabama. He is married with three children.

Miller is the author of *State versus Gentry in Late Ming Dynasty China, 1572-1644* and *State versus Gentry in Early Qing Dynasty China, 1644-1699* and is the translator of *The Gongyang Commentary on the Spring and Autumn Annals*. *Southern Rain* is his first novel.

yellowcraneintherain.blog